SHORE BREAKS

MIKE WALKER

INK START MEDIA
5710 W Gate City Blvd Ste K #284
Greensboro, NC 27407

DEDICATED TO *CASSIDY JORDAN WALKER*

"We are more powerful than we are damaged, and

we will rise from any abyss,"

-Nikita Gill

TABLE OF CONTENTS

SHORT STORIES INFLUENCED BY EXPERIENCES DURING THE ERA OF COVID.

In honor of the heroes of Covid, our medical professionals who worked day and night to help heal and treat their fellow citizens, and to the families who lost loved ones along the way.

BEYOND THE BREAK

We moved to Surf City, NC in 2010, leaving Boston due to Eddie's new job... senior sales associate for Pharmaceutical Product Development, one of the area's biggest employers. We knew no one; sight unseen. But after 15 years in the Boston suburbs we grew tired of the congestion, cost of living, cold winters and commuting in and out of the city. The only reprieve from the stress of Beantown was the summers on the Cape. But moving to the coastal south would ensure we would still get our fill of beach days.

The first eight years here were a breeze. Then in 2018 came Hurricane Florence, and in 2019, Hurricane Dorian. Florence was especially tough. Our yard was trashed, fence was destroyed, and the pool was full of debris, but by hurricane standards we made out ok. Compared to other people in the region, we survived both storms relatively unscathed.

In 2018 our oldest daughter, Jordan, finished college at NC State, met a boy, and was living at home and working locally doing data processing. The first year of Covid, spring of 2020, she and Remy moved to Raleigh. Our youngest daughter, Chase, was in her senior year at UNC when Eddie went to pick her up mid-March to bring her home. The impact of the first wave of Covid on her, as it was on countless others, was palpable.

"Hey sweetie, ready to go?" Eddie said standing at the door of Chase's apartment just off Chapel Hill's campus near Franklin Street. The same place where she lived since moving out of her dorm after freshman year.

Eddie could see the answer was *no* based on the look on her face.

"Are you sure they're cancelling the whole semester, dad? I mean, couldn't I just stay here and take my classes online? I've got to go all the way back to Surf City?"

"Trust me, I know it sucks. All I can say is the letter from the university says there will be no in-person classes the rest of the semester, and everything on campus is closed and everything in town is shutting down. Until we know what this pandemic is doing, it's safest for you to be home with family. In two weeks, this will be a ghost town."

Eddie hated having to give Chase the reality of the situation, as he knew she was looking forward to all the senior year traditions and, of course, graduation. Little did she know, even the ceremony was probably a no-go.

As Chase's mom, I tried to lend her ample support and called her as soon as they loaded the truck and were on Interstate 40 heading home. But my attempt at solace rang empty with her.

"Hey sweetie, are you ok? Dad called and said the loadout was tough. I'm sorry about the timing of all this with school."

"Thanks, mom. Hey, let me just talk to you when I'm home, ok? I'll be fine."

The next call came from Jordan. Also just an attempt to cheer Chase up.

"Hey sis. Are you ok?"

"Not really, but I get it. This fucking Covid shit, or SARS, or Coronavirus, whatever it's called. If I wanted to stay in Surf City I would have just gone to school at UNCW." Chase gave a half laugh given neither her nor Jordan took any interest in attending their local university.

"Come to Raleigh and finish your classes online from here. The view from our balcony is amazing and the breweries are right around the corner. Remy is still going into work and is holed up in our room every night taking his classes on Zoom. So it's just me and Rizzo most of the time."

"Dad says before long no one will be going to work. Those breweries are probably about to close their doors, girl. I'll call you when I get home. Tell Rizzo I said to stop pissing on your floor. Thanks sis. Love you."

They shared a laugh and then got back to their respective priorities- Jordan petting her Yorkie Rizzo on her lap while plowing through processing background checks online, and Chase making sense of what the hell was happening to her world.

Chase got home and unpacked, and over the coming days we did our best to help her settle in. Eddie continued to work at the office, then early-April was ordered to work from home. As a real estate agent, I had always enjoyed the ability to work from home anyway. So Covid was no change for me.

By April the global infection rate topped one million, and most businesses shut their doors forcing the real estate market to also go on hiatus. Too much uncertainty with the economy, and people unwilling to risk having strangers in and out of their homes. So the ambiguity of Covid was a big, black storm cloud to a real estate market that otherwise had been booming.

The agency told me and the other staff to continue to work from home, generate leads, and wait things out. My commissions from sales last year along with Eddie's salary would stabilize us for the time being. As I followed the news, it was clear others were not as fortunate.

Chase got settled at home, but her despair intensified despite our persistent efforts to cheer her up.

"Eddie, maybe see if Chase wants to tinker around upstairs in the music room. I'm sure she misses performing, and it's been a while since you guys played together," I suggested.

"Good idea, Ike. Let me see if she is up for it later after I finish work and she's done with classes."

I smiled and left Eddie to his laptop. I loved when he called me by my nickname, something he started in college after we first met, associated with my maiden name- Eisenhower.

Eddie played guitar as a hobby on and off since college, and Chase was a vocalist and performed in musical theatre since elementary school, and majored in dramatic arts. We knew a creative outlet for her especially now would be a good diversion from the stress of leaving school.

The first several days of being at home full-time without visits to the agency, without seeing clients or doing showings, and without scheduling or traveling to closings was nice. After 20 years of having work activities every day and chasing kids around, the break was welcomed. I woke, walked our two golden retrievers, read the paper over coffee, dug into a few books, and binge-watched my favorite Netflix series.

Eddie passed through the living room consistently each day for coffee refills and snacks, and always stopped along the way for a customary kiss on my cheek and to describe whatever I was watching on television as *blather*.

Chase was catching up on her sleep each morning and started doing music with Eddie a few evenings a week. Jordan was planning to drive home for Father's Day since the hassle of flying during Covid was becoming a pain.

Unlike many others who were losing their jobs or getting infected, by all accounts we were making the best of things. As usual, we felt blessed.

Late May came news our local gym was closing. In our mid-40s, Eddie and I used the gym as a routine outlet for well-being, to spend time together, and to stay in shape. Eddie also jogged around the neighborhood, so his back-up to the gym was an easy shift.

A competitive swimmer in college and whose main workout consisted of thirty minutes in the pool at least four days a week, this news was more troubling for me. So after dinner one night, I checked in with Eddie on an alternative to the gym.

"Hey, so do you want to surf with me in the morning? We can go back to our spot near Sea-N Topsail." Looking up from his nightly game of Euchre on his iPad, he seemed surprised at the question.

"Surf? We haven't surfed in two years, and even then it was like twice that summer. Sure, I mean if there are waves. But I'm gonna be rusty."

I chuckled before replying, "You mean even more rusty than in your prime, big guy? It's just that since I can't swim for now, I thought it would be a good back-up plan."

As was often the case whenever I tried to talk to Eddie while he was looking at a screen, I could tell he was only half-listening.

"Uh, sure babe. Yes, just let me know how it goes." His eyes were already back to being fixed on his game.

I entered the garage to check on the condition of our boards, both resting in carry bags and setting idle on the surfboard racks along the wall. Not unlike the mower, neglected kids toys and other stuff we accumulated in the garage, I walked past them 10 times a day without notice.

Eddie's nine-foot McTavish was a great craigslist find, and for half the price he would have paid retail for the popular longboard from Australia. The deck was solid white with a beautiful sky blue wave in the middle, and bright yellow speckles along the rails. The rocker was rounded and it featured adaptable one or three fin options.

Eddie surprised me with a Channel Islands board for my birthday several years ago. He had it designed specifically for my height, weight and ability. A medium-sized board for advanced surfers with a pointed nose and custom-painted design on the bottom, featuring the astrological symbols of Chase and Jordan with their birth dates in my cursive handwriting.

The top of the board included a beautiful stringer, the long center bead down the middle, made of cedar and splashed with my favorite color, pink. The center of the deck featured a light grey shark's fin with a splash of Carolina blue ocean water scattered toward the rails.

Eddie's board was nice, but my board was a marriage of function and form. As much a piece of art as it was a conveyance.

Though not very good initially, Eddie fell in love with surfing the first time his board hit the water. He confessed he wasn't a "surfer," he just knew how to surf a wave. But over time he got good enough to enjoy it and, even when there were no waves to catch, he loved being out on the water.

By comparison, the sport came much easier to me. I grew up skateboarding and snowboarding in the Northeast. So versus Eddie who grew up in Indiana and was not familiar with board sports of any sort, the motion and movements of surfing were much more intuitive for me, and my training as a swimmer made paddling somewhat effortless. After a few lessons it came easy, and was fun.

I checked the garage fridge and to my surprise there was still one bar of surf wax left from our last outing. I grabbed it, threw it along with my rash guard and a towel into my beach bag, and hung the bag on the rung where the board lay still.

I unzipped the surf bag enough to peek in at the beautiful design on the smooth surface, and ran my hand along the rail. *Tomorrow morning, be ready*, I softly spoke to her.

I set my alarm for 5:30am, enough time to check the waves on SurfChex, an online video system that live-streamed the local beaches. I usually hit Sea-N because it was a straight 12-minute drive from the house, but if the waves were better at other nearby spots I could quickly divert and drop in there.

As the sun rose over the horizon, the video showed the beautiful image that was also the one I least hoped for. Flat. Flat as a lake. Not a single bump.

"Shit," I said aloud.

I had been so pumped about getting back out. A good session on the water even permeated my dreams the night before, so I woke with great anticipation of hitting the waves again.

I considered grabbing our stand-up paddleboard and making the best of it, but that would have only made for more disappointment. Much as I liked paddling, it was just not the same rush as surfing.

While looking at the conditions on my phone, I strolled out to the curb with the dogs on my heels, grabbed the newspaper, and returned to the kitchen. A few minutes later, Eddie made his customary beeline to the Keurig.

"Hey, I thought we were surfing. You didn't wake me."

"Zero waves. We can try again tomorrow."

11

"Ah, Ike, I have a 7am conference call with some clients, so I have to pass on tomorrow. Hit me another day," Eddie said as he made his way to his laptop to start his day.

I looked back at the image on my phone; now 10 minutes past sunrise I noticed the beauty of the sun coming up over the horizon. The tiny images of gulls and terns, razorbills and massive pelicans scattered above the water. As the camera angle turned to scan the beach, there were many people walking or jogging on the water's edge. Some taking pictures of the sunrise and others just sitting and staring out at the magnetic ocean.

As I viewed the serene images, I recalled the number of times after we first moved to the Carolina coast that Eddie and I took walks on the beach, some mornings waking early enough to catch the sunrise.

We tried a number of different entry piers, but eventually found a favorite spot at Sea-N where an old pier jutted out from a Tiki Bar, and where a sand bar made for easier surfing for Eddie because he could stand and then pop on his board versus float and paddle.

But like most fads, we hadn't seen the sunrise in a long time. Much as we cajoled the girls to come with us periodically, they expressed interest the nights before, then come morning rolled over and told us to go on without them.

Though disappointed in today's conditions, I was resolute in trying again tomorrow. And since I knew full well that the ocean tides could for many days straight fail to offer surfable conditions, I decided to have a back-up plan.

I heard about ocean swimming a number of times from people I met at the gym. Some swam the intercoastal waterway in the morning, but I always worried about the dangers of swimming a channel at dawn with passing fishing boats and where the water was murky and unclean.

I sometimes saw people swimming along the shore in the ocean, but I always worried about jellyfish and rays. Sure, sharks too, but less so as most surfers divorced themselves of worry about such intrusions given the statistical unlikeliness of being bitten.

By the time I read the morning paper and finished my coffee, it occurred to me how bored I had already become with so many successive days at home. I was already feeling cooped up, and had to get out of the house.

I yearned for more human interaction and exposure to nature. I needed a purpose, and a break from the allostatic load the pandemic produced, as well as the monotony of my cell phone, iPad, laptop and TV. The screens were closing in on me. I needed to get my blood pumping.

So I committed to rising at 5am every morning, Monday through Friday, as if part of a new job routine. The coffee maker was set to have my java ready at 5:05, and after throwing on my swimsuit and rash guard, my board would go in the back of Eddie's old Ford and I would make my way to the ocean. Waves or not, this is how I would start my day. I added my swim goggles to my bag so that if there weren't surfable waves, I would instead do laps along the shore.

I woke the next morning, June 1, 2020, and sprung out of bed. A swish of mouthwash, a splash of cold water on my face, I grabbed my coffee, phone and keys, and was out the door. I threw my bag and board into the truck and my brain and eyes came to life as the headlights illuminated the still dark roadway leading toward Sea-N.

As I pulled in the lot near the entry point marked Plauck Pier, I was surprised at how many other cars were there. I assumed this probably meant surf's up. I excitedly grabbed my bag and board and ascended the wooden steps gradually making my way over the arching pier and toward the ocean.

Every step east on the pier brought an accelerated heartbeat and anticipation of the beauty that awaited. My eyes and brain consumed the contrasting images as they unfolded. First a thin, bold line of the distant horizon, like the curve of the top of an eyelid; then the crystal navy blue water and passing birds; then the white-capped waves rolling toward the shoreline; and a few steps later- the beautiful shoreline and beach.

As the full view of the tides became clear, the waves looked outstanding. A dozen or more surfers littered the surf line and were dropping in one after the other. Best yet, the waves looked perfect for my skill level. Anything too small and my time would be mostly spent paddling and floating. Anything too extreme, and I'd have to work hard to drop in, or possibly risk an injury. But waist to chest high was my jam.

Same as always for me at the beach, the effect of the surroundings was uplifting and energizing. Perhaps similar to an astronaut leaving Earth and entering the stratosphere, and looking down at the breathtaking and shrinking blue orb below her. The beach and ocean had the same effect on me. Any worries, stress, any negative thoughts were washed away.

Each time I visited the spot at Plauck Pier, the more it seemed people were drawn there. Most staring out at the water in earnest, looking to find something. Some looking at their past, others looking to the future. Drawn to something bigger and more infinite than themselves.

The sun was starting to peek over the horizon, already illuminating the area before making its grand appearance. Like someone slowly pushing up the toggle on a dimmer switch, the dark blue night sky gradually gave way to the orange and reddish rays rising over the water.

The clouds above became a beautiful canvas of colors, changing every second that the sun pushed upward for its full recognition. And at one point when the sun was halfway up, the beautiful, mirrored image of colors between the sky and ocean were identical.

I dropped my board on the sand, gave it a few strokes of new wax, threw on my rash guard, and leashed up. I thought to myself how lucky I was to be in a space of such beauty and peace- 44 years old, 140 pounds; not necessarily in my "athletic prime," but still lean and fit enough to surf.

Given it was two years since my last outing, I was planning to be careful; the ocean and I had a mutual respect for each other, so we understood the limits of one another when united.

Before plunging in, I stood on the shoreline a few ticks to view the full sunrise. Years ago I may have ignored this aspect of the experience and eagerly submerged, but as I grew older I worked to slow things down, and to appreciate the beauty around me. And since the average sunrise from the point the top of the sun's iris punched through the horizon's darkness to the last point that the bottom of the orb pushed off from the ocean's line was a mere 34 arcminutes (4 minutes of real time), it was worth the wait.

Once the perfect orange sphere illuminated the navy playing field, I made my running plunge into the surf. The water was a tepid 72 degrees, plenty warm enough without a wetsuit jacket. The top of my rib cage felt the unfamiliar firmness of the solid board beneath, something that would take a few weeks to get used to before the discomfort of that region of my body would pass.

Back arched and head up like a Cobra, my smooth paddling along the rails fell right back into perfect harmony. Perhaps no better match for a surfer than one who grew up as a competitive swimmer. Unlike other surfers who may lose their wind after a few rides or whose upper body may call it quits while there were still good rides to be had, I could surf for hours without tiring.

I waved at a few nearby surfers and positioned my board horizontal to the beach. The muscle memory of every aspect and technique quickly fell right back into place. My legs effortlessly blender-kicked to turn the nose of the board toward the beach as the first good swell made its way toward me. A few strokes of my arms deep into the water and one last stroke when the energy of the wave met me, and I popped up with ease.

"Yes!" I smiled and spoke aloud as the joy of claiming my first wave in a long time consumed me. Knees bent, athletic position, and a nice ride left to right before the wave gave its final push and collapsed. I spun the nose back to the horizon and paddled back out for the next offering.

The exhilaration and impact on my mind and body was just as I anticipated. Between rides and shooting some nice curls, I sat or lay on my board and took deep breaths, working to connect with my center and replenish my soul.

The pilings from a pier destroyed by Hurricane Hazel in the 1950s appeared just as they were when I last surfed here two years ago. The tallest two remaining poles, upon which the end of the pier once sat, were occupied by large gulls lazily watching over the line of surfers, as though they were carved into the top like tribal totem poles. My beloved Hoosier Eddie always said the gulls perched on the poles reminded him of touchdown Jesus watching over Notre Dame stadium.

Ride after ride provided me just what I hoped for in the way of getting my salt fix, and after an hour and as low tide neared, I rode one last mellow, spilling wave all the way to the shore. I unvelcroed my leash from my calf, wrapped it around the fin, and smiled while seeing the girls' horoscope signs beneath the board.

As I exited the water, a small child on the beach bounded in front of me on his tip toes evading his parents, walking and laughing like a miniature Herman Munster. One final splash of water tickled my heels, perhaps the ocean's way of saying *I'll see you tomorrow*, before my feet sunk deep into the warm morning sand.

I paused as a pack of Plovers scurried in front of me, pecking at the sand for food, and hopping over the billowing, white sea foam rolling in from each wave.

"Ike, is that you? How were the rides?" Eddie peered out the door of the den into the kitchen as I entered.

"Hey sweetie. God, euphoric. I can't believe we stopped surfing for so long. What were we thinking?"

"I know. Hard to believe. I bet you fell right back into it."

"You've *got* to start coming out with me some mornings. I mean the sunrise was stunning. I am totally committed to Monday through Friday, so at any point set your alarm and grab that Cadillac of yours."

No response came, but I assumed he heard me and was back into his work. I always joked with Eddie about his longboard and named it *The Cadillac*, because it was by most standards a stylish but massive board that just sort of provided Eddie slow cruising on the waves.

Eddie was a family man but also a workaholic. He seemed pleased I was intent on some new rituals to help ease the stress of stay-at-home monotony, but he didn't seem overly interested in getting back into surfing. I think if he did make it out one morning it would be to appease me, but we were always happy both when we were together and when we were independent of each other.

Jordan called to check in and I shared with her my excitement about getting back to surfing. We talked a bit about Covid stuff and how Remy was liking his new job. Their puppy Rizzo was keeping Jordan busy when she was not working or at the gym. I couldn't help but inquire about how things were going in terms of her relationship with Remy.

"Has he popped the question yet?"

"Mom! Why not just come right out and tell me what you're thinking," she replied, scoffing at my directness.

She continued, "I think he wants to get through school first. But the relationship has been great and we're getting along well. And something about living alone without our parents hovering about has been great for our sex life."

"Good for you. Just be careful. I don't think your dad wants to walk you down the aisle with a bun in the oven."

"Don't worry. We're being careful but he sure has a higher need than I do, if you know what I mean."

I appreciated Jordan and I could always have these sorts of mother-daughter conversations.

"I always told you and Chase this about men and women and sex- For men, sex is like dinner. They eat, and soon after they're hungry again. For women, it's more like dessert. We don't need it every day, but when we get it we sure do enjoy it."

Jordan laughed and we hung up as Chase came into the kitchen.

"Dad's having some friends over tonight to play music, and I'm gonna sit in. We must have played for two hours last night, so my voice is a little hoarse, but I'm looking forward to our little jam session."

Chase at 21 was a beautiful girl, tall and with long, straight, jet black hair. Most people said she favored Eddie who also had dark features and was tall and lean, though his previous black hair was long gone. But by bald standards, Eddie was still handsome and most people mistook him for being much younger than his age.

Jordan and I also resembled each other more and more. Though she was not an athlete per se, she had taken to weightlifting and was currently a bit of a gym rat since moving to Raleigh. Each photo she sent appeared to show not an image of the little girl we raised, but of a confident young woman in incredible shape and with the beauty of someone who could easily fall into a career in modeling. She didn't use much make-up to promote her beauty, she just sort of shined a light that exuded happiness; when she smiled, heads turned.

The following morning I was still feeling the buzz from yesterday's session. I again woke at 5 and excitedly made my way to the spot. But the cloud cover made for a less impressive sunrise, and the ocean was again flat and offered only shore break.

Other than people on boogie boards and skimboards along the shore, there would be no rides today. But the conditions were perfect for swimming.

Abandoning my board in the truck bed, I grabbed my goggles from my bag and went through my usual pre-swim stretching routine. Various versions of a progression of stretches were the same as those I learned at swim camp when I was eight, through rec league swimming, travel team meets, high school competitions and college. The intensity was lower than before, but the cycle of stretching the legs, core, upper body and limbs was fairly similar.

"You come here all the time to swim?" A woman's voice from behind me caught my attention.

"Hi. Well, I do, but not to swim. I prefer surfing but of course not today. What about you?" I asked as her goggles dangled from her wrist while she also stretched a bit. A pretty woman a bit younger than me, short, blonde hair and stocky proportional to her height, with solid lats and very muscular legs.

"Good for you. I swim here a few days a week. We live close but of all the places to greet the morning, this is my favorite. No surfing for me, though. On the days I don't swim I sometimes paddle my SUP out. I work afternoons at the hospital, unless I pull overtime and also work days, so the mornings are usually the best time for me to exercise. Plus the view here is unreal. I'm Cathy. People just call me Cat."

She smiled and extended her elbow as the new customary replacement for shaking hands during Covid, so I introduced myself as Britt and we chatted a little further before walking toward the water. I wasn't expecting to make a friend during my new morning routine, but she seemed very nice and highly knowledgeable about ocean swimming. As we walked together toward the water, I gathered some key info from her.

"The Jellyfish aren't bad this time of year. Later in the summer they can be, so just keep moving and if you feel one near you just go around it or push it aside like you would push a basketball away from you. Just don't grab the tail. I get stung a few times a year and it's not that bad."

I was drawn to Cat's incredibly friendly demeanor and boundless energy, especially to a complete stranger during Covid. She continued speaking as we entered the water, and I became a bit intimidated by my first ocean swim.

"The best spot to go back and forth is just after the first break. You're a surfer so that part will come easy. Since obviously you swim north and south along the beach, you don't need to worry about tow once you're beyond the break. Just be careful coming back in as some days it can be strong. I do about 50 yards north just past the old pier, and then 50 yards back."

As she spoke it occurred to me I really had no plan for how I was approaching things, so I found her suggestions useful.

"How many times do you go back and forth?" I asked.

"Well I don't count laps, I just swim for 20 minutes without stopping. Some days I push it to 25 or 30, so it just depends on how things go. When the current is strong or the waves are big I tire more quickly. I just keep an eye on my watch."

Cat pointed to the thick black surf watch strapped to her left wrist, and as she made her way into the water I decided fate had brought us together in order for me to start my ocean swimming routine out right.

"Wow. That's awesome. I believe a 30-minute swim is about a mile, right?"

Cat smiled and nodded yes as she pulled her goggles down over her brown eyes, the sort of eyes that smile independent of one's mouth.

"Listen, I don't want to get in your way, but any chance I could just follow behind you this first time? Would just give me a sense of the yardage." I hoped she didn't mind the request.

"Oh my gosh, Britt, of course. But I don't go very fast, so if my pace is too slow feel free to pass me and do your thing." Cat seemed thrilled to have a swim companion.

With that, she made her way directly east swimming from the beach toward the horizon, over a few small waves, then under a few larger ones. I let her get ahead a bit, then followed her line. Once past the break, she was already turning right and swimming south at a faster pace than I expected. I plunged in and followed stroke for stroke with her, freestyle as I assumed she would also be swimming.

The southern direction made for a nice view of the sky, even though the sun sat dense behind the cloud banks in the distance. But every time my head turned left for a breath, like the shutter of a camera, my eyes captured a different view. Each cloud shape, image of the sky meeting the water, type and size of birds, and occasional jumping fish made for a brand of swimming I had never experienced. Pool swimming makes for only one view, that of the wall along the pool. Not too exciting, so this was quite different.

I looked ahead to see Cat's distance between us increasing, so I dug in and accelerated a bit to close the gap. Soon I caught glimpse of her making a wide turn left toward the heart of the ocean, then looping back north in my direction but about 10 yards from me. As I passed her our eyes met while catching a mutual breath, and she appeared to smile.

A few more yards and I made the same turn, now again trailing directly behind her.

Heading north, the views as I turned my head to breathe were different. Visual snapshots of people on the beach, the sky above the land, and the colorful houses and condos facing the ocean. A little boy using a toy shovel to fill a green bucket with sand. A small group of women in warrior pose doing yoga.

As was the case yesterday, I felt exhilarated. I settled in and focused on my breathing, my strokes, my form including my kicks. I looked ahead to see Cat now very much ahead of me, and my intuition was to catch her. *It's not a competition, silly. Just relax and have a good workout.*

But the thought of swimming for fun versus to win was counterintuitive to me after years of training and racing. So the need to kick it up a notch fueled my adrenaline and quickened my pulse.

I lost track of how many times we went back and forth, and without a watch on I tried to get a sense of how long we had been out there. The thing about swimming is that time sort of stands still. What feels like 10 minutes may actually only be 5 in real time. So breathing easy and going at a good pace are important.

Each lap offered new views and images, and several times heading south not far from me large terns or gannets plunged from high up in the sky and splashed into the water, coming up with fish in their bills. At times it felt like swimming in a pool while watching a beautiful panoramic movie on the wall. It was relaxing and rejuvenating.

I glanced forward to check on Cat, and noticed she had switched to butterfly stroke. While not my favorite stroke after competing mainly in freestyle and breaststroke in college, I certainly could have followed suit. But *butterfly stroke* in the ocean? I mean, who the heck was I swimming with?

After a final turn I noticed Cat gradually making her way at an angle toward the shore. This was smart given what she said about the currents. A straight line back is where one could get caught in the tow, while a gradual line back was the same as swimming more horizontally through any undertow that existed.

I followed her line and by the time I was back on the sand she was already toweling off, smiling and waving at me.

"Hey. Whatcha think?" she asked as she bent at the waist forward and flipped her head up and down to help dry her hair. She wasn't breathing hard at all, and I noticed my breathing was much more labored. I put my hands on my knees as I bent down to pull my towel out of my bag.

"Ok. First of all, where did you swim in college?" I asked her while patting the perspiration from my forehead. "I mean, I've seen people swim out here, but butterfly?"

"Well you kept up great. I just finish the last lap with a different stroke just to break things up. Stanford. I swam at Stanford on scholarship for four years."

Still catching my breath, I grinned and threw my goggles into my bag.

"Well that makes me feel better. I mean, I was cruising at a good pace but there were times I had to dig deep just to stay with you. I must have made you feel like a tugboat pulling a broken down ship."

Cat's eyes brightened and she seemed flattered by my recognition of her abilities.

"That's nice of you to say. I've actually lost a lot since competing and having a daughter. But you know how it is, it gets in your blood and you just keep coming back to it. Did you swim competitively?"

"Yes, but nothing like Stanford. But I also love it and think it's the best form of exercise. Have you ever tried surfing?"

"My wife and I have SUPs, but we don't seem too interested in converting to surfboards. We just like the easy pace of paddleboarding, and the exercise aspects, and the beauty of what the ocean provides. Is this not the best spot on the coast?"

"Agree." My breathing was settling back as Cat began to gather her things. "And this part of the beach is my favorite of all," I said.

Cat wrung her hair through her towel and replied, "Right? Something about the sunrise here is totally addicting."

"I don't want to hold you up, Cat. But listen, thanks so much. I hope to see you out here again and would love to shadow you if that's ok."

"Oh my gosh, Britt, I would love that. Really, I have been hoping to find a swim partner for a while. Susan usually stays back to get our daughter Rosie ready for day care, but with Covid now, she's home. So it's often just me out here doing my thing. Here, take my number down and text me any time you are here. We live on Pinfish just up Tennessee Ave, so I can be down here in minutes."

"Thanks again. By the way, my friends call me Ike. See you soon."

"Makai!" she said as she waved back to me and headed off the beach.

I texted her my number, scooped up my things, and made my way back to the truck and home. My body felt much like it did back when I swam meets, tired but energized. My brain was also swimming in many directions having felt the incredible highs of two different ocean experiences in one week, but also from meeting a new friend and falling into what was looking like a great new morning ritual.

Over the next several weeks, each morning at the beach offered up a different experience. A mosaic of amazing sunrises, interesting people, exceptional surfing, and other mornings perfect for swimming. Though Covid was ravishing society, the beach seemed to provide a respite from all the stress and worry, a sanctuary of sorts.

And each day my affinity for the ocean intensified. My senses were awakened by the smell of the salt air, the morning dew on my body, the gradually warming sun on my face, and the impact of being in the water on my spirit.

Even the days the waves were weak, the ocean calmed me and helped me connect with my center. Some mornings I entered the surf and eagerly caught my rides. Other mornings I lay on my board looking toward the horizon, studying where the ocean meets the sky in some attempt to differentiate the two, while lazily watching the sun and clouds as the slow, silky waves rolled under me.

Some mornings the colors were distinct with the strip of brown sand meeting the flat blue sea beneath the light blue sky. Other mornings the waves offered beautiful, sporadic white caps, popping up toward billowing grey and white clouds of various shapes and complex layers of colors- as if intermingled by a universal paintbrush of pink, orange, and red hues.

No matter the weather, every day my senses were punctuated by the ocean breeze and subtle smell of salt air, mixed with scents from the nearby pink, magenta and violet beach peas, yaupon hollies and wax myrtles.

Most mornings Cat was there, swimming not far from where the surfers put in. Whether I was surfing or swimming, each morning we struck up a conversation and quickly felt like kindred souls... similar in age, I with two daughters and she with one, both having competitively swam in college.

Cat was open about her life as a lesbian and very open about her wife and their life as a gay couple in Surf City, and she spoke of it with great ease sensing my total acceptance of her identity.

One morning when dark clouds brewed above and the sky over the distant horizon flashed with heat lightening, we chatted while sipping coffee under cover of the lifeguard stand. Miles from the shore over the ocean, stark grey curtains of rain sheets fell.

The conversation illuminated for me the terrible conditions for the healthcare professionals managing the Covid sick.

"I've been in healthcare since graduating from college, and I've never seen anything like this. I mean, the waiting rooms are jam-packed, family members can't enter to see their relatives, and anyone with a predisposed health condition is in such a fragile state right now."

I leaned in and listened intently as Cat described what I had only read about or seen on television.

"I mean, the U.S. is already above 300,000 deaths and there is no slowing in sight. Pfizer and J&J appear to be feverishly working on a vaccine, but until then we are totally at the mercy of this pandemic. It's terrifying," Cat said while staring up at the darkening sky.

"Wow, Cat. I'm sorry you have to go through this. How are the staff holding up?"

"A lot of people are quitting, especially those worried about infecting their families. The other day we treated a boy dating my wife Susan's niece. Serious TBI from a freak golf cart accident, and his poor family couldn't even come in with him. We can't hire enough help right now. I could pull an extra shift every day if I wanted to, but if I don't pace myself I'm going to be fried."

Long, vertical bright white lines of lightning flashed from the clouds to the ocean's surface in the distance, with thunder booms reaching our ears seconds later. I felt like I needed to perk her up a bit, though she seemed very secure in her approach to it all.

"I'm sure your morning swims help keep you centered. I know that if it weren't for these mornings at the beach, I would go stir-crazy at home. There's just something about the ocean that seems to draw people in. No two days are alike, and people are here for so many different reasons. But they seem to leave happier than when they came. Plus, I really cherish our time together."

She sipped her coffee, her eyes and mouth smiling in unison as they did every morning we connected. Then she bumped shoulders with me, expressing her gratitude for our friendship.

"Thanks. Meeting you and having a swim partner has been a true blessing. The ocean sure has a purifying effect, doesn't it? For me, it provides glimpses of the images of my life," Cat said.

She continued, "I see babies taking their first steps, little kids building sandcastles, teenage girls gossiping, boys rough-housing, lovers snuggling, and loners staring out in search of something. My favorite sight though is older couples holding hands as they steady each other into the water. All the phases of life can be seen here."

We appeared to have so much in common as she talked about her interests, and even the tone of her voice was, like her personality, warm and reassuring. The sort of person you would want with you when things went wrong, but also with you to share the joy of things going well.

Cat stood to get up and said, "By the way Ike, Susan and I were talking about having you and your family over for dinner one night after the pandemic clears."

I had mentioned the same to Eddie, ironically, and said, "Of course. We would love that. Besides, if I keep trying to keep up with you out there, I'm going to need the carbs!"

Week by week the group that connected at our spot at the beach became less strangers and more a community. People happily greeted each other *good morning*, while also keeping a safe distance apart. A few people wore masks, but most felt ok being outside in the open air without them. Cat gave me a few hospital grade N-95 masks, and kept me updated on various issues related to Covid and on progress toward a vaccination.

As the pandemic grew in impact, the bond of the beachgoers intensified. It was a beautiful paradox in every respect, and I found the regulars taking more time to connect, talk, and discuss their struggles.

One couple shared of their loss of the man's father who succumbed to Covid-related illness. Others talked of losing their jobs in the surrounding food service and entertainment industries due to plummeting patronage. Others just talked about the stress of being cooped up inside, Zoom fatigue, and the increasing fear of human interaction in close proximity.

I continued to manage my own stress related to it all, meanwhile my surfing evolved in a great direction. Eddie came out with me a few times as I kept telling him about Cat and the amazing people who were using the beach as a means of getting through the pandemic.

As Eddie and I made our way out of the water after a surf session, he remarked about my surfing.

"Dang. You were good before. Now you're sort of kicking ass. Should we get you on tour?" His longboard looked like a massive log draped under his armpit.

"Ha-ha. Actually, the morning swimming is helping a ton. It makes my entry into the waves easier, and I conserve more energy because the paddling takes less strength. And my cardio is phenomenal. I guess I owe it all to Cat."

Over the next several weeks, Cat and I connected nearly every morning on the beach.

Most mornings were better suited for swimming versus surfing, but even the few mornings when the surf was decent, I elected to swim with Cat instead.

On my birthday, a Friday, as we met just before dawn, she surprised me with a gift.

"Makai!" she greeted me as we threw our bags on the sand.

"You said that to me when we first met. What does that mean?"

"It's a friendly Hawaiian greeting that also means 'toward the sea.' Hey, I noticed on Facebook today is your birthday. I got you a little gift." Her sheepish smile suggested she was up to something.

"I hope it's a motorized propeller so I can start keeping up with you out there!"

We sat on our towels as I opened the beautifully wrapped box.

"Cat! This is too much! You didn't need to get me anything. Really, your friendship is gift enough."

"I figured you could use it on the days I'm not here. I wouldn't want you shortchanging your workouts." She smiled as I strapped the new waterproof surf watch to my wrist.

"This is so nice. I've been thinking about getting one and put it off, so this is perfect."

That morning was one of the most beautiful sunrises yet. As the sun rose, the sky turned a majestic pink, then slowly transitioned to shades of lavender, violet and purple.

Instead of hastily making our way into the surf, we sat and talked well beyond the sun's ascent into the sky, feeling its gradual and increasing warmth on our bodies and faces.

Cat looked up the beach and saw a crowd of people gathering about 30 yards from us. We rose and walked over to see what the fuss was.

"Sea turtles hatching! Oh my God, what great timing," Cat said as we got closer.

I had never seen turtles hatch, but I was aware they nested in the area and were looked after by volunteers who guarded the nests against people and prey.

As we watched, Cat expertly explained the process to me. She said the mother turtle was here several months ago laying up to 100 eggs, then she returned to the sea never to see her babies. When the sand dropped a few inches on the nest several nights before, it signaled that hatching was a day or two away.

"Isn't this amazing? This is rare because normally they hatch at night in order to avoid predators. Now they will slowly make their way to the water, where unfortunately most will not survive. The majority will be eaten by larger ocean species or birds. Sort of a regrettable survival of the fittest thing. No mama around to help them into the world and protect them. But the process is amazing."

Cat was enamored by the little hatchlings as they poked their tiny brown noses from the shells and slowly and awkwardly made their way toward the surf, their miniature propeller legs less suited for traversing sand than water.

The nest watchers, who wore special shirts, reminded the on-lookers the turtles were not to be touched or assisted to the water, but an alley of sand with small berms built by the watchers the night before helped guide the babies directly to the ocean.

The watchers also helped keep an eye on the large ospreys circling above, knowing seahawks are more interested in a quick meal than celebrating the turtle parade.

We watched many of them dart toward the water, each receiving cheers from the beach-goers. As the last one tumbled into the surf, a long line of giant brown gulls descended from the clouds like roller coaster cars rolling from a top hat. Each gull tickled the tip of a wave with its shore-side wing, with no interest in the hatchlings.

We took a few photos and made our way back to get our morning workout in. Cat was effusive in her focus on my birthday, asked what my plans for the weekend were, and didn't bring up work or Covid once, though I know it was weighing heavily on her.

"Hey, why don't you lead today birthday girl? Give your friend Cat the day off so to speak."

I laughed since we both knew she was a far better swimmer, and many days I caught her in the lead looking back to make sure she wasn't too far ahead of me.

"Ok. But just because it's my birthday, doesn't mean I'm gonna slow down and wait for you. I've got my new watch on, so I'm feeling especially buoyant today!"

We caught ourselves in a mutual smile that only the best of friends exchange. I wasn't clear why the universe intersected our time and space weeks ago when we first met, but the timing for both of us with all the craziness in the world couldn't have been better.

It was a great session that morning, and taking the lead was a nice change. I got to decide how far to go between turns, when to slow a bit and enjoy the ocean and beach scenes, and I made sure each time Cat and I passed each other to give her a little wave or playful splash of water. Being with Cat was like being at middle school recess with a best friend. It was the highlight of my day each time we were together.

That weekend, Eddie and Chase and a few friends gathered at a safe distance at the house to live stream a set of music dedicated to the healthcare providers assisting with Coronavirus.

Jordan helped by setting up a Go Fund Me site to accept donations that would go toward families with excessive Covid medical bills. The event was a hit, and raised over $5k. Eddie got me several pairs of new swim goggles for my birthday, and the girls pitched in for a few new rash guards and bars of wax for my surf sessions.

Coming off a great birthday weekend high, more than ever I looked forward to my beach mornings that week, and being with Cat and asking her how things were going at the hospital.

Monday's forecast was excellent, so I arrived a full 15 minutes before sunrise to stretch and hopefully catch up with Cat before we swam. As I arrived and scanned the beach, I noticed she was not there yet. The sun rose over the distant horizon line, and still no

Cat. I found this a bit odd since especially on nice mornings she was usually eager to swim.

I figured she likely pulled an extra hospital shift and might be resting, so I didn't bother texting her. But two more days, and still nothing. On Thursday a massive thunderstorm hit before daybreak, way too unsafe to be on the beach. So I assumed for sure I would see her Friday morning.

Friday morning I arrived and waited, but she never showed. I skipped my swim and returned home, then texted her to check in- "Cat, it's Ike. Hey, missed you the last several days. Everything ok?"

It was a few hours before I received the reply from Susan using Cat's phone.

HI BRITT. CAT HAS TOLD ME A LOT ABOUT YOU. LISTEN, SHE SAID TO TELL YOU SHE'S GOING TO BE OUT A BIT. SHE CONTRACTED COVID FROM A PATIENT AT THE HOSPITAL. SHE'S IN ISOLATION AT HOME WITH WHAT SEEMS LIKE FLU SYMPTOMS. WE WILL KEEP YOU UPDATED.

My fingers flew into motion to reply- THANKS SUSAN. PLEASE TELL HER HI, AND LET US KNOW IF SHE NEEDS ANYTHING.

I spent the weekend worrying, but kept trying to reassure myself that Cat would be fine. I wasn't in the mood to surf Monday morning, so I skipped the trip to the beach altogether. Tuesday I slept through my alarm and again stayed home. I woke Wednesday morning and Eddie was already up reading the paper.

"Hey. Are you heading out this morning? I noticed you've skipped a few days. Do you want me to go along? Looks like the sunrise should be great around 6:20."

"Nah. I'll be ok. I'm just worried about Cat but I don't want to bother Susan. I'm gonna go just in case the others are worried about her. Or maybe someone has news of how she's doing."

I made my way to the spot and the usual crowd was there. It was still mostly dark, with the sky above the impending sunrise beginning to lighten up and provide its gradual, magical glow. Long, hovering clouds began to make their slow transition from white to pink to orange to red as the rays from the horizon intensified in strength and beauty.

The surf conditions were good, but I decided to swim instead. I felt doing so in some small way would keep my mind on Cat and send positive vibes her way. I dove in and swam with greater intensity than usual. First freestyle, then breaststroke, then back to freestyle.

Forgetting briefly she was not there, a few times out of habit I looked forward to gauge Cat's distance from me. As I made my final turn back south with my eyes toward the ocean, several yards from me a school of dolphins emerged from the water.

At first I was startled, but then worked to keep pace with them as they submerged, then made their slow arching break above the water's surface, before plunging back down. In total it appeared there were five of them, and I switched to butterfly stroke and followed along their side for several minutes before they drifted further east into the ocean's depths.

I exited the water and decided this interaction must be a sign. *Cat's ok. Everything is going to be ok.*

As I toweled off, I felt the silhouette of someone approaching me. A woman I had not met but who seemed to know me.

"Ike?"

"Uh, yes. I'm Ike."

"Hey. I'm Susan. Susan Dewey. Cat's partner."

"Oh. My gosh! So good to meet you. I would give you a hug but..."

"I know, of course," Susan said as she gave a slight wave from a few feet away.

"Listen, Cat asked me to come down and say hi for her, and give you an update."

I could see based on Susan's strained face that the news was not good. I pulled my goggles out of my hair and patted my towel over my mouth, in part to stifle the worry that was coming over my face.

"We're not sure what's wrong with her. I mean, she tested positive for Covid, but the flu-like symptoms have worsened. They admitted her to the hospital over the weekend, and her breathing is very labored. The doctors, of course she is a nurse on the staff so they all know her, they are giving her the best attention. I think she will be ok, but she really wanted me to come in person and tell you hi and not to worry."

I wanted to be strong for Susan, so I restrained my natural reaction which would have been a clear look of concern or possibly tears.

"Susan, my gosh, thank you for coming down. Cat is so strong. I'm sure she will be ok. Are they letting you in to see her?"

At this, Susan sat on the sand and buried her head between her knees, then raised her head while wiping tears from her cheeks. She breathed a heavy sigh that blew the hair on her bangs back, then mustered words difficult to speak.

"That of course is the hardest part. When she needs me the most, I can't be there. The doctors have let her Zoom with me a few times, but they are not under any terms permitting visitors."

I wanted to hug Susan as I would anyone in such grief, but I couldn't. Instead, I knelt on the sand several feet directly in front of her. The morning sun now shining directly on her face and intensifying in heat and brightness, I positioned myself so my shadow would give her some relief from the glare.

"Listen. Stay positive and I'm sure she will be ok. Eddie and I go to church on Sundays, and we will start a prayer circle for her. Cat is not someone who is going to let something like this beat her. Let me put your number in my cell so I can check in with you, if that's ok."

I didn't have the words to make her feel better. After all, at this point none of us knew much about Covid. We knew it was especially dangerous to the elderly or those with other medical conditions if exposed. But Cat was young and healthy and strong. *No way this was going to be that bad, right?*

Back at the house Eddie tried to cheer me up, but he too didn't have the answers to such a new and peculiar puzzle as Coronavirus. That evening, we sat at the kitchen table and he handed me a glass of wine to try to keep me calm.

"Ike, she will be ok. How about if we see if Susan needs us to send her some food? I mean, maybe we can cater a few meals to her just to show support."

"Sweetie, I'm not concerned about feeding Susan. The gesture is nice, sure. I'm really worried about Cat. She is the most amazing person I have met since moving here. Heck, maybe one of the best people I've ever met. Her soul shines in a way that very few people are capable of. She only knows one approach to this world- to help people. This is so unfair."

I was feeling my emotions getting the best of me, so I took a generous sip and exhaled.

"I need to be more positive. She's going to be fine," I said half convincingly and stood from the table. "I'm going to step outside and call Jordan. Do me a favor and check in with Chase after her night class ends."

Jordan answered and could tell something was wrong.

"Mom, you sound worried. What's going on?"

"You remember my friend Cat I have been talking so much about? She has Covid and her wife is really worried about her. So am I."

It occurred to me that for the first time I was relying on my kids for support and advice versus providing it. The role reversal felt sort of nice.

"Mom, I'm sure she will be ok. I can tell you made a connection with her because of how much you brag on what a great lady she is."

"I've almost given up surfing just to spend more time with her swimming in the mornings. She's that sort of person. She just draws you in with her strength and care. I really hope, I mean I really can't wait for you and Remy to meet her. She's an amazing spirit."

I peered into the bottom of my wine glass and noticed it was empty. Slipping back into the kitchen from the back deck to refill my glass, I finished the call sitting on the kitchen counter.

"Anyway, just keep her in your thoughts and prayers. We miss you and Remy and little Rizzo. Give them hugs, please."

That night, sensing a tension in me he had not seen in a long time, Eddie gave me a back massage as we prepared for sleep, then made love to me in the most caring way. After, I drifted into a deep sleep and dreamt I was sitting at the beach with Cat at my side.

On Sunday, Eddie and I stood when it was our turn and asked Pastor Victor and the church to support Cat Regan and her wife Susan Dewey in their fight against Coronavirus. It seemed every week in church more and more families were seeking such support.

Later that day, I texted Susan to check on Cat. No change. Still in the hospital and still with various symptoms including shortness of breath.

May 25th came the terrible news of the killing of George Floyd, followed by social upheaval and the woke movement. Layered with the pressures of the pandemic, it felt as though the United States was on the brink of implosion.

I continued my morning swims, mostly for introspection and meditation, consistently leaving my surfboard on the rack in the garage. Cat needed my energy to help her through this, and it seemed that energy was best derived through the activity she loved the most.

I ended each morning's swim with her favorite butterfly stroke, and each time I exited the water it took great effort to prevent myself from collapsing on the sand and crying.

As I pulled into the lot for the final swim of the week, Friday morning just before dawn, I could see Susan sitting on the bench atop the pier. She was facing the water, but even in the partial darkness I knew it was her.

I jogged across the pier to where she was seated, fearing the worst but also hoping she was coming in person to deliver good news.

My breath was heavy as I approached her, and my heart pounded in my chest.

"Susan, hey. How is Cat?"

I could tell before her reply the news was bad. It was on her face. It was reflected in her posture and her eyes. It was consuming her. She sobbed before getting a word out, and despite my better judgment about social distancing, I pulled her in for a hug.

I could feel her pain through her heaving sobs which permeated my upper torso. I hugged her with great strength, then sat next to her holding her hands as she tried to calm herself enough to speak.

"Cat is on a ventilator. We Zoomed yesterday and she seemed the same as before. Just someone in a hospital bed with the flu. But they became concerned about her breathing last night, and then this morning they called and said she is not able to breathe on her own."

I continued to hold Susan's hands and elected not to speak. There were no words capable of bringing her comfort. Sometimes human touch is the only way to aptly express support for those in pain.

We sat for what felt like a long time without speaking. Susan continued to cry, and I made the greatest effort to contain my tears, at least for now. I felt them welling up inside me much like the waves that propelled my surf sessions, or like the momentum of Cat's swim lane that enabled me to smoothly swim behind her. I wanted to be strong for Susan, so I resisted the impending catharsis that I knew would come the moment we parted.

We spoke for a bit with me mostly being present for her and reassuring her that Cat would pull through. I offered for Eddie and I to stop in to see her; she was thankful but declined.

Their own daughter Rosie, whom Cat spoke about whenever we chatted, was only five. So fortunately Susan was not contending with having to help her understand the inconceivable impact of what her mom was going through. She just knew one of her moms was sick. That was all a five-year-old needed to know at this point.

I updated Eddie and the girls, and they began to worry for me as much as they worried about Cat. The strong connection I had with her was obvious to them, and they knew that if Cat didn't pull through I would be devastated.

I texted Susan every day for updates and to lend support. The news was about the same each day. Cat was fighting for her life, and getting the best of care. Rain or shine, I continued to swim each morning for Cat, though it took great energy to stay focused.

Several times I stopped mid-lap, floated in the ocean water, and stared up at the sky. I didn't pray out loud, but I was doing my best to ask the universe to step in for Cat... to spare her so she could continue to help spare others.

Though the beauty of the morning sunrises should have inspired me and motivated my optimism, they became almost an annoyance. How can I be happy and see beauty while my friend is fighting for her life?

Several more days, and no change. Another Sunday and another vigilant prayer circle convened at church, listing the names of now 40 friends or family of our congregation battling Coronavirus. Then on Monday at 4:30am, before my alarm sounded, a text from Susan came.

ARE YOU GOING TO BE AT THE BEACH THIS MORNING? I CAN COME DOWN AND TALK TO YOU.

I hastily replied, YES. SEE YOU SHORTLY.

I hopped out of bed, left a note for Eddie, and grabbed my keys. It was still pitch black, and I left the house without grabbing my bag or wallet, and in my haste left my cell on the counter. I steadied myself as I drove, several times catching myself distracted, exceeding the speed limit, and veering off.

Calm down. She's probably just wanting some support. If the news was really bad, she would have called versus texted.

I spent the entire ride to the beach rationalizing various scenarios, while also talking directly to God. *Please, please don't take Cat. I beg you. Please help her.*

I pulled into the lot just before 5, and the street lights were still on. This was the earliest I arrived here since my new morning ritual, and the sun's rays were nowhere close to offering first light to the sky. The night dew still set thickly on the pier.

As I made my way to the bench where I last comforted Susan, I noticed how luminous the surroundings were. The full moon still pronounced itself brightly above, like God holding a flashlight from heaven to check in on me.

I tilted my head toward the sky to accept the offering, noticing that the moon above the beach looked very much like a glowing yellow balloon dangling from the beaconing north star hovering over the ocean to the east.

Though I was anxious for Susan's arrival, to steady myself I slowed down to take in the beauty of the surroundings. Large yellow corn spiders dangled from their webs between the pier and local flora, some swaying in the light breeze like kids on a swing set.

Bright purple Morning Glories bobbed up and down excited for the new day, gladly pestered by yellow moths and bumblebee intrusions. Beautiful orange Beach Plums aligned the length of the pier.

I sat on the bench and looked at my watch, the watch that every time I checked the time reminded me of my bond with Cat. Susan's text did not establish a meeting time, so it wasn't clear when she would arrive. No matter, I sat alone picturing Cat's smiling eyes and graceful presence.

I slowed my breathing and closed my eyes several times, almost in a semi-meditative state. I needed to stay calm, and whatever the news Susan would provide, I needed to be ready.

I nervously checked my watch again. 5:30. Still nothing. A few minutes later I heard footsteps of someone ascending the pier steps and making their way toward me. I turned to see an elderly man walking his dog.

Can't believe I forgot my damn cell phone! Had she texted me something about a change of plans? Should I go home and grab my phone, and risk not seeing her?

I rose from the bench and prepared to return home, and turned to see Susan making her way up the steps and onto the pier. I approached her mid-pier as I needed some sign, some read on her body language to prepare me for the impending news.

As I got close to her, it was clear why she came in person. This time she grabbed me and hugged me, then pulling away from me held my hands and smiled- "Cat is going to make it! Cat's awake!"

Before she could continue, I hugged her with greater strength than either of us was prepared for. All the worry and emotion I had suppressed in order to be strong for her in case the news was bad now burst out of me. I fell on my knees to the wooden planks of the pier, and buried my head in my hands.

"Just give me a minute. I'll be fine," I blubbered as I wiped my tears while Susan stood over me, lightly resting her hand on my head. She started laughing, which caused me to intercept my crying with laughter of pure relief and joy.

"Cat is going to be ok. I heard those words. You said Cat is going to make it!"

I looked up at her and by now the sun had begun to brighten everything around us, as if God orchestrated a crescendo of beautiful light while the news was shared. The sun illuminated the nearby wet and bright green sawgrass, as though encouraging it to join in the exuberance of the moment.

I stood and we began to walk each other toward the bench. But I wanted to be closer to the water, so I instead led her to the lifeguard stand where so many mornings Cat and I talked about our lives and our families over morning coffee during sunup.

"Do you mind if we sit here? This is Cat's favorite spot," I said as we hopped from the last step of the pier onto the sand, then a few more feet toward the ladder leading to the lifeguard platform.

"I know. She told me it was her favorite thing to do. Even preferred her talks with you over swimming."

This started me crying all over again.

"So the doctor called last night and said within the last 24 hours all her vitals improved. Her blood pressure, her temperature, and most importantly her breathing. Soon after, they pulled her off the ventilator. Around 4am this morning they called and said she was awake and asking questions. She's tired, but still they are amazed at the sudden turn."

As I listened I was energized by the news, but also felt exhausted by the combined emotional toll that Susan and I had experienced over the last several weeks. I felt like I just emerged from the water after a two-hour swim... depleted but exhilarated.

"Any sense of when she will be released?" I asked.

"Not sure, but they said if she continues to make progress it could be soon."

"I can't imagine how hard it's been not to be there with her. I mean, the thought that millions of Americans are going through the same thing right now with their loved ones is devastating. Thank God for her, and I'm so happy for you and Rosie."

She smiled, and sitting beside each other we leaned our heads together while looking out over the ocean. I couldn't imagine a better place in the world to hear such great news.

"I guess we should get back to social distancing now? Don't tell Cat. It will be our secret," Susan said.

"Please call me the minute she is home. And tell her when her strength returns, I expect she will be back out here for our morning swims. She's got a lot of distance to make up."

I stood and helped her down from the lifeguard platform, and she brushed herself off and began to head toward the pier. Before she got out of earshot, I yelled in her direction, "And tell her I said Makai!"

TAP

Sitting at the desk in his bedroom, Neil stared at the news on his laptop in a daze. March of 2020, and after only two months of SARS- which was now officially named the *Covid-19 Global Pandemic* by the World Health Organization- his reality was shifting.

The news was awash with strange occurrences and terms... *The Chinese Flu, Coronavirus lockdown, pivot to work-from-home status, social distancing and 6-foot spacing, Zoom meetings, mask requirements...*

Hospitals were staffing up as the U.S. hit 100,000 cases by mid-spring. President Trump and Chief Medical Advisor Fauci were sparring over what should be done. It was all starting to look increasingly bleak.

Neil rhythmically tapped his fingers on his lap, a nervous habit formed years ago he repeated a thousand times a day, unconsciously.

Jackie entered the room with the same pace as usual- fast, fleeting, like a ping pong ball. Flailing her arms about to empha-size her current crisis.

"Neil, my laptop keeps freezing up. Can we *please* get a new modem so I can do my work? The principal called a Zoom meeting for ten."

This snapped Neil out of a daydream, and he offered his usual response.

"Sure babe. Just a minute."

Rising from his chair, he paused to notice his mid-section. For the first time, the flesh around his belly hung slightly over the band of his pajamas. Six feet one, always around 190 pounds, 41-years old. Lean frame, high metabolism. Moderate exercise and a smart diet kept him in good shape. But the midnight shift at the grocery store was becoming less favorable for his overall health as he aged.

The gym he belonged to closed last week due to spikes in patron infection rates, and working nights meant lots of access to snacks at off hours. As he headed for the kitchen to reset the modem, he considered whether a decline in his health was normal for men his age.

"It's rebooted. I will go offline for a bit and you should be fine. I'll finish my orders after your meeting."

With that, Jackie continued her work and Neil headed back to his desk. Their modest ranch house in a suburb outside Chicago was always plenty for just the two of them. About 2,000 square feet including three bedrooms, two baths, a nice kitchen and breakfast nook, and a fenced yard with a patio for relaxing and grilling.

The second bedroom, which they commonly referred to as "the practice space," housed Neil's drums, and the third was all set for the new baby's arrival in August. They already knew it was a girl, and decided *Selena* would be the name of their first born.

Jacqueline Dewey and Neil Abrams met in college. For all intents and purposes, a storybook romance. She a cheerleader who coming out of high school had her sights set on competitive gymnastics, until an awkward tumble and blown out knee at States her senior year negated any chances of her competing in Division I gymnastics. Instead, she opted for a modest cheer scholarship to Eastern Illinois University.

Neil noticed Jackie immediately when reporting for summer marching band camp as a freshman at EIU. As the August heat and humidity caused his long mane of wavy, sandy blonde hair to drip with sweat on the practice field, he peered through his perspiration at the stunning brunette on the cheer squad.

Though he never seriously dated in high school, he took quick notice of her, and a few weeks into camp mustered the courage to approach her during one of the rehearsal breaks and ask her what she thought of the Panther Drumline. Best he could recall, the first interaction went something like this:

"Hey. I'm Neil. I'm, um, on the drumline...I assume you're dating the quarterback or something?"

"Nah, jocks are self-indulged egomaniacs. Are drummers just as bad?"

"Oh, we're worse actually, because we *know* we're talented and don't need to score touchdowns to prove it," Neil joked as he tapped his fingers nervously on his pants pockets, thumbs hooked into his belt loops a bit like a cowboy.

Jackie laughed and smiled at Neil and felt her heart skip a beat. His looks, his openly geeky demeanor, his sense of humor, his piercing blue eyes. It all added up for her in a way that each time she interacted with him she felt a gravitational pull toward wanting to be with him.

A few days later they had their first date, and several years after graduating from EIU in 2000, they were married in a beautiful little chapel in Long Grove, Illinois.

Jackie became a high school English teacher, taking a job about an hour outside Chicago near their house in Arlington Heights. Neil got his degree in Music Merchandising, but after graduating found there were limited positions in the industry as the Internet took over the market for music stores. Even the recording industry was adversely impacted by software programs musicians could download to produce their work versus booking time in traditional studios.

Eventually, Neil began working as assistant manager at several grocery stores while playing in a string of bands and doing gigs in the Chicago area. Though talented, he grew tired of the club scene and all that went with it. Packing his gear, unloading, setting up, playing to drunk patrons until 1am, then re-packing and re-loading, and not getting to bed until 3 or 4am. Only to draw shift work at the store and sometimes need to drag his tail in on several hours of sleep. In his 20s he could pull it off, but having eclipsed 40, it just wasn't appealing. It was nearly ten years since his last gig.

Neil's cell phone chimed his favorite ringtone- a clip from Rush's song *Spirit of the Radio*. Terry, his nice but somewhat overbearing boss, was calling.

"Hey Neil. How's it going?"

"Good, T. What's up?"

"So, bad news. Martha has Coronavirus and she's going to be out for a bit. Not sure how bad it is, but she tested positive and said she feels like a truck hit her. I'd like you to cover permanent days for a while versus the night shift. I need a manager who has their shit together and figured you could use the break anyway. Good?"

"Well dang, I was sort of getting used to the permanent graveyard shift and you guys throwing all those vampire jokes my way. 'Gool of Jewel,' and all that, right? Yeah man. Thanks. I'll take it. See you tomorrow."

As Neil headed to share the news with Jackie, he passed by his covered drum set looking abandoned as it had for many months in the practice space. He stood in the doorway and stared at it, calculating the last time he sat and played. *Easily been six months. Shit, closer to eight?* He shook his head discouragingly and yelled for Jackie.

"Good news, babe. Well, not for Martha, she's got the Vid- but I'm gonna pull regular days for a while."

Jackie was happy for Neil and said it would be nice to have a few free evenings to spend together, continue to plan for Selena's arrival, maybe even get back to some date nights.

It occurred to Neil that the day shift rotation at Jewel was prime. Four days on, then three off. 6am-4pm. He could get regular sleep and work around the house, or maybe even pick up his sticks again.

In the spirit of the good news, Neil felt a burst of energy that needed managing. With more time inside the house other than going to work due to Covid, his months-long drumming drought was pecking at has creative conscience of late.

"Babe, can you put your headphones on so I can practice a bit?"

"Practice? Your drums?"

"Yeah. I'll close the door and keep it at a reasonable level."

Neil exhaled and headed toward the room that housed his neglected six-piece Ludwig drum set; a space he had not entered in many months.

Neil's parents put him in drum lessons when he was eight, around the time they first noticed some persistent hyperactive tendencies in his behavior... his constantly fidgeting and tapping on tables and countertops. When they inquired about this behavior with Neil's pediatrician, the doctor said, "Just put some drumsticks in his hands. He'll be fine."

So whenever Neil's mom or dad noticed him anxious or hyperactive, they told him to go "drum it out," and Neil would hit the skins. In fact, he heard this instruction so many times as a kid, the phrase stuck with him.

From that point through high school, Neil stood out with drums and percussion. He took lessons, raced home to practice each day after school, and started his first garage band at 13. It was *what he did*, and it was his total identity.

There were jocks in his school known for putting a basketball in a hoop, hitting homeruns, and scoring touchdowns. Neil was known for his prowess at drumming. Although far less popular by comparison to athletes, Neil drew respect because he was good at the drums. Actually, he was *great* at it. Even the kids at his high school who didn't know his name knew him as, "that drummer kid."

As Jackie had been a phenomenal gymnast at her high school on the north side of Chicago, at his west side high school Neil was the man. He got multiple band scholarship offers for college- Northern Illinois, Southern, Eastern, and even the flagship University of Illinois. But a number of his high school buddies picked EIU, he liked the band director who promised him captain of the drumline by his sophomore year, and it would only be a three-hour drive to and from Charleston if he wanted to come home on weekends.

Before making his college choice, Neil did his homework on drumlines in the state. Besides the University of Illinois whose Big Ten band was over 350 players with a drumline of around 40, EIU was one of the best around. One of the best in the Midwest actually. Their line of 35 players regularly traveled to compete at regional and national drumline competitions, often outperforming lines of much bigger and more notable schools.

Neil heard that last year Eastern's drumline was runner-up to Michigan State at the Drum Corps International (DCI) competition held annually in Washington, D.C., so this motivated his choice of EIU for college.

Other than pledging Sigma Pi fraternity and spending all his time with Jackie, Neil's entire college experience was devoted to the drumline. By the time he graduated, his best friend and fraternity brother Tony was getting some looks from the NFL, which made Neil feel like kin to a celebrity.

While at EIU, Neil helped elevate their drumline to new levels. Word spread that Neil and a few other exceptional drummers were on their line, which resulted in even more talented percussionists from the Midwest and beyond enrolling there.

At one point their snare line was reputed to be one of the best in the country. Twelve snare drum players locked in and playing with amazing chops and speed, sounding like a single drum with cacophonous power. But it took many hours of sweat and toil to get to that level.

The drumline practiced for three hours a day before reporting for full marching band rehearsals, which were another two hours. As they strapped their drums on to get ready to rehearse, there was laughter and stories of who each player was shacking up with, what their plans for the weekend were, and which concerts they were buying tickets for. But when practice started, it was all business.

Thirty minutes of stretching and warm-up drills, followed by 30 minutes of rudiments at various speeds and volumes, all while marching in place. Neil participated, but periodically unleashed his drum so he and the other section leaders could freely walk the line and give feedback to the players. Detailed input on form, stick height, grip, and musical precision.

It all mattered, and to the judges who would be evaluating the line's performance at DCI at the conclusion of each football season, it was *all* that mattered.

The line worked to first be solid in its sound, then in its choreography, then on melding sound and choreography so the projection of sound and the imagery of the line's formations would bring both percussive elements and showmanship to each performance.

Creativity was also important, so they added non-traditional percussion instruments and sounds to their shows- one player dragged a garden rake against a steel oil drum, another dropped a sledgehammer on an iron plate, and several clanged railroad spikes together like metal claves.

At the conclusion of one of their performances, a cymbal player threw her cymbals to the ground in perfect time with the end of a verse, then pulled three baseballs from under her hat and threw them in perfect triplicate rhythm in succession against the top of a timpani to end the song.

The balls sprung off the timp like bottle rockets into the air, and the crowd went wild. They were the talk of the campus, and they delighted crowds every time they performed.

At each rehearsal, they worked to refine their skills, but also added new elements. They practiced for hours rain or shine incorporating and perfecting challenging stick twirls in perfect harmony, and flipping sticks and mallets between players on the line. They knew such complicated and flashy movements would please audiences and impress judges come competition time.

When the line got solid at matched grip, it switched to the more challenging traditional grip. Eventually they incorporated both styles on snare within a single performance. This too was abnormal for most drumlines.

Before every rehearsal they were each responsible for properly tuning their drums, so there was no variation in pitch on snares, and perfect variation in pitch on the tenors. Twelve snare drums sounding like one was the goal. A line of six bass drums tuned in perfect harmony from a 16" high treble to a massive 28" low bass, with the body type of each player mirroring their instrument.

Five quad drums were played by drummers with ripping chops, incredible speed and accuracy, and a line of eight cymbal players punctuated the end of phrases with a powerful splash, or stood in front of the snare players with their cymbals horizontal so the snare line could use them as hi-hats.

A pit of marimba, xylophones, and several timpani provided the musical elements on top of the rhythms of the battery players. Musicians of the highest skill and focus. A band within the band.

After serving as section leader of the snares his freshman year, Neil was promoted to captain of the line. He approached this responsibility seriously, most of the time taking on the role of a focused teacher and mentor to the other players, but when necessary as a drill sergeant.

If a drummer's stick height varied from the rest of the line, it meant that player stepping out of formation to go correct the abnormality, before returning to the line apologetically and getting it right.

The exact placement of striking the stick on the drumhead was also highly relevant, as it impacted pitch, volume, timbre and appearance. All such minutia was critical, and was something each drummer focused on both at rehearsals and while practicing on their own.

It was not uncommon that any given night after the marching band departed rehearsal, the drumline stayed even longer, fine-tuning any aspects of their playing or marching that needed perfecting.

Trumpet players, saxophonists, flutists, and the dance and cheer squads quickly left the practice field for other endeavors. The drumline stayed put, honing their art at the highest level.

As captain, Neil elevated expectations of the line to a level higher than ever before. Snare drummers would split parts of the song, picking up at the exact measure and beat where a fellow drummer stopped playing.

The line knew that at any point in rehearsal Neil may stop and turn to any player and ask them to start at a particular measure of a song that they had already learned, a little game Neil played to ensure each player completely locked every song into memory.

As tough as he could be on his fellow drummers, Neil ended most rehearsals with positive messages to the line- "Way to drum it out. Tomorrow let's be even better. Go home and pound those pillows."

Pounding pillows in drumline vernacular meant spending time each night practicing rudiments on a pillow to improve arm strength and speed. To Neil, for the line to be great every player must consistently be practicing, or at least be *thinking* about drumming.

To the freshman players on the line, he would say, "You are what you think about. So you plebes better constantly be thinking about drumming on this line, or I'm going to be on your asses all season."

And the line was as diverse as it was talented, with male and female drummers, White and Black and Brown, broadly representing the Midwest, but also states as far as California and several other countries.

Neil and the line of drummers morphed into an amoeba of awesome power, sound and artistry, and approached drumming with great alacrity and passion.

They mutually respected the craft of drumming and pushed each other to their individual and collective limits. There were band geeks, and then there was the drumline. They were the equivalent of band geeks on steroids- amazing control, ridiculous speed, and solid musicianship. *Grace under pressure.*

After winning the Midwest Regionals and taking third at Internationals his freshman year, then placing runner-up his sophomore year, they claimed the Drum Corps International title Neil's last two years at Eastern. At that point, it was well known by all college bands and drum & bugle corps that the EIU drumline was irrefutably the best line in the country.

For their final performance the year they defended their title, the line pulled off *La Villa Strangiato*, a highly complicated Rush standard that no drum corps, nor most highly rated drummers, would ever dream of attempting.

So by the time he graduated, Neil's drumming chops were at an all-time high. Four years in a top Division I drumline had maximized his skills.

After graduation and marriage and landing jobs, life took over. Neil played in several respectable cover bands around Chicago in the early 2000s. But around 2010 he stepped away from it so he could spend more time with Jackie, and begin to focus on having a child.

Neil closed the door to the practice space and pulled the bed sheet off his kit. The dust puffed into the air as he threw the sheet onto the floor, not unlike a collector uncovering a prized antique Corvette in his garage.

He bought the kit in high school with money he saved from bagging groceries on weekends. It was still in pristine shape, and as he sat on the throne his heartbeat elevated.

He kicked off his shoes and socks and grabbed a pair of 7A sticks from the stick bag hanging on his floor tom. His pulse quickened, and the feel and contour of wooden sticks in his hands woke his senses. He wacked each tom once to test their tones.

"Geeze Neil," he said aloud, disappointed at how badly out of tune the toms were. Some quick adjustments with the tuning key and they were back to the perfect tone he was used to. A tight crack on the snare, and a tonal and sonorous thump of each tom, along with a deep and muffled boom on the kick drum.

He plugged his headphones into his cell and cued up some random songs from Pandora's classic rock channel.

Neil was surprised at how rusty he was. Anyone entering the room watching him would have been impressed, but by his standards it was a mess. Sloppy timing. Poor dynamics. Weak power. Low mobility and hunched posture.

Ten minutes in and his forearms were already achy. He paused after just two songs and stood to stretch his legs, torso and arms. He sat back down, shook his head and tightened his ponytail. *I'm in worse shape than I thought*, he nearly said aloud.

He cued up a few more songs, but the humbling reality check on his current skill level compared to where he once was felt both frustrating and disappointing. Feeling like a runner who didn't log enough miles before a big race, after another 20 minutes of playing he set his sticks on his floor tom and turned off the light.

"Done already?" he heard Jackie call out as she heard him close the door.

"Gonna need some time. I guess not all things are like riding a bike," Neil replied as he headed back to his work, glancing down at the scar on his left palm that was partly the cause of his long respite from his last period of serious drumming 10 years ago.

The next day he returned home from work committed to lowering his expectations of his playing. *Give it time. Go back to the basics,* he told himself.

He made his way to his kit, but was again frustrated with his mastery of the basic strokes. He reached for one of his regiment books, *Haskell Harr's 26 Rudiments*. As he had done a thousand times before, he started with each rudiment and worked it over and over.

Flams, flam taps, ruffs, 5 and 7 and 9 stroke rolls. Drags, paradiddles and double paradiddles. Ratamacues. Long stroke rolls. His brain brought his focus back to the countless hours of practice that started when he was a child, intensified in high school, and became as rote as walking by the time he was in college.

Over and over. First slow, then faster. First quiet, then a gradual crescendo. Accents alternating on various strokes. Focus on his grip, his forearm position, his fulcrum around the sticks, and stick height. Alternating left and right starts and stops, then alternating from snare drum to toms, then adding in kick and hi-hat. A million combinations, a million possibilities. An endless forest.

Neil learned early on that drumming is about precision. It's about filling time and intersecting space with sound, or the accurate absence of sound. It's about opening the creative portal of one's heart and soul and using the brain and muscles to collectively dictate a range of reverberations. Best yet, to produce sounds that evoke feelings and emotions in listeners and get people's bodies in motion.

Most serious musicians agree the drummer is the quarterback of the band. It's the beat of any song that people dance to, setting pace and feel. Those who study music learn early on of the genesis of percussive instruments. Since prehistoric times, drums evolved as the most primitive form of communication, and helped prepare men to hunt, to march into battle, or to dance in celebration.

As Neil paused again to stretch his arms and wrists, he thought back to a conversation with his college buddy Tony. When Neil wasn't practicing with the drumline and Tony wasn't on the football field, they were hanging out together.

After EIU solidly pounded Eastern Kentucky just before Thanksgiving their freshman year, the crew met back at the Sig Pi house after the game to celebrate and congratulate Tony on his dominance.

"Dang, Tony. You tore it up today. Eastern Kentucky never saw you coming."

"Thanks bro. How was the halftime show? I was in the locker room getting my ribs taped up after that sack I took in the second quarter."

"All good. We ripped it as usual and the crowd went wild. You know, we have more in common than just being frat brothers. I mean, you're the quarterback of ten other guys. But the drumline has three times as many players to keep in line. So technically my job is harder than yours!"

Tony laughed, his boyish dimples deepening as he replied, "Sure, but those guys aren't having to keep other guys from ripping your head off, drummer boy."

Neil got back to his exercises until Jackie opened the door and worked into Neil's line of sight to get his attention.

"Burst of energy, sweetie? You've been drumming it out nearly three hours."

"Dang. Sorry. Yeah, just working out the kinks. They say both good and bad habits are hard to break, so I'm trying to get back into it. My chops are for shit compared to where they were. How about I come help you with dinner?"

As usual after playing drums, Neil's hands were pulsating and clammy to the touch. As he switched off the light he reached for Jackie's hand and put his other hand on her protruding and now very pregnant stomach. Within the next 5 months they would have a daughter, something they had been praying for since their wedding.

Several weeks into the new day shift, Neil bumped into Terry as they were getting ready to open the store.

"Hey Terry. Thanks again for moving me to days. How is Martha doing?"

"She resigned. Her symptoms are mild now but she wants to find work from home after she recovers. From what I read, a lot of people across the country are doing the same. Keep things in order here during the days, Neil, and if it works out we will see about your options. She leaves me with an associate manager position to fill."

"Got it. You bet. But listen, about the mask requirements for customers. This wasn't a problem on the night shift because almost no one came in, and we weren't really enforcing it. But the memo you gave me from corporate seems to indicate we have new rules. Can we talk about all this?"

"Yes. That's the topic for tomorrow morning's staff meeting. Be here an hour earlier, 5am, and all the managers and supervisors will be in the break room and we will clarify everything. I'll cover breakfast."

Terry walked away as this last statement trailed off. A bald character of round proportion who, with a pencil behind his ear and usually holding a clipboard, looked very much the part of a grocery store manager.

"It's a grocery store, Terry. There's food everywhere!" Neil yelled down aisle 11 in Terry's direction, while twirling his pen between his fingers as he did whenever his hand clutched any implement that resembled a drumstick.

The next morning Neil rose early to get to the store on time. The prospect of being named associate manager on permanent days was very appealing. A higher salary, improved benefits, new responsibilities, the ability to hire and train new staff, and most importantly- no night shift.

The associate manager even got an additional 20% off on groceries. This gave him a pep in his step he hadn't felt in years. Coupled with a renewed commitment to using his evenings for practicing drums and looking forward to having a daughter, by all accounts other than the pandemic, Neil was riding high.

Increasingly, the morning traffic was lighter and lighter as more and more people stopped going in to work. Neil furrowed his brows as he noticed several cars on the road with bumper stickers with the Covid symbol that, ironically, read, *Stay Home!*

Still dark as he hopped out of his Chevy pickup at the store, Neil held a black hair tie in his teeth as he reach around his head to tie his blonde mane into its usual ponytail. Along with the other shift supervisors and store managers, he made his way into the employee entrance around back. He grabbed a mask from the box outside the break room where the meeting was about to start.

As Neil plopped a K-cup into the Keurig, he noticed a newly formed blister under the forefinger of his right hand. He smiled and pumped on it with his thumb like squeezing a marshmallow, knowing that the sign of blisters meant the forming of new calluses, which meant toughening the skin on the hands and enabling longer durations of playing.

The calluses would come and go, but the scar was a daily reminder of how delicate a drummer's appendages are. He flashed back to the day at the store ten years ago when he carelessly cut his palm with a box cutter while opening some boxes and stocking shelves, an accident that knocked him out of drumming and began his long hiatus from his beloved art form for far too long.

He grabbed his coffee, snagged a banana and a blueberry muffin off the side table, and took his seat with the others. Claire, a fellow supervisor who sometimes spent time socially with him and Jackie, leaned over to Neil.

"Turning over a new leaf, huh Gool?"

Neil smiled and whispered back, "Yeah. I haven't slept with Jackie this many nights in a row since breaking the dorm rules at Eastern. I sort of like it."

Terry started the meeting with his usual rushed and officious approach. As always, his goal was to meet, communicate the issues, and get the staff back onto the floor to prep for opening. A few staff chuckled as Terry pulled down his mask in order to speak.

"Alright, settle down you maniacs. Listen, we have to start taking this pandemic seriously. WHO says there are now over one million cases globally, so corporate is serious about this Covid stuff. There will be bottles of hand sanitizer at all check-out stations, and multiple sanitizer dispenser stands at the front entrance for patrons. When the clerks are not at registers, they must wipe down all the carts with disinfectant. All staff are required to wear masks at all times when in the store. Absolutely no exceptions, starting today. Patrons must also wear face coverings or masks upon entry. We will have boxes of masks at the front doors and at the service counter for anyone who needs one. Masks must be worn above the nose and cover the mouth."

As Terry made this last statement, he raised his eyebrows and pulled his mask back above his nose which evoked chuckles from the staff.

Neil tapped his fingers on the documents from corporate that lay before him, rhythmically adding some momentum to the meeting as it all started to feel so heavy. Terry continued...

"In front of you are the new protocols. It includes recommendations for your healthcare and protection with the pandemic. Go to the Jewel website for more details. You will all need to be tested and provide me a copy of your results. If you test positive, you will have to go into isolation protocols and then test negative again before returning to work. If you feel any related symptoms, or if you are exposed to anyone who is known to be Covid-positive, you must leave the store and go into quarantine protocols and give me the results of a negative test before you are cleared to return. There are no exceptions."

Neil was already feeling annoyed with his mask, pulling at it to keep it from stifling his breathing.

"What about when we're on breaks?" Claire asked.

"The break room is part of the store, so masks in here as well. If you take a break in your car, which of course I would recommend, you can take it off. But, if you're in your car and a customer approaches you with a question, it goes back on."

Terry rolled his eyes as he spoke, but it was also obvious he was serious about compliance. He pulled at his mask similar to Neil and started walking toward the door signaling the meeting was over, then turning back toward the staff said, "People, I'm sure this thing will pass in a few weeks, but for now let's just make the best of it and follow the rules."

Claire stood then gave a playful tug on Neil's ponytail, and whispered, "Between that mask and your hair, you're going to be the prettiest staff we got."

As others left the room, they joked with each other about how to properly wear their masks. But for the most part, it appeared they were on board. By this point in the pandemic, most businesses in Illinois were following suit; so the employees of greater Chicagoland Jewel store number 23 didn't feel singled out.

Two days later, Neil began to feel the impact of the new rules on Jewel's faithful patrons as he approached an elderly gentleman who entered without a mask.

"Excuse me sir, as the sign reads we're under a mask mandate at this time." Though he made the best effort to sound upbeat, Neil was surprised at the hostility of the response.

"Listen you fucking hippy, I know my rights under the law. And you can't require me to wear anything to shop in your little fucking grocery store. I don't have Covid, so leave me alone."

Neil's head drew back a bit and he pulled on his mask to give his mouth a little air before he replied.

"Sir, this isn't my rule. It's a rule in compliance with operating a public food service business in the State of Illinois at this time. It's the same rule you will find at any grocery store, so..."

The man stopped walking and turned and got in Neil's face, interrupting-

"Call the cops if you want me out, you fucking Nazi. Then I'll wear your mask. On second thought, I'm not giving you my business. I'll order my fucking groceries online and all these little local stores will crumble. Happy?!"

As the hostile man shouted, he stormed out of the store. Other patrons who had stopped to view the exchange returned to their shopping, and Neil shook his head and watched as the man briskly exited while still muttering to himself and flailing his arms.

"Jesus. What a prick. Nazi? I should have let him know I'm Jewish," Neil said under his breath.

Neil headed to the break room to cool off over a mid-morning coffee. As he sat drinking and reflecting on his exchange with the nefarious customer, his fingers tapped on his cup.

Fact is, Neil incessantly and unconsciously tapped his fingers most of the day- an involuntary behavior that plagued him and probably countless other musicians. The connection between the brain and previous rhythms buried in the recesses of the mind, which without prompting are called back to the surface during times of stress or even just when the body is otherwise at rest. Or whenever a good tune is playing over the store's sound system. A strange and cathartic signal sent out like morse code from a ship in distress. Even when no music was audible, Neil's brain interrupted his focus with random patterns connected to some previous score.

Several weeks passed, and while Neil continued his new job content with normal working hours, the rigors of doing the work during a global pandemic created more stress than when he pulled night shifts.

Staff were on edge, and customers were on a *razor's* edge. The economy was shifting, people were being pushed out of their offices and forced to work from home, and everyone had to adapt to learning new technologies such as Zoom to stay connected to their jobs.

Customers frequently stopped each other and spoke through their masks about knowing others who were getting infected, some describing how packed the hospitals had become, and several mentioning sick loved ones.

Neil noticed a strange divide occurring where the pandemic was increasingly becoming politicized. The left side pushing for greater restrictions to enable a higher level of healthcare protection, and the right side arguing that the politicians weren't doing enough to find a cure for Covid and that the government was intruding on individual rights by requiring tests and masks.

Liberals in favor of vaccinations and boosters, and conservatives dead set against them, while all parties demanded a quick end to what was feeling like a new normal. The Internet was even awash with conspiracy theories espousing that the pandemic was manufactured by the government.

As Neil tried to manage the stress of it all, drumming became his primary outlet. He channeled a heightened focus into getting his playing back to form. But it was slow in coming.

His age and the distance between his last period of regular playing and now had robbed him of the muscle memory needed to play at a level he deemed acceptable. Nonetheless, he found himself drumming it out in his practice space almost every day after work, and for several hours on his days off.

Along the way, he discovered his new best friend- YouTube.

When Neil was last in a gigging band, whenever they decided to add new songs he had to listen to the song on a CD or download it from Napster. But in 2020, Neil could YouTube any song he wanted to learn, and ten drummers would appear on video showing exactly how to play the song.

This made learning and practicing new music incredibly easy. It showed the proper pace, sticking, dynamics, accents and fills, as well as multiple variations of each tune. And because repetition is a drummer's best friend, he could play any song over and over until the brain and body adopted the motions as permanent- what drummers refer to as *locking in*. Having been a drummer his whole life, Neil knew of the joy of locking songs in. He knew this was when drumming became fun.

During one of his practice sessions, Neil glanced into his stick bag and saw his old marching sticks. Massive Lincoln Logs compared to the sticks he was now using to play his kit- 2B, solid hickory, 17" with large oval beads and short tapers to improve strength and durability.

He pulled them out and broke into some of the snare cadences the EIU line played as the band marched into starting formation for games.

As he took a break from playing to grab a snack from the kitchen, his brain took him back to some of the fondest memories of his college days. The parties after the games, how much the fans loved the halftime shows, and especially the showcase performances by the renowned drumline, and the power he felt as captain.

As was the case when he was section leader his freshman year, once he became captain his job was to make sure all drummers on the line showed up on time and knew their parts. If the line got sloppy in their playing, he tore into them. And for the neophyte drummers on the line, hazing rituals to indoctrinate them into the proper frame of mind to earn the right to play with the best drummers in the country were commonly used.

Neil recalled standing over the freshman drummers who failed to memorize their parts, barking orders and making them do pushups on their knuckles while grasping their sticks. As the pushups were performed, Neil always yelled out the same thing- "An actor doesn't dare take the stage without knowing his lines. On my line you will NOT fail to memorize your parts and embarrass this line, or you will do pushups until you puke!"

He recalled the time he made the entire cymbal line hold out their cymbals at a 90 degree angle, arms straight out parallel to the ground, for five minutes straight because one of their players dropped his cymbal during a performance.

Neil returned to his kit and played intensely for several hours non-stop, with great focus and precision. Song by song, his body temp increased and his clothing dripped with sweat. Around mid-afternoon, after several more hours of high-energy playing, he connected with his kit at a level he had not experienced in many years.

He felt an out-of-body experience and borderline euphoria that only a few people on any sort of natural high get to experience. Long-distance runners have described it as being at the point in a race when their breathing takes a relaxed pattern and running becomes effortless, and when the runner looks down and sees their sneakers kicking out in front of their body but their legs and feet somehow seem detached. Almost like watching oneself on TV.

The same happens for drummers. At least for some, if they're lucky. When the body and brain are in total harmony with the craft, the drummer views their own performance as somehow disconnected from it. The brain shuts off and the body takes over. Arms and hands and feet effortlessly act in perfect synch but feel independent of their owner. When the artist gets to truly enjoy the ride at a surreal level.

Neil took another break and placed his hand on his wrist to feel the pace of his heartbeat. On the Eastern line, he taught the other drummers that the average human heartbeat is the same as room temperature- 72 beats per minute.

For fun, Neil would bring a metronome out to the practice field, set it at 72 clicks per minute, then each player would have to call out a song that was played at 72bpm and the line would play the song along with the nome. Neil's favorite two were Bohemian Rhapsody by Queen and Dream On by Aerosmith.

Having totally lost sense of time, after an eight-hour session Neil looked through the window to see Jackie's car pulling in.

When they sat down for dinner that night, Neil decided to raise an idea to her. An idea that as his drumming was coming back into form was less an idea and more of an inevitability.

Several times as he prepared to start the conversation, he noticed his incessant tapping on the table, and worried he might reveal his anxiety about broaching the topic with her. Then again, she had long ago blocked out his tapping habit. Like someone living near train tracks, the sound became unnoticeable to her over time. Other than when sleeping, Neil's body and brain were always in the mode of drumming.

"How was your day, babe?" He eased in.

"Not bad. But the kids refuse to keep their masks on. The parents are complaining, and the staff are stressed. I gotta tell you, we couldn't have picked a better time to have a baby. I cannot *wait* for maternity leave. I think you had the day off. What did you do? Let me guess, *practice*?"

Jackie smiled as she plopped a second scoop of Hamburger Helper onto her plate, unapologetic now that she was eating for two.

"Yeah, with all the work stress I have been hitting the skins more than ever. I have to say, I think even at my age I'm hitting my stride. I'm just more disciplined about what I'm doing. And the Internet makes it easy to try new exercises and play different stuff. I even played along to a clip from Buddy Rich from like 1950 today. It's fun again."

"That's good, sweety. I'll just pretend to know who the heck Bobby Rich is," she smiled as she ate. Then she continued, "Don't forget you promised to get an electric practice kit for quiet rehearsing once the baby comes. If you land that new associate manager salary, you have my permission to jump on Amazon."

"Yep. No doubt. *Buddy* Rich," Neil laughed and reached for his glass of wine as he prepared to pitch his idea to Jackie. Before becoming pregnant he could have plied her with a few glasses of wine to coax her support on just about anything. But in a sober state, he was a bit worried about her reaction.

"Listen, I was looking on craigslist and there are a few good bands out there looking for drummers. With my new hours, I'm thinking maybe it's time to see about getting back in the saddle."

Jackie, always supportive of Neil's playing, reached for her glass of water and took a sip before responding.

"What are we talking about though, like regular practices and gigs or just something for fun? I mean, of course when the baby comes you might not have as much time for that sort of thing. But for now I'm not opposed; I know you love it. I knew a long time ago I married someone with drumming in his DNA."

She smiled adoringly at Neil given in her heart of hearts, she always loved being married to a drummer. It was who she fell in love with, and what for years kept her highly attracted to him- his drive, his talent, his tenacity.

Neil was happily surprised at the response, but also felt inclined to clarify his position. He already knew if he landed some-thing with potential, he would be all in.

"Well, nice thing is that we both have family in the area, so even if I end up with weekly rehearsals and do some selective gigs we have coverage. I mean, I'm not trying to quit my day job of course. I just think I have some good playing years left in me, and lately I'm feeling gripped by it again."

"You know how much I always love watching you play. Those smoky bars and those girls gushing at you until I got in their face and told them you're spoken for. You know, I sort of miss those days too. Sure, do your thing. Just keep me posted on where it goes. But any extra gig cash must land in her college savings account."

Jackie smiled seeing how happy Neil appeared with her sup-port, then put her hand on Neil's and leaned over and kissed his cheek. She turned over his hand after feeling the rough calluses.

"Geeze. You *have* been chopping wood, rockstar. Any issues with the scar?"

"Not at all. As the doc said years ago, another quarter inch deeper and the tendon could have been severed and it would have been lights out for drumming. But it's been fine."

Neil did the dishes and agreed to watch Netflix with Jackie. He was conscious to make sure he was being as attentive to her as he was to drumming. Though, as was usually the case, while they watched TV he rapped his hands and fingers on a couch pillow. His mind was only half on the show. Most of his brain was now squarely focused on finding a good band.

Later that night after Jackie crashed and after scanning the Musicians Community on craigslist, Neil perused a range of openings for drummers. He texted three bands who placed ads. One, an Indie band looking for a player wanting to create and play originals. Then a cover band from Skokie looking to rehearse three nights a week and gig most weekends. The last band looked enticing: "Seeking a rock drummer with drive and a solid pocket. Must send a video of your playing ability."

Within days, the first two replied they were not interested. For the third, Neil considered sending old footage from his previous band. But those camcorder videos were now over 10 years old with weak video and audio quality by today's standards. He coaxed Jackie into using her cell phone to capture him playing a few songs in the practice space. Not professional quality, but good enough to give them a sense of his skill level.

He sent the video to the link, and waited. Several days passed, and still no word. Then that weekend the reply came—"Sorry. You're not what we're looking for."

Neil considered himself the sort of person who worked hard for everything he achieved. Modest upbringing, music scholarship for college, and significant equity in his solid marriage to Jackie. But rejection was not something he was accustomed to, especially not related to drumming.

That night, Neil fell into a deep sleep and found himself standing in a dark cemetery. He knew he was dreaming, but the dream felt very real.

An obscure figure approached him from behind, and at first Neil was afraid. But as the ghostly specter approached, Neil felt drawn toward the spirit feeling confident it presented him no harm.

The apparition got very close to Neil, motioned toward the tall, grey tombstones protruding from the mist, and began to speak.

"This is the goal."

Neil was confused by the statement, and replied, "The goal is death?"

The figure waved his hand back and forth, and said, "No. The goal is reminding yourself that this is where you will end up. That your mortality is inevitable, therefore time is fleeting."

Neil did not reply, and after a few moments the figure spoke again.

"The only way for your legacy to be known, is if the shadow you see on the lighted stage is your own."

With that, the spirit floated into the smoky mist and disappeared.

After waking, Neil had a vivid memory of every aspect of the dream, and began to try to make sense of its meaning. Was it a warning about his health, about some impending horrible acci-dent, or was the dream a reminder that he needed to make the most of his life while he could? He couldn't help but associate the message in the dream to his fervent pursuit of a drumming career.

As Neil dressed that morning, the dream reminded him of a line from a poem he read in college by Henry David Thoreau- "The mass of men lead lives of quiet desperation."

All day long while at work the dream plagued Neil, and he reflected on what the spirit was telling him... *Be passion-ate about your life. The journey is beautiful but ephemeral, so extend yourself beyond the boundaries of common men. Reach for the unreachable.*

Neil came home from work and practiced with a greater zeal than before. Whether from the feeling of dejection from the bands he tried to join, or as a result of the dream, he felt com-pelled toward a vision quest unlike anything he ever pursued.

He pulled out old set lists from his previous bands and cre-ated a Spotify list of songs and played them one after the other. First note for note, then with his creative spin. Stick twirls, compli-cated tom fills, ghost notes, replacing 8th notes with 16th notes, and adding triplets in places where typically there were none.

His heart rate elevated as he settled in and successfully played one song after another. Though not certain he would find it, he chased the drummer's high he felt several days ago and which he knew would sometimes return if he got back to playing full gigs.

Thumbing through YouTube, he stumbled onto a John Bonham tutorial and devoted a solid 2 hours to replicating Bonham's signature style and triplet grooves.

He retrieved from the closet where his equipment was stored his double kick pedal, which was essential for properly playing many of the more challenging rock songs. This alone required many days of practice to wake the muscle memory between both legs and feet in order to cleanly play certain songs. But in no time, he was blending double kick rhythms in perfect timing under complicated percussive patterns and cross-sticking.

Day after day, he attacked his practice sessions with incredible discipline, honing on any conceivable weakness in his craft. The first hour strictly going through the 26 rudiments on snare. First each one matched grip, then traditional grip. First slow, then faster. First *pianissimo*, then *mezzo piano*, then *mezzo forte*, to *forte* and sometimes *fortissimo*... delicate to moderate to explosive. Intentionally fine-tuning all the dynamics a professional drummer would need to play any song.

He bounced from genre to genre, devoting an hour to swing rhythms, then an hour to jazz or R&B, then an hour to ska and punk, then an hour to reggae, and always a final hour to standard rock. Pandora and Spotify channels made it easy to randomly cue up music from any genre, and to go back and replay the more difficult arrangements as he learned them.

He focused on Gerritsen's Four Ps of Drumming- Posture, Pace, Precision and Power, and began to note how long he could play consecutive songs without needing a break.

His stamina got better and better. Where weeks ago he tired after 20 minutes, then 40, eventually he played 90 minutes without needing a break. By even professional drumming standards, most drummers never play more than 90 minutes without an intermission or the band playing something acoustic to give the drummer time to hydrate and stretch.

Neil recalled from his previous bands how important it was to focus on his cardio training so that he wouldn't get winded or cramp while playing. He also recalled keeping pickle juice in his gear bag for the times he needed to chug it to relieve cramps that emerged in the middle of outdoor summer gigs when his body temperature soared.

As his rehearsals advanced, Neil took things to a different level, a level compared to many pro drummers. On his days off when he had longer durations to rehearse on his own, he would play for an hour, then hop on the treadmill in the garage and jog for 20 minutes to elevate his heart rate, then jump back onto the kit for another 30 minutes, and back to the treadmill. Once a week he rearranged the drum set so he would be forced to lead with his non-dominant hand, essentially playing the kit backward.

Carter Beauford from DMB, Yonrico Scott with Derek Trucks, Travis Barker with Blink, and Taylor Hawkins with Foo Fighters. All the best drummers were ambidextrous, able to play open-handed with the left hand leading on the hi-hat, or vice versa. Both hands equally strong. No discernable weakness in their playing ability. Neil pined for the same.

He again opened the ads placed on craigslist for drummers. This time he noticed an ad that read, "Established professional classic rock cover band looking for in-the-pocket drummer. No drugs and no drama. Just come ready to have fun and play some good gigs. Contact The Kickin' Aces for details."

Neil's heart pumped, as he was well aware of the reputation and quality of The Kickin' Aces, one of Chicagoland's best bands out of Schaumburg. They had been playing some of the bigger bars and clubs in the suburbs and downtown before Covid hit.

He contacted The Aces, and they sent him a partial set list of fifteen songs and asked him to come to the audition that week-end ready to play five. By the time Neil received the list it was 10pm, way too late for him to practice while Jackie slept.

Neil made his way to the couch and downloaded all 15 songs. Sitting on the sofa, he placed two larger seat back pillows on the coffee table as toms, two smaller pillows above them as crash cymbals, and used his thighs as the ride and snare.

He was somewhat familiar with all 15 songs, well known covers from classic rock bands from the 70s, 80s and 90s. Around half of the songs on the list he played in previous bands, though it had been years since he worked through them.

With his headphones in and trying to be delicate with his power, he played each of the fifteen on the makeshift sofa drum kit, then played them again, then played them again. His thighs stung a bit from the persistent strokes, but he was like a kid in a candy shop.

After spinning the list for the 5th or 6th time, Neil looked up to see that the clock showed 2:15am. He was tempted to go a few more rounds, but instead elected to sleep so he could get through the workday fresh and come home and play them on his regular set.

"Sweetie, I'm leaving. See you tonight after work." Jackie's words permeated Neil's sleep and he woke the next morning to her face nearing his and received her customary kiss goodbye.

Neil rubbed his eyes. "Hey. Yeah, have a good day. I'm heading out shortly myself."

Before his feet hit the carpet, his brain began downloading last night's data. Each song he was learning, each rhythm, each pattern. He looked at his alarm clock and knew in order to make it to work on time he would need to be out the door in 25 minutes.

Not unlike a student who gets out of bed on the day of a big exam and contemplates whether an excuse can get him off the hook, Neil suddenly was terrified at the thought of going to work-paralyzed by the prospect of waiting another nine hours before he could come home and rehearse. He threw his feet onto the floor, tapped his kneecaps a few times to gather his thoughts, and grabbed his phone from the nightstand.

Without capitulation, the decision was made and his hands were scripting the text to Terry that would within seconds be sent. After all, Neil was the guy who rarely took vacation, always showed up on time, and never called in sick. So he had plenty of equity with Terry to spend on one day of hooky.

HEY T. DON'T WORRY, I DON'T HAVE COVID. BUT I ATE SOMETHING LAST NIGHT THAT DIDN'T AGREE WITH ME. GONNA TAKE A SICK DAY AND BE BACK TOMORROW. THANKS.

As he clicked SEND, Neil felt exhilarated. *A whole day to rehearse!* No work. No nasty customers. No haggling over mask requirements or listening to everyone bemoaning Covid stuff.

He splashed water on his face, grabbed a cup of coffee, and scooped his sticks off the couch to head to the kit.

Each run-through of the fifteen songs that The Aces sent him took about 45 minutes to play. The audition wasn't until the weekend, so there really was no hurry. But he ran through them one after the other for several hours, stopping briefly to throw a sandwich together, then continued to play them all day.

He especially focused on the same genre as the band he was auditioning for, playing songs from Boston, Journey, Styx and Reo Speedwagon. Though he was holed up on the kit since early morning, he couldn't believe where the day went. Compared to where he was when he pulled the dust cover off his set weeks ago, he was satisfied with his progress. He couldn't wait for Saturday.

Neil arrived at the address provided for the audition and, as usual, he had modest expectations for both the space and the quality of the musicians. This was always the best way to approach an audition versus getting his hopes up. He donned stone washed jeans, a black tee shirt and flip flops, and his hair already tied back.

The property was a large lot with a white farm style fence in front, a nice ranch house toward the road, and what appeared to be a large, red, enclosed pole barn setting at the back of the property. Ten minutes earlier than his scheduled audition, the guys greeted him at the door.

"Hey. I'm Neil Abrams. Nice to meet you."

The first guy, clean cut wearing jeans and an Umphrey's McGee tee shirt, extended his hand and ushered Neil into the cavernous space.

"Hey Neil. Glad you could make it. I'm Kip, and that's Trevor who plays bass, Lee on guitar, and Mark, keys. I play rhythm and sing."

Neil didn't let on that he already knew their names having looked them up online.

"Got it. Great to meet you guys. Wow, nice practice space." Neil's eyes spanned the cavernous barn-like structure, and he was taken by the size and amenities.

"Yeah, well we've worked on it over the years; it's padded pretty well and we're not too close to the neighbors. We're in a good neighborhood so we feel ok leaving our stuff here and not worrying about it walking away. We rent it from the guy who lives out front."

The space had high wooden ceilings, two large circulating fans above, and several external A/C vents that were blowing in cool air from an external source. The walls were decorated with posters of various bands, and in the corner were several couches, a few end tables, a long picnic table, and a refrigerator and sink. A flat screen TV hung on the wall, above a very modern stereo.

Neil's previous band practice spaces mainly consisted of dingy, unfinished suburban basements, damp and dank; or musty and humid garages smelling of sweat and gasoline. By any standard, this space was superior.

Neil glanced over at the silver Tama drum set with a range of Zildjian cymbals and fully mic'd on a large stage adorned with a backdrop of colorful tapestries, including The Kickin' Aces logo on a banner, and oriental rugs on the floor; plenty of PA speakers and monitors, and a bank of modern stage lights, rounded out the well-equipped playing area.

Seeing Neil examining the kit, Kip said, "Oh, right. Most importantly we have our own drums so our drummers never need to bring their stuff back and forth. They just show up with their sticks."

"Nice. Drummers plural? Do you have more than one?" Neil was surprised and curious about this statement.

"Ah, no. But because we play out frequently and sometimes play as many as forty-five songs in a night, we have gone through drummers every few years. You know, rigors of playing long sets of rock music. So we do have a few on standby who can always sit in if our regular guy needs a break. Our last drummer just moved to Ontario for work, so here we are."

As Neil made his way behind the kit, he heard a toilet flush and a short, dark-skinned guy made his way out of the bathroom. Neil waved and the man shouted over, "Yo. I'm Jeremy. Band manager. Good luck, bro." Neil sat as the guy continued toward the corner of the barn and started fiddling with the soundboard.

Then Jeremy yelled over, "Hope you don't mind we are recording each audition in case we need to go back and listen. No pressure though." With this statement, Jeremy smiled in Neil's direction and gave a thumbs up.

Kip slung his guitar over his shoulder and the rest of the guys took their positions. They looked over at Neil curiously as he kicked off his flip-flops.

"You play barefoot?" Trevor asked.

Neil took for granted that new players might not be accustomed to such a habit, so he explained, "Uh, yeah. Ever since college I only play barefoot. It helps enhance my feel and connection with the kit. Hope that's ok."

Kip snickered and looked at the others, then turned to Neil and said, "If you're a solid drummer, you can play naked for all we care."

The others smiled as Neil proceeded to make a few minor adjustments to the set, then Kip said, "Ok. Just call out any five from the ones we sent you and let's see how it goes."

While the true caliber of their play was unknown to Neil before they started, he already felt at ease with the players and the space. He knew that finding the right band was as much about personality as it was about talent. As he got set to start, he was happily surprised he wasn't more nervous.

"Roundabout." Neil called out the first song.

Kip turned toward Neil with a surprised look given Neil had just called out one of the more complicated songs from the list, a well-known classic from Yes. Trevor and Lee smirked at each other as Kip reached for his acoustic guitar instead of his electric. Neil clicked them in to start, lightly tapping his sticks in perfect meter to the song's subtle beginning.

As the song progressed, Neil brought his focus back to where it was when he played at Eastern and the various bands he gigged with after. Emphasis on pace and dynamics, providing a tight pocket with the bass player, and establishing a launch pad for the guitarists and vocals. Clean playing, with good chops but not overfly flashy. Just solid from start to finish.

After Roundabout ended, The Aces smiled and turned to Neil, each complimenting him on his playing.

"Thanks. Sounded good," Neil modestly replied.

"Dang, that was tight already. What's next?" Trevor asked enthusiastically.

"Do you have another person coming after me to audition, if I could ask?" Neil said.

Kip replied, "We had one person earlier, but you're it for today."

"Well depending on how much time you have, I can do any on the list."

Lee looked somewhat aghast at the others, then approached Neil.

"You learned all fifteen? For an audition? Are they all as tight as that one?"

Neil didn't want to appear arrogant, so he was a bit guarded with his reply.

"I had some extra time this week, and I've played a few of these before. So really, whatever you want to try I'm ready for."

Kip tilted his head and raised his eyebrows, then turned to the group on stage- "Ok. Let's just start at the top and see how far we get. Next one after Roundabout is REO, Keep the Fire Burning. Click us in, Neil."

Like clockwork, Neil and The Aces made it through all fifteen songs as though they had been rehearsing for years. A few tempo hitches between the players and Neil as they adjusted to each other's nuanced styles, and a few issues with outros, but otherwise by most accounts the set could have been performed live with great reception.

The guys shook their heads positively as they put their equipment up.

"Very solid, Neil. Can you sing back-up?" Kip asked.

"Sure, within reason depending on the song."

"So listen, go grab a beer out of the fridge and give us a minute to huddle. You sounded really good, but we just want to compare notes a bit before you leave." Kip rested his guitar against his amp, then took a seat with the others on the front of the stage.

As he made his way to the lounge area of the space, Neil knew it went well. Frankly, he knew he was at or above the skill level of the entire band. He wasn't cocky about his performance, he just did what he always did as it related to drumming. He prepared. He respected his art and had his shit together. Unless Stewart Copeland was the person who auditioned earlier in the day, he was confident he would be their choice.

As he passed the soundboard, Jeremy gave Neil a fist-bump and whispered, "Way to rip it, dude."

Like a jury who only needed a few minutes to deliberate, he didn't take the second sip of his beer before Kip called him back to the playing area where The Aces already concluded their huddle.

"Listen, we think you could be just what we're looking for. Your chops are tight, your tempos are solid, you drive with a sense of dynamics, and if you can sing back-up on a few songs it's an added plus. We would love to do some more rehearsals and, depending on this Covid thing, get you out on a few gigs with us to see if there is a match. What do you think?"

Kip tried to be honest while containing his enthusiasm for their new prospect. Truth was, it was clear Neil was much better than anyone who auditioned so far. It occurred to the band that he could even be better than *all* their previous drummers.

"Likewise. You all sounded tight, and your set list is songs that people want to hear. I like to have fun with this stuff; I don't take it too seriously but I don't flake out. I show up on time and ready to go. So if this is a no-drama thing, let's do this."

Neil smiled and shook hands with each player, knowing he softened his response a bit. Fact was, he took his drumming *very* seriously. Same as always. And he expected they would do the same.

Neil shared the good news of the audition with Jackie. She was ecstatic for him, and saw in Neil a renewed zeal for his craft. It wasn't lost on her that a happy husband is good to have around, so there was limited downside to endorsing his passion for music and a new band venture.

Terry made the offer to Neil for associate manager, which included a $10,000 pay raise, incentives for overtime, and additional vacation and sick leave.

By June of 2020, The Aces were practicing two evenings a week and working through around forty songs. But the closer they got to being ready to book gigs, the fewer venues remained open due to Covid. The timing for live music couldn't have been worse.

Jackie finished teaching mid-June, and spent the remaining weeks of summer mostly indoors to beat the Chicago humidity in her third trimester, and to avoid Covid exposure. The second week of August she gave birth to eight-pound Selena Jordan Abrams, a beautiful baby girl with a sprout of black hair just like her mom's, but with her dad's piercing blue eyes.

Jewel remained open as Covid continued to mostly keep the American economy shuttered, and which brought more social restrictions. Jackie was informed that the school would not resume in person when the students returned in September. She would be teaching from home online, which frankly she was ok with given she could also spend more time with Selena while Neil's and her parents took turns coming over to lend a hand.

Neil was feeling positive about his family, his job and his music, but the Coronavirus numbers were soaring and causing him and all Americans great worry.

"Have you guys thought about doing some outside shows or just having friends come see you in the practice space, masked up of course?" Jackie asked from the rocking chair in the living room as Selena slept in her arms.

"Not really. Two of the other guys also have kids, so they don't want to risk infecting their families. That's a definite concern for me as well with you and Selena. No one is even booking outdoors now either. It's all a waiting game."

As the fall Chicago weather turned cold, the Gamma strain emerged, and by November the U.S. reported over one million total deaths. Infection rates across U.S. hospitals and healthcare facilities soared while the FDA feverishly pushed to test and approve vaccines.

By Christmas 2020, the U.S. became the first country to report over 10 million cases, and the new Delta variant was announced. But as 2021 came, the FDA approved Johnson & Johnson as well as Pfizer to distribute millions of vaccines. The global death count exceeded 2.5 million.

Neil and Jackie insisted their parents be especially careful because they were coming over to help take care of Selena. All agreed to consistently use sanitizer and masks even in the house, and periodically take Covid tests to confirm their status.

Because Neil's job was around the public, he was particularly worried about contraction. He used hand sanitizer every time he touched anything in the store, and was religious about properly wearing his mask and insisting staff and customers do the same.

Other than the occasional disgruntled customer spewing their political ideologies about conspiracy theories associated with Covid, the world by now was doing its best to get through the pandemic, and Neil did everything in his power to keep his family safe. He continued regular rehearsals with The Aces, and the barn made for sufficient social distancing.

The headlines early spring of 2021 were initially depressing- "Covid-19 is the leading cause of death so far in 2021"... "U.S. Covid deaths higher than many other countries combined."

But by April 2021, between those who already survived their infections and over one billion vaccines given worldwide, herd immunity was achieving gradual control over the spread. Covid rates began to decline and restrictions slowly loosened.

Neil continued at the store, and was resolute in his commitment to drumming. He practiced almost daily at home, and several days a week with The Aces. They even had a few virtual gigs they streamed to friends and family.

At a practice session early May, Kip announced The Aces were scheduled to do a Covid fundraiser at a public park in Schaumburg in June. Two sets of 15 songs each.

Neil was thrilled with knowing they booked their first live performance as a band. Once they agreed on the 30 songs they would perform, in normal Neil fashion, he practiced them obsessively.

By now he took less time to warm up, his arms and legs didn't get tired at any point, and his playing was excellent in every respect. Timing, tempo, dynamics, fills and locking in with Trevor on bass were solid.

There was no conceivable flaw in any aspect of Neil's playing, and even he was aback at how far he had come since picking the sticks up after so much time off. His vocal harmonies were also at their best ever.

When he wasn't playing The Aces' songs over and over at home, he was online messing with other songs that were new and challenging to him. He watched tutorials of other drummers as they played classic standards and complicated genres. Polyrhythms, double bass patterns, complicated cross-sticking, songs with off-speed signatures and charts with complex drum solos. It all kept him challenged to expand his abilities to new levels.

The new Alesis electric mesh kit meant he could play through his headphones with almost no external noise other than the light thumping of his right foot quietly permeating the house. So even as Selena slept, Neil could practice.

He worked through songs by bands with insanely good drummers that would have taken other drummers weeks to replicate. Neil nailed them in hours. He expanded his use of Facebook in order to invite more and more followers to view The Aces' shows online.

One day he noticed a number of online tutorials by Todd Sucherman, drummer for the rock band Styx. Neil was already familiar with Todd given Todd grew up in the Chicago area and had been playing for Styx since 1995. Neil and Jackie saw their shows several times before Covid, and Neil was always super impressed by Todd's drumming.

Neil noticed a Facebook ad pop up for registering for an upcoming master class with Todd while Todd was in town for a gig. A Chicago music shop was hosting the class, limited to 20 local drummers.

He had never attended a master class, but figured this would be a good chance to test his skill level with a pro and other drummers. So the weekend before The Aces' Schaumburg gig, Neil took a trip into the city for the three-hour workshop at the Chicago Music Exchange along the Lake Michigan shore.

When Todd strolled out in front of the students, they stood and roared with approval and applause. Todd, wearing a faded Chicago Cubs hat, jeans and an old Styx tee shirt, appeared incredibly modest from the start.

"Hey. Thanks. Listen, this was an easy one. I get to do shows tonight and tomorrow night in the best city on the planet, then hang out with family and friends. And eat the shit out of some deep dish pizza and hammer some Goose Island beers!"

This drew laughter and claps from Neil and the other drummers as they took their seats.

Todd sat behind the drum set and continued, "Really though, I've been doing these workshops for a few years and they're a lot of fun. The drumming community is amazing, and I am learning as much as I'm sharing. The only rule today is to relax, have a good time, and express our love for this amazing art form with each other."

The room was set up with a practice pad in front of each participant, and one drum set facing the set that Todd sat at.

Neil was at ease given how informal Todd was, and he scanned the room a bit while Todd did his intro just to see what the range of local drummers looked like. Men in their 20's through 60's, a little boy around 12, two high school girls, and a little girl who couldn't have been more than eight. A broad cross-section of people paying homage to the best instrument on the planet.

"So we're going to start with something that always terrifies my students, but doesn't need to. You will each come up to the set in front of mine and play any 16 bars of drumming you want. Any genre, any style, any pace. I don't need you to prove any- thing. This isn't an audition [nervous laughter from the students]. I just want to hear you lock in for 16 measures so I can give the group some collective feedback after."

Neil scanned the room and saw the panic on the others' faces, most of their knees already nervously bouncing up and down. Neil's mind started racing. Not that he was worried about keeping time for 16 measures, nor about being in the pocket. But there were just so many options to choose among.

Was Todd looking for someone to play a rhythm from one of Styx's hits, or just light up the kit, or just hang back and create some- thing original? Worst yet, Neil was only two chairs from the front, which meant he would go third and have little time to plan.

Neil nervously tapped his fingers on his knees, then caught himself and stopped so as not to appear anxious. Not because he couldn't go up and nail 16 bars of drumming. Of course he could. But had he known this was to be part of the class, he would have spent countless hours perfecting a 16 bar riff to blow Todd and the others away, and to separate him from the pack.

But he quickly settled down and reminded himself what Todd just told the group- the class is for fun. The little voice in his head helped settle him down... *Take it easy. Just go up and let it rip, and be the solid player you know you are.*

The first guy, a slower-moving man of around 60, was pretty sloppy. While Neil would never admit it, this sort of put him at ease. He also finished two bars early, which Todd quickly pointed out when he finished. "Not bad. But you owe me two measures!"

The second player, a Latin woman in her 20's, went up and played 16 bars of swing, pretty tight but without much flair. Todd shook his head supportively, graciously giving a thumbs up.

Neil was next. He still hadn't really decided how to approach his turn, and whether to play matched grip or tra- ditional. He started with a fill on the toms he developed years ago and used for some of the songs with The Aces. Matched grip to start.

After a few measures and recalling that Todd is among the most talented traditional grip players on the rock circuit, without skipping a beat Neil switched to the more challenging traditional grip and worked in some off beat hi-hat pops and complicated rhythms, with contained volume in perfect time.

Using a 4/4 scale made it easy to remember when to stop after 16 bars. Neil took care to be solid, not too showy, but to just do what he always does behind the drums- grip and rip.

Neil finished and was the first to receive applause from the others. He stood, patted his right hand on his heart, and extended it to Todd. A sign of respect for being in the same space as such a talented musician and rock legend.

Todd smiled and paused to remark on Neil's playing. "You're no beginner I see."

Neil was cautious to be humble in his response. "I probably started playing around the same age as you, but then stepped away from it for a while. I'm knocking the rust off and getting back into it."

"Your playing is very disciplined. Let me guess- you came up in drum corps?"

"Yes. High school and then Eastern."

"Very cool. One of the things I'm going to emphasize today is getting the drum corps players in the room to loosen their grip for better speed and less fatigue."

Neil felt affirmed by the comments and took his seat, then watched the others in the room take their turns. Other than a few stand-outs among them, Neil was several levels above them all.

The little girl who introduced herself as Stella, age seven, and who said she started playing at age four, stole the show to the great joy and applause of the group. Though she could barely touch either foot pedal, she ripped into 16 measures of the drum riff from Wipeout that was close to spot on. The place went nuts, and any tension in the room around ego or pressure to perform from that point vanished.

After each drummer took their turn, Todd spent the next two hours combining stories of his life on the road with Styx, talked about his formative training as a percussionist, and exposed the group to a range of exercises and techniques they could use to improve their skills.

Neil intently watched Todd play, in his mind checking off the patterns and riffs that he knew he could also perform. Todd taught them about posture, breathing, control, pace, dynamics, and most importantly, how to break the "monkey grip," which Todd explained as over-gripping the stick and disabling fluid play and limiting the highest comfort and speed.

By any respect, Todd's drumming was unbelievable. Amazing speed, accuracy and power. As Neil observed Todd's skills, his favorite childhood book popped into his memory- *Jonathan Livingston Seagull*. Todd very much emulated JLS as a teacher, but also displayed the virtues that Neil sought in his life... peace, introspection, and the quest for self-perfection.

But as impressed as Neil was by Todd's abilities, he knew he was capable of reaching a similar level. He knew he could exceed his own capabilities by sheer will and determination, driven by the intense love for this art form.

By the end of the class, Neil felt even more confident about his playing, and his hunger to improve heightened to yet another level. Todd's comments at the end of class especially resonated with how Neil lived his own life...

"Thanks for spending some time with me today, and I hope the class was useful to each of you. Remember, your craft as percussionists and drummers is about more than banging a drum. It's about creative expression, about connecting with the rhythms of the people and lives around you, and it's about the cadence of your journeys through this world."

"Hey babe, how was the class?" Jackie asked as Neil set his keys and phone on the kitchen counter. He kicked off his shoes, and after a quick kiss was already heading back to his kit.

"Amazing. Todd is legit, and such a nice guy. I just need an hour to refine a few things he talked about. I'll jump on the quiet kit though."

Within minutes she could hear the light thumping on the floor that emanated whenever Neil used the practice kit. She chuckled, then opened the door as he was already intently applying what he learned in class.

"Your parents are watching Selena for the day, remember? You can use your loud kit if you want." Jackie knew this would be music to Neil's ears, and before she could finish her sentence Neil hopped from the practice set to the full kit, causing Jackie to rush out of the room holding her ears before the force of his playing overtook her.

The June gig the weekend after the master class was a huge hit, and a solid turnout of patrons hungry for live music after being cooped up for months due to Covid showed up in large numbers. The Aces were back to form, and they began booking out dates into the fall most weekends, both in the city and in the surrounding suburbs. They got invited as an opening band to play Summerfest in Milwaukee later in the summer, a highly sought gig by any band in the region.

Not only was Neil's drumming on point, his back-up vocals were strong. A non-smoker, Neil's vocal chords were well maintained and his knowledge of music and pitch enabled him to blend his harmonies with the others to elevate the group's overall sound quality.

In his mind, he knew that any decent band needed drummers who could sing back-up, which took incredible focus and many hours of additional practice. Getting four appendages to move independent of one another was hard enough, but doing so while singing was a significant added challenge. For most drummers, singing and playing drums simultaneously was too counterintuitive to do well.

At the June shows, the band drew solid applause, and the crowds that followed The Kickin' Aces created a buzz around

Chicago that quickly spread. Neil often looked up while playing to see the fans focusing on him, pointing and whispering and cheering. Though he was modest as a performer, it was gratifying for him given all the effort he put into respecting his art at the highest level.

Somehow the combination of his age, his drumming IQ, and the quantity of time spent rehearsing on his own- and rehearsing and performing with the band- resulted in a quality of playing that exceeded his natural abilities.

One morning early July, Neil arrived at work to open the store and received a direct message via Facebook from an unknown number. The message read- HEY NEIL. IT'S TODD SUCHERMAN. CAN YOU REPLY TO MY MESSAGE WHEN YOU HAVE A MINUTE?

Neil laughed and looked around the store. *Claire. What a clown.*

He ignored the message assuming it was his co-worker pulling his leg. Though he attended Todd's class, there was no exchange of numbers, nor anything to suggest he and Todd hit it off on a personal level.

After the class, Todd just hopped into a black limo that pulled up front of the music store and rushed him off to the stadium for their gig that night, which they were sharing with fellow musicians REO Speedwagon. They had been doing a national joint tour with REO for several months.

Around 4pm that afternoon as Neil was getting ready to clock out, another message came- HI NEIL. I KNOW WE HAVEN'T TALKED SINCE THE CLASS, BUT THIS REALLY *IS* TODD. HERE IS MY CELL IF YOU CAN GIVE ME A CALL.

Neil stood still and tapped his fingers on the side of his cheek, still perplexed. He had seen Claire several times today and she didn't say anything about a prank message.

Shit. Why not play along? he thought to himself. *Maybe Jackie put someone up to it.*

Neil exited the store and jumped in his truck and dialed the number. A male voice on the other end immediately picked up.

"Neil. Hey, thanks for the call."

"Yes, but who am I talking to?"

"It's Todd. I found you on Facebook and was able to send you a direct message."

Still not totally convinced it was really Todd, Neil replied, "Hey. All good. I really enjoyed your class and the adjustment to my grip has made such a difference."

"Ah, very cool. Thanks for that. Listen, you probably know we are touring through next year with REO. Confidentially, their drummer Bryan Hitt has to step away from the tour for a bit, so the guys asked me if I have recommendations on talented drummers to audition. I pulled up some of your Facebook videos from your recent gigs with The Kickin' Aces. I don't think you perhaps understand how solid your playing is."

Neil's brain was racing and still trying to keep up with the information he was receiving. But at this point, he realized he actually was talking to Styx's drummer.

"Any chance you might want to audition with REO? Whoever they pick will tour with them, and Styx, for at least six months until Bryan might be able to return."

Todd stopped speaking and noticed a long pause.

"Neil, you still there?" Neil stared in a daze at a skinny high school kid straining to push a long chain of shopping carts across the parking lot toward the store.

"Yes. Sorry, yes, I'm here. I'm just trying to make sense of this. You're telling me I can audition with REO Speedwagon and possibly go on tour with them?"

"That's what I'm saying. Hey, I even pulled up some old footage of you guys winning DCI at Eastern. Your chops were fucking unreal!"

"Wow. Thanks Todd. Coming from, uh, you, that's very humbling. Tell you what, let me check in with my wife on this tonight, and I will get back to you. I've watched enough of your drumming videos online that I can tell by your voice it actually is you, which I have to admit freaks me out a bit. Anyway, thanks for the call. This is quite an honor."

"You bet. The auditions are next weekend downtown. They're moving fast so we don't have to cancel gigs. They will only audition around a dozen prospects, so once you have the set list you should come prepared. I'm guessing that's not an issue for you."

Neil ended the call and looked at his hands tightly locked on his steering wheel. He relaxed his grip and his fingers intuitively sprung into their usual frenetic tapping. He glanced at his piercing blue eyes in the rearview mirror, then tilted the mirror down to display the image of his broad smile.

"Holy shit. HOLY SHIT!!" Neil said aloud as he started the engine and pulled away.

The ride home was a blur and Neil's mind was racing. *Was this really happening?* His brain worked to process the situation. Was it possible that all the hours of practice, lessons as a kid, hours and hours of time on the Eastern line, and the recent revitalization of his passion as a drummer could have him on a professional tour? And with one of the biggest and most popular rock bands in the U.S.?

Jackie sat rocking Selena in the living room as Neil entered.

"Hey. How was your day?" she asked, as Selena drank from her bottle.

Neil reached his hands behind his head to tighten his ponytail, smiled at Jackie, and gave the only reply that came to mind- "I believe it's time for us to fly!"

VENTURA HIGHWAY

Of course I could save him. That wasn't really the question at all. The real question was, what would have the best outcome? Sometimes saving a life answers prayers, but isn't the best thing really.

Most agree that some are better off moving on than staying. For example, a 90-year-old suffering from cancer is an easy choice. Others, not so much. A 10-year-old girl in a coma after being hit by a car while riding her bike. A soldier with a head wound and missing a limb while serving his country in combat. A 60-year-old who just retired, diagnosed with cirrhosis of the liver.

They're all a bit different, and all are a judgment case. And for every one of them, the prayers pour in. Religion doesn't matter. Catholics work their beads, Hindus chant, Muslims kneel on prayer rugs facing East... Heck, even the atheists and agnostics try to talk to me. That's why I make the big bucks I guess, spiritually speaking.

This one was interesting. I actually had to think on this one for a bit, and it truly was a close call.

As I viewed it, from 10,000 feet so to speak, it certainly would have been tough to bring Jay up. His parents obviously would have missed him. His friends of course, and his Marine unit for sure.

But the Dewey family, they were another story altogether. Especially Reagan Dewey, his fiancé. I'm careful about what I define as "tragic," as the term is so subjective and often gets overused. But this one, yes. The case of Jay Gomez definitely would have qualified as a tragedy by any and every form of the definition. This would have been nothing short of a Romeo and Juliet, epic tragedy had I taken him.

So while I get to make these decisions every day, technically every second of every day... who stays, who goes, when, how, where, etc. They're all difficult. This one no less so.

The day started like so many others. Quiet. Simple. Predictable. Only difference was, it was Matt and Stacy Dewey's 27th wedding anniversary- June 5, 2020. Covid-19 was raging and the United States was a mess with Trump wrestling with how to manage the virus as well as address racial unrest and protests.

I don't get political in my line of work of course, but in addition to all my other jobs, keeping an eye on the United States to help ensure it didn't implode into a total state of disarray was wearing me out.

Anyway, it was a Friday as I recall. Matt took the day off just to keep their options open. He and Stacy got up around 7, walked the dogs, made breakfast, then floated in the pool. She lazily leaned over the edge doing the crossword puzzle, while Matt did his daily laps- an unflattering, half freestyle stroke of sorts. Now several months into working from home due to Covid, they did whatever necessary to try to make each day feel a little different from the previous.

As Matt came up for air at the shallow end of the pool where she stood with the paper, Stacy tapped him on the head.

"Hey Aquaman, how about we grab lunch at Dockside? Harper has to work at 11 anyway, and Reagan and Jay are heading to the beach in a bit."

"Sounds good. Give me about 30 minutes after this to check some emails, then we can go."

By noon they were enjoying an appetizer and glass of wine on the Wrightsville intercoastal waterway. One of their favorite waterfront restaurants provided a beautiful view of boats and birds on a gorgeous, sunny day- much like the day they were married 27 years before. This was always one of their favorite spots to unwind, and they were happy to set their face masks aside while they sipped their favorite Sauvignon Blanc.

I always took a liking to the Deweys. They were straight-shooters, hard-working and by American standards bred from the ground up. Both first-gen college students who met in college and worked hard for everything they had- a nice house, a pool in the yard, a few dogs, etc. Not rich, but stable and, best yet, Christian. Though they were what I call "Eastermas" churchgoers, they were kind to others, charitable, and good-natured. In my book, they had done enough to warrant my support. As I told my staff as we consulted on the matter, "They have plenty of equity in the goodwill jar."

I smiled as I saw them holding hands at their table that day, a ritual they practiced frequently over 34 years of friendship and nearly three decades of marriage. Matt did his best to make the moment with Stacy special, though his type A personality gave him a proclivity to always want to rush to the next thing.

"This is so relaxing. Are you hungry? I could do lunch or apps if you're up for it," Matt stated the obvious in hopes Stacy would bite.

"I know sweety. You can *always* do lunch," Stacy chuckled as she squeezed his arm. She loved that Matt was always in a mode of relative hunger, which enabled her to try out new recipes on him.

"It's nice to see you relax a bit, Matthew. Sure, lunch sounds good. I could do a beer with lunch as well. Corona or Stella, please."

She only called him Matthew on occasion, usually when she was giving him a hard time about something. I smiled as I watched Matt kiss her hand before putting his facemask back on to head inside to order their food.

So there they were, having one of those quintessentially beautiful moments at their favorite, tranquil waterfront spot. Matt laughed to himself as he headed inside the restaurant to place their order, thinking *after all this time and she's still telling me which beers to order her.*

Matt knew the pecking order by heart- Corona Light. Stella. Amstel. Modelo. Heineken Light. For wine, always Sauvignon Blanc or Pino Grigio for whites; Cabernet or Pino Noir for reds. They knew each other's favorite food and drinks. In fact, most of the time they finished each other's sentences.

They were there around two hours, ignoring other patrons in line impatiently waiting for their table, filling the time with funny stories from their long marriage.

After grinding it out through college and, for Matt, two graduate degrees; after living in the hectic D.C. area for twelve years; after raising two daughters and moving to Wilmington, they were as happy as any two people could be. Before leaving, the last subject was the one they were talking so much about recently-Reagan and Jay.

"Matt, I'm really going to miss them. When they talked about leaving for Chicago after Jay finishes his service with the Marines, it felt like it would never get here. Now it's a month away. I hope they are ready for such a big move."

"Well, remember we were only 25 when we left Chicago for D.C. Sight unseen, we didn't know a soul and had no idea what we were doing. But we figured it out."

"Yeah, but you know Reagan doesn't like change much. I'm so thrilled they found each other, don't get me wrong. But I just worry about them being able to make it on their own."

"I know, Stace. But they've been dating for two years. They love each other, and Reagan is 26. She's ready. He has family there and so do we, so they have a support base. Plus, we can be the obnoxious parents who pay them surprise visits all the time."

Back at the house they put music on and floated in the pool. The Bichons chased each other around the pool deck, and the weather offered up a perfect afternoon for relaxing. About 80 degrees, low humidity and sunny.

By 3pm Jay and Reagan returned from the beach, joining them in the pool.

"What's up, Marine? How was the beach?"

"Nice. A bit crowded. But no one was wearing masks, so I'm sure it was a damn super spreader."

Jay eased into the shallow end of the pool holding a beer and with his signature headband on. Part Mexican, his tan skin and toned physique made Matt think back to what it was like to be 22.

Being around Jay always seemed to make Matt more youthful. Given they both grew up in Chicago, loved Chicago sports teams, and enjoyed the same things- sports, grilling, beer and music- Matt took a liking to Jay the day his oldest daughter introduced them.

"You want to throw some bags?" Matt asked Jay. Cornhole was their favorite backyard game, though Jay's game was, as Matt often reminded him, a work in progress.

"Definitely. Just don't go easy on me this time. I want to beat you straight up at some point."

As they finished their second game, Stacy came outside with a tray of snacks and said, "Matt, the Crew is gathering at Tom and Lori's tonight. He finally finished the tiki bar and wants to christen it. Should I tell them we're in?"

Matt threw his last bag into the hole as he replied, squarely beating Jay 21-6, "If Reagan and Jay want to go, sure. We can Uber there and maybe Harper can meet us after she gets off work."

"The Crew" were the Dewey's closest friends, a group that lived in the same neighborhood near Snow's Cut Bridge near Carolina Beach. Tom and Lori Kole, Jane Harris, Brad and Jennifer Hyland, and Trina and Taylor Everson. These were the touchstones for the Deweys that they spent many weekends with- in their pool yard, on the beach, or sometimes hopping around their favorite local watering holes.

The Uber rolled up at 8pm and dropped them off at the Kole's house by 8:15. They walked up the driveway to the house, and Matt removed his mask and whispered to Stacy an observation about the driver.

"Did you see the dent in that guy's head? Explains why his speech was so slow. Poor guy, most have had some sort of accident or something."

"You notice the strangest things, Matthew," Stacy replied.

As Matt walked up the driveway, he caught sight of a golf cart parked next to Tom's truck.

"Whose wheels?" Matt asked Tom as they greeted each other in the driveway.

"Taylor's friend let him borrow it for the weekend. He's been giving little Winnie rides around the block and helping everyone with their coolers." Tom put his arm around Matt's shoulder and led him toward the backyard.

They greeted the group and as usual the Deweys doted on little Winnie Everson; Trina and Taylor's six-year-old daughter. Having raised two daughters, they took a liking to her early on. Smart, precocious, and with whirlwind energy.

Every meeting with the Crew started with hugs and high fives. They were the closest of friends, and the closest thing to family the Deweys had in the Wilmington area.

Jay and Reagan set their cooler near the new tiki bar, and held hands as they settled into two Adirondack chairs in the corner of the yard. It was one of those perfect early summer evenings that everyone dealing with the Covid crisis needed.

"Wow. Tom, you did a great job with this! You did all this yourself?" Matt, himself quite handy, was blown away by how great the bar and yard looked.

"Yep. Finally finished it. The bamboo around the bottom is real, and I had to cut it into halves to nail it flush along the base. I used stainless steel pipe for the foot rail, and Lori got the stools from a local antique dealer. The nautical wire was the hardest part, but makes for a nice touch along the deck. Of course, here's the topper..." Tom reached behind the bar and flipped a switch, illuminating the entire bar with brilliant white lights that lit up the entire yard.

"Dude, nice job." Matt swatted away a bug as he reached for the lighter to light the tiki torches. "We're going to need these tonight. No-see-ums are tearing me up!"

A few other neighbors arrived, and by around 9:30pm the group was helping break in the new backyard paradise. Matt finished his second beer and noticed the golf cart pulling up with Taylor and Trina and Winnie returning from a ride. It was not completely dark yet, and the streetlights in the small cul-de-sac made it bright enough for a ride around the block.

"Marine, let's go for a ride." I noticed that Matt always called Jay "Marine" ever since they met. Appeared it made Matt feel cool to be connected to someone serving their country, and Jay appeared to like the nickname.

Jay excused himself from conversation, and quickly made his way from the backyard down the driveway and into the cart. He put two beers in the cup holder and launched Pandora on his phone to provide some music for the ride.

Jay didn't do much without music, and Matt and he- though 30 years apart in age- shared a common affinity for classic rock.

"What a nice night, huh? Is Reagan having a good time?" Matt eased around the neighborhood and already knew the answer that was coming.

"It's nice to be outside where we don't have to wear masks, so of course. Plus, she's out with you guys, she got some sun at the beach today, and tonight she got to dress up a bit. And she's hav-ing a few cocktails so trust me, she's in her element."

In just two years, I watched a bond form between Matt and Jay uncommon for men not related by blood and so far apart in age. Best I could tell, this was a product of them having a lot in common, and because Matt never had a son, and because Jay's dad traveled a lot. Marine or not, being far from home at 19 wouldn't be easy on any young man.

It seemed in many ways their relationship resembled that of father and son, but also of two good friends, and- of course- of that between the father of a daughter and the young man she was dating.

While not officially engaged, it was understood that there would be a marriage at some point after they made the move to Chicago in a few months. Understood in Matt's mind at least.

"Ok, grandpa. Pull over and let me drive," Jay said as he placed his phone in the cupholder, increasing the volume on Sugaree, his favorite Grateful Dead song.

"Ok, Marine. But take it easy. I don't want to head back to the party too soon. Look at that sky." Matt pulled over and they switched positions so Jay could drive.

Jay floored it and they sped off. The cul-de-sac was a rectangle of about ten houses on each side, with only one way in and out to the main road, so there wasn't any traffic. But the corners were a bit sharp, and though the cart wasn't moving too fast, Jay was approaching his turn at the wheel more like driving a go-cart than a golf cart.

"Alright, Mario. Let's not wreck this thing. I gotta hit the head, so one more time around and back to Tom's." Jay floored it and headed toward the house, singing in unison with Jerry Garcia as they pulled up- "Shake it, shake it, Sugaree. Just don't tell them that you know me!" Matt exited the cart and headed up to the bathroom, as Jay returned to the yard.

By the time Matt came back down, Jay was back at the cart with a few others, including Reagan's younger sister Harper who knocked off early from the restaurant in order to see everyone. This was obviously going to be a thing for the rest of the night, taking turns on the cart for a night cruise under the stars.

"What's up, girl? How was work?" Matt kissed Harper on the cheek and gave her a hug.

"Putting my degree to good use, dad. Four years of college to have to come home early, no graduation ceremony, and now to be serving pub food to the locals. A dream come true!" Harper did a dramatic bow as she often did when she was being sarcastic.

"Ah, you're all good. You're making good bank and it's only for a while, kiddo. The world is still your oyster."

Matt loved his daughters equally, but they were different in so many ways. Reagan at 26 independent, in her first serious relationship and very much in love, and always a bit of a worrier. A talented violinist, and finally with a boy she could trust and whom she adored with every fiber of her being.

Harper at 22 just finished college, with an anticlimactic end wrought by Covid, and with a business degree waiting for the economy to spring back while deciding her next move. Possibly an MBA in a big city.

"C'mon. I'll take you for a spin," Matt said as he hopped back into the driver's seat mainly to avoid letting Jay drive. But also because, as Matt often did, he liked to be in control. Not unlike the trips they took each summer to visit Stacy's family on Cape Cod, Matt would rather drive tired than be in the passenger seat.

As Matt turned the key, one of Tom's neighbors Pat jumped in the front passenger seat. Harper hopped into the rear seat with Jay, then Tom jogged down the driveway and plunged into the back middle seat.

"Shit, anyone else? We're gonna bottom out!" Matt said as they plodded forward. Jay played music on his phone again, this time "Sympathy for the Devil" by the Stones.

"Grandpa, step on it!" Jay yelled from the back.

"Marine, you hear that noise? That's the frame grinding on the axle. This thing is barely moving with five people on it. It's going to be a '*slow ride... take it easy.*'" Matt sang the end of this phrase, inserting song lyrics as he often did.

"It'll buff, Matt," Jay said, peering through his Malcom X-style glasses and wearing his favorite Chicago Bears hat. He often used this description for compensating for anything that presented a challenge.

Harper, always good for a laugh, began playing tour guide with the group- "Ladies and gentlemen, thank you for joining us on Matt's motley moat. Welcome to the greater Wilmington area. As the sun sets behind us to the west, replaced by a beautiful sky-line over the tidal region, we make our way up the block. Please buckle your seatbelts..."

I can't really fault anyone for what happened next. Like most things, no one could have seen it coming. It simply was what people who have such incidents often say afterward- *it was an accident.*

Though not going very fast, as they rounded a corner Jay's hat blew off. He stood to try to catch it, and his feet slipped off and caught the concrete. His legs tangled, and in a flash he fell off the cart and onto the street.

"Matt, stop the cart!" Tom yelled. "Jay's off."

"He's off?" Matt slowed the cart as he turned around to see Jay sprawled on the pavement as the others dismounted to run to his aid.

Matt quickly hopped off and followed the others toward Jay, at first assuming it was a playful tumble and Jay was goofing around.

"Nice job, Marine. Get your ass up."

But as he approached Jay and observed his condition, he knew this could be more serious. Jay was barely moving on the concrete street where he so awkwardly landed.

They immediately tended to him. Jay's flip-flops lay on the street near him, and his legs were tangled and crossed as he lie motionless on his back. His glasses had shifted down to his chin, and Matt took them off and put them in his pocket as he called out to Jay, whose eyes fluttered open and closed.

"Jay! Jay are you ok? Can you hear me?"

Tom held Jay's head and continued to talk to him.

"Jay, open your eyes. Jay, we're here with you," Tom said.

As they checked on him, Tom noticed blood dripping from Jay's left ear. Matt reached down and helped cradle Jay's head to keep it off the concrete.

"Call 911 right now!" Tom said to Harper with a panicked look.

Harper dialed the phone and began talking to the dispatcher.

"Our friend fell off a golf cart. Please come now. His head is bleeding. No, we don't see any cuts but there is blood dripping from his ear. He's not speaking, and his eyes keep closing. He's moaning a bit. Oh my God, please hurry!"

Harper gave the closest address visible and Pat moved the cart to Tom's driveway. By now, the guests from Tom's yard and a few other neighbors came out.

So just like that, as those I try to help frequently say, *life turned on a dime.*

As the ambulance arrived, the Deweys jumped in their car to go directly to the hospital.

"Jesus Christ, Harper. What the hell happened? We weren't even going that fast." Matt looked in the rearview mirror at Harper in the back seat. Harper's eyes were welled with tears and her complexion was pale. Next to her, Reagan sat staring silently out the window.

"Dad, I don't know. He just stood up and reached for his hat, then he was off. Tom tried to reach over to pull him back down, but it was too late. I heard his body hit the pavement hard. And his head hit really hard."

Harper reached over to put her hand on Reagan's shoulder. But Reagan remained catatonic and still.

They arrived at the hospital and began to inquire about Jay. The charge nurse reminded them to keep their masks on in the lobby and to be patient with updates.

"We're slammed with Covid cases, so everything is taking longer. He's in the ICU, so he is getting immediate care. Someone will be out to update you soon."

Matt spoke through his mask, "Can we go back and see him at some point?"

"Are you immediate family?" the nurse asked.

"I'm his girlfriend, and I am going to need to see him." These were the first words Reagan uttered since Jay's fall.

"Let's see what happens. If you do go back it would be just you. We're very strict right now on visitors with the pandemic." The nurse stepped away from the desk as this edict was provided.

It's funny how I get called into action when people are in need. Outside of church, my name gets mentioned during the strangest of times. Either people are angry and use it in blasphemous contexts involuntarily, such as when a carpenter swings his hammer and misses the nail and smacks his finger instead- "God Dammit!"- as though I somehow caused such a thing to happen. Or when someone needs something- "Dear God, *please* help me."

But whatever the context, I don't get offended. It's all part of the job. But it's ironic that many people only call on me when they need something. Either way, I have to make all the big decisions on things that will impact people for their entire lives.

The Deweys sat in the ER lobby for several hours before anyone came out. The Crew texted them to check in and offer support, but they had no updates to share.

Matt and Stacy reassured Reagan he would be fine, mostly to try to convince themselves. Reagan didn't see Jay fly off the cart, but Harper saw the whole thing. So each was managing a different level of trauma around the situation- Reagan because it was her man who got seriously hurt. Harper because she saw him flail off the cart and onto the unforgiving concrete street below.

Finally, a bespectacled doctor in his 60s with the usual white coat and white hair approached them.

"Hi. I'm Doctor Stevens. You are friends of Jay?"

They all popped up and eagerly approached the doctor. Matt spoke first and intuitively reached out to shake Dr. Stevens' hand, then pulled it back.

"Sorry, yes, Jay and my daughter are dating, and he lives with us on weekends when he isn't on base at Lejeune. How is he?"

"He has significant brain trauma. The nurse said he fell off a golf cart. Did any of you see what happened?"

Matt replied, "There was a group on the cart, and he was in the back. His hat flew off and he stood up to try to catch it and he fell off. We weren't going very fast at all."

"We're going to do more tests and he's resting now. But he isn't conscious, and he has a serious traumatic brain injury which is why you saw blood coming from his ear. His brain is swelling and hemorrhaging, so we have to monitor him closely so that the brain doesn't expand and press too hard against the skull and cause further damage. There really isn't anything you can do for him here tonight, so leave your information with the nurse and we will call with updates."

With that, Doctor Stevens turned and exited the lobby as swiftly as he came in. Like a ghost with bad news and limited emotion who briefly emerges then quickly vanishes. Matt stood motionless as if he didn't understand what was just said. It all just felt like a bad dream.

"Dad, what does all that mean? Oh my God, what's happening right now?" Reagan grabbed her dad's arm with both hands.

This was the first sign of true panic from Reagan. She let out a loud sob as her knees buckled and she fell to the floor. As others in the lobby looked over, Matt scooped her up and they guided her back to a nearby seat.

"We're ok. Shit, this is unreal." Matt tried to be calm but his own reaction to the situation interrupted his attempt to reassure his family.

"Dad, I don't want to leave here. I'm NOT leaving here without Jay."

"I know, Reagan. Stace, how about you take Harper home to get some rest, and I'll stay here with Reagan. We can Uber back later if necessary, or you can pick us up. Whatever. But I'll stay here with her."

Harper and Stacy gathered their things and headed out, as Matt and Reagan sat back down. Reagan, now sobbing, leaned her head on her dad's shoulder and curled her knees up to her chest.

"Say some prayers. Say lots of prayers for our boy," Matt said as he stared up at the bright red EMERGENCY sign above the nurse's station. His brain wrestled with how it happened, why it happened, and whether or not he was to blame.

Reagan drifted off to sleep, mostly out of exhaustion from worry. Meanwhile, Matt got up to use the bathroom, and looking at himself in the mirror felt the weight of the world on his shoulders. As he prepared to wash his hands, he spotted several blood stains on his palms from attempting to help Jay hours earlier. With no others in sight, he buried his head in his hands on the sink and wept.

No updates came through the night, and Matt never slept. But as the hours ticked by he pleaded to me for help, bargaining as all souls do to try to motivate the outcome they seek.

While he spoke to me, his memory drifted back to when he knelt at the foot of his bed in his pajamas as a little kid, head bowed and hands clasped before going to sleep each night. He recited the prayer his mom taught him and which was hung in a little frame on his bedroom wall.

As Matt prayed for my intervention, he apologized for not talking to me as much as he did when he was a child. Even still, I considered us closer than many of the souls who call upon me for help. Since he was born, whenever I checked in on Matt it appeared he was doing my work- selflessly helping others, spreading joy, and trying to be the best version of himself.

As I looked down on him and Reagan in the waiting room, I saw not a father and child, but two children. Small, humble, frail.

Several times through the night Matt silently repeated the prayer over and over, speaking directly to me with great urgency. Then again, they all do when it comes to situations like this.

"Angel of God, my guardian dear. To whom God's love, commits me here. Ever this day, be at my side. To light, to guard, to rule and guide."

Between prayers and occasionally pacing the lobby floor, Matt's mind raced with various outcomes. *He'll be ok. He's tough. Nasty concussion, but he will be ok.* But Matt was also a smart guy, and he kept reflecting back to Stevens' words- *Traumatic Brain Injury. TBI. What if he isn't himself again? What if he doesn't make it? How will I ever look at Reagan again? What am I going to say to his parents?*

Matt began to think about what time to call Jay's parents. He looked at his watch... 5am. Just then he got a text from Stacy asking for an update. He called her back to check in.

"Hey. No updates, but I'm going to have to call Jay's parents soon, and his base so they know. I have no idea what to tell them honestly. I'm hoping to have more detail on his condition before I start making calls. I'll call you when I know more."

Matt fell into a half sleep for a bit, then a different doctor approached them. She tapped Reagan on the arm to wake her up.

"Hi. Dr. Stevens is off duty. Not much change for Jay. We have intubated him and are trying to drain the blood from his brain and have induced him into a comatic state so he can rest while his brain continues to swell. The next 24 hours will be important in terms of his status."

Reagan grabbed Matt's hand tightly as Matt turned to her and they briefly locked eyes.

"Reagan, let me talk to the doctor alone for a second."

Reagan drifted back a few feet as Matt walked the doctor away from her.

"Thank you. Tell me though, is he going to make it? I mean, that is Jay's girlfriend over there. I have to know... I mean... do you think he's going to pull through? I need to call his family and his Marine base with an update."

Matt pulled his mask back over his nose as the doctor responded.

"It's hard to say this soon. Again, the brain has been traumatized and is bleeding. We've been able to relieve the pressure on the skull by extracting the blood, and he's young and in good shape which will help. But it could go either way. You can give his parents our number to get updates, and you can tell them he has a TBI. We're not letting anyone into the ICU at this time, so no visitors."

"I understand. What does intubate mean?"

"It means we are using a tube to help him breathe."

The doctor departed as Matt prepared to update Reagan. He knew he would have to play it straight with her in case things turned for the worse. He didn't want to give her false optimism.

"Reags, not much change. It is serious, but these types of injuries take time. So we will head home because I need to make some calls."

"Can't I just stay here? I'm afraid if I leave I may never see Jay again."

"Don't think that way. You've got to be positive. Keep praying, and as soon as they have more details they will call us. I texted mom. She's on the way. You need some food and rest."

Stacy came shortly after to pick them up, and Matt got settled at home and started making some calls. First to the group from last night to update them and thank them for helping out.

Then to Jay's best friend and fellow Marine, Jason, so he could inform the base. Then, most difficultly, to Jay's dad.

Jay's parents were separated, and Matt hadn't yet met his mom, so he only had Jay's dad Frank's contact info.

"Frank, this is Matt Dewey."

"Hey Matt. How's it going?"

"Not so well. So I need to update you on something. Jay had an accident last night and he's in the hospital."

"Oh no. What happened?"

"He fell off the back of a golf cart and hit his head."

"How bad, Matt? Matt, how bad is it?"

"Not sure. But he's in the ICU and they want you to call them. They won't share detailed updates with me since I'm not immediate family. I'll text you their number. But we're here for him and will try to get in to see him if they will let us. With Covid, they're pretty strict, so they may not let us in at all. I know you're up in Pennsylvania working right now so we will do whatever we need to."

"Oh man. Ok. Thanks for letting me know. I will call them right away. Does his mom know?"

"I don't think so. I don't have her number."

"I'll call her and give her the hospital's number after you send it. She may call you though if she has questions."

"You bet. Thanks Frank. I'll keep you posted. Please do the same."

The brevity of the call was good, but it exposed a pain in Matt that he had not yet felt in his life. That of a parent with a seriously injured kid. His daughters had their bumps and bruises, but never anything serious. Never anything that would cause Matt or Stacy to fear the worst. That was a feeling Matt never had, and never wanted to have.

He was relieved Frank had no detailed questions on the accident, and very relieved Frank offered to share the news with Jay's mom instead of asking Matt to call her.

Reagan was a wreck, so was Harper. The day after the accident the hours ticked by like a clock with weak batteries. Several calls to the hospital yielded little detail on his condition. The same response was given over and over- "He's resting, and we're watching his condition. We will call you if we need to."

Life outside the house ceased to exist. There were no plans made, no trips to the store, no joy, and certainly no smiles. They held vigilant to hopes that Jay would pull through, and that the nightmare they had stepped into would end.

Around dusk, Matt's phone buzzed. It was Frank.

"Hey Frank. Any news?"

"Not really, but I think it might be good for me to come there." This statement only elevated Matt's worry, given Frank was getting more intel from the hospital than the others. *What did he know, and how bad was it?*

"For sure. When, and are you driving or flying?"

"I was planning to fly in tomorrow. I can rent a car and get a hotel."

"Of course not. I will get you from the airport and you are welcome to stay with us. Absolutely."

"Thanks. I appreciate that. Paula may want to come too if that's ok. We will make sure to mask-up."

Matt agreed to help in any way, but the thought of having Jay's parents at the house as they waited for news of their son's status would be tense. They had met Frank already a few months back when he was visiting Jay at the base. Nice guy, hard-working and easy to be around. But they had not yet met Paula, and wondered if there would be any tension between them.

The next day, Matt picked up Frank from the airport and the following day did the same for Paula. They agreed to use separate guest rooms and seemed to be ok in each other's presence.

After Paula unpacked, she stepped onto the front porch to smoke a cigarette. When she came back in, they all sat in the living room to chat.

"Matt, can you tell us what exactly happened? The hospital only says he fell off a golf cart. Was he out golfing somewhere?" Paula asked.

Matt sat next to Stacy on the couch across from Jay's parents, with Reagan and Harper sitting in chairs in the nearby kitchen.

"No, actually we were at a friend's house. Stacy and I had lunch earlier in the day for our anniversary, and we drove over to some friends for the evening. Reagan and Jay had been at the beach, then we all went together. The people there were taking turns with golf cart rides around the neighborhood. We weren't there two hours and had taken a few rides when it happened. Jay was on the back of the cart with Harper, and he stood up and then just fell off. When he fell off, he hit his head on the pavement."

"The cart wasn't going fast at all. It happened so fast," Harper interjected. Paula held her hands on her cheeks and became flush as she listened. Then asked the question Matt was most dreading.

"Who was driving the cart?"

Matt answered without hesitation-"I was."

"Matt, was he drunk?" Frank asked directly.

"No. I don't think so. In fact, we were with him from the afternoon on and I only saw him have a few beers. It was just a freak accident."

Harper interjected, somewhat to her dad's defense- "Mrs. Gomez, I got there after work, and no one looked drunk. The cart was full, but there was nothing reckless. We were going around a corner, and Jay's hat blew off and as he stood to reach for it he tumbled out. As we tried to grab him and tell him to sit down, his flip-flops tangled and he was on the street. It just happened so fast."

Matt added, "I was looking ahead so I didn't see him, but no matter what I'm sick about the whole thing. We've been with Jay every weekend for several years. When he's not on base, he's here. I consider him part of this family. So we feel awful about this."

Matt and Stacy did their best to make the Gomezes feel at home. But the lack of information on Jay's status and their collective worry made for a constant tension that filled every space of the house.

They kept busy prepping meals and checking in on the girls, while Frank and Paula mostly stayed in their rooms save the occasional trip to the front porch for a cigarette. But each time the Deweys checked on their guests, the worry and tension they observed in Jay's parents was palpable.

Matt and Stacy started taking daily walks to get some fresh air and talk in private. Today, June 9th, it was raining, so Stacy decided to stay back.

"I'm gonna go for a jog, sweetie. I don't mind the rain. See you in a bit."

Matt tied his shoelaces and threw a raincoat on and started a slow jog out of their cul-de-sac. As he did, the rain came harder. About a half mile out, Matt's worry overwhelmed him at a level that overtook his body. He stopped, put his hands on his knees, and wept profusely.

He tried to control his emotions, but the pain became too great. Now several blocks from his house, Matt stood in the middle of the road and let out a primal cry that echoed through the surrounding homes and trees-

"AAAAAGGGGGGGGGHHHHHHHHHHH!"

His face was awash with tears and rain, and he sobbed much like people do at funerals. Heavy, uncontrollable sobs with loud heaving motions and pitiful noises. The sort of sobbing that emerges from a place unknown, but that comes with the cathartic purpose of retching out all the pain that a body and soul can no longer bear.

Matt's mind raced between the accident and all the memories with Jay and the girls, including all the one-on-one time he and Jay spent together. Their long talks around the firepit in the yard much like a father and son would have... military service, world events, philosophy, and frequently about music.

Matt and Jay had a connection whereby each would do anything for the other, and- if asked- where each would describe the other as one of their best friends.

He steadied himself and continued his run, and the rain came harder and completely drenched him; he couldn't help but feel the entire universe was now weeping for Jay. As he ran and glanced up at the slate grey sky, it occurred to him that the sun had not appeared since the day of the accident.

As mentally and physically exhausted as he was, instead of turning for home he turned back up the road and quickened his pace. He wasn't running for exercise or to calm his nerves. He was running for Jay.

Several miles into the run, Matt turned onto a street where new construction was underway. He switched from the street onto the newly paved sidewalk along which as many as 50 new homes would be built in the next year.

As Matt looked down at the new sod that was planted between the sidewalk and street, his eye caught something moving in the grass. He stopped to observe it more closely.

The newly planted grass was covered in thin green mesh to help keep the sod intact, and entangled in the mesh was a beautiful snake. Black and red in color, with yellow rings around the black sections of its body. About three feet in length.

As he observed it, its wriggling only made it more tangled. It was clear the snake was desperately trying to free itself, and wasn't going to do so without assistance.

He looked around, seeking the help of something or someone. His first inclination was to leave it alone and keep running, but for some reason he felt compelled to try to help the little creature. The torrential rain continued to pound even harder.

Matt knelt and attempted to delicately free the snake from the mesh, but in doing so the snake only flailed further and became more entangled. There were several sections of the snake where the plastic mesh tightly constricted its body, and it appeared to be suffering. Time was crucial.

"Dammit." Matt knew if he tried to rip the taut mesh with his hands, he would only risk injury or death to the snake.

"Got to find something," Matt said aloud as he looked around.

Most of the lots on the road were vacant dirt plots, but further up the road several homes were under construction; Matt sprinted toward them in hopes of finding a tool or anything sharp he could use to cut the plastic mesh to free the snake.

As he scanned the construction area, he found nothing other than large piles of wood. He started to look for a sharp rock, but the driving rain made seeing anything very difficult.

The more he searched in vain, the more he became committed to helping it, to *saving* it. For the moment he had forgotten about Jay, and freeing the snake was his singular mission.

Finding nothing that could work, Matt headed back to the snake, when within several yards of being back near it he looked down and spotted a long metal screw. *This would work. This could cut through.*

He grabbed the shiny, silver object and approached the suffering creature.

It was not moving, and Matt thought perhaps it was dead. But as he knelt down and cupped it and the ensnarled mesh in his hands, it began frantically wiggling again, like a nightcrawler on a fishing hook.

Matt spoke to the snake aloud as though it could hear him. As though it were a person.

"Take it easy. We got this. You're gonna make it."

Like a surgeon with a scalpel, Matt carefully cut each small square section of the mesh around the snake's body in order to clear the sections that were suffocating it. At one point the snake stopped moving again, and Matt yelled, "Don't you fucking die on me!"

Careful not to stick the body with the point of the screw, Matt continued to meticulously cut through each piece of plastic twine with great care, one by one freeing more sections of the snake. After a few minutes, the last section was cut and the mesh fell away.

Matt stood with the snake in his palms, not afraid of it, and the snake's body heaved in and out as it tried to regain itself. Matt's body and heavy breathing mirrored the same movements, and tears fell from Matt's eyes and he wept again as the raindrops pummeled him and the creature he cradled.

He walked to the nearby wood's edge and carefully set the snake on a bed of leaves. While he was tempted to leave and resume his run, he instead stood there for a long time just staring at the snake. Watching its slow and labored stomach rise and fall, he didn't just want the snake to live, he *needed* it to.

As Matt watched the breathing continue, soon the tail started to twitch back and forth, then the head perked up off the leaves, and the snake's little pink tongue emerged, licked the air a few times, then in an S-shaped pattern it slowly slithered off.

He put a piece of the green mesh and screw in his pocket, wiped his face, and turned toward home. He felt tired but vindicated. Small as the occurrence was in the grand scheme of things, it was the first positive experience for Matt since the accident.

Matt silently talked to me on the run back, continuing to plead for my help, somehow hoping saving the little serpent would cull favor from me. The Saints and I chuckled over this, finding the whole thing quite ironic from a biblical perspective.

On most days when Matt experienced strange things, he would immediately share them with Stacy. He got home from his run, and didn't mentioned a word of it to anyone.

Later that day, Matt got a call from Jay's sergeant at Camp Lejeune.

"Mr. Dewey, this is Sergeant Stafford from Lejeune. Jason Smith gave me your number. How are you sir?" Matt was immediately intimidated by the call, as Stafford fit the bill as a Marine drill instructor.

"Good, sergeant. Has Jason given you detail about what happened?"

"Some, but we've sent staff to the hospital to be there. I'd like to send two of my staff to stop by your house to talk. Sir, are you going to be there tomorrow?"

All the sir talk made Matt even more nervous.

"Yes. I have taken the week off of work to be here with Jay's parents. I'm working from home due to Covid anyway. Jay and my daughter have been dating for several years now, and..."

Stafford interrupted, sounding somewhat rushed to end the call.

"Very good sir, then they will see you tomorrow. Private Smith provided your address already. Pearson and Grady will be there around zero nine hundred. Take care."

Matt ended the call and let the others know staff would be coming by from the base tomorrow. Shortly after, the group made what would be its twice daily check-in with the hospital, gathering on the couch with Frank's phone on speaker so all could hear. Still limited progress, and today's message from the nurse on call was similar to yesterday's...

"He's still intubated and resting. He's fighting hard and he's strong, so we're hoping for the best. You can call once each morning and once each night for updates, and if anything changes we will call you."

It was starting to feel like different hospital staff were reading from the same script each time.

Reagan pulled Matt into her bedroom out of earshot from the group.

"Dad, what do you think will happen? I mean, it's good he hasn't gotten worse, right? But do you think he will ever wake up? I don't think I can make it if he doesn't."

To this point Reagan had held it together pretty well, with Harper supporting her and trying to keep her calm. But it appeared to Matt her hope was weakening and she was starting to crack. Matt put his hands on her shoulders and looked directly into her eyes.

"He's a strong kid, Reagan. We have to pray hard, and ask God to bring him back to us. He's our boy. We need him here, and so do his parents. Stay positive. We're gonna get him home, I promise."

Matt hugged Reagan and kissed her on the forehead, then checked on Harper.

The next day after breakfast a large, white Ford pick-up truck pulled in their driveway. Matt greeted the man and woman at the front door, both in dress clothes versus uniforms; but it was very clear they were military.

Both officers wore camouflage medical masks adorned with the U.S. Marine Corps seal, and the female officer extended her hand first.

105

"Mr. Dewey, I am commanding officer Pearson, and this is first sergeant Grady."

"Hi. Please call me Matt. Nice to meet you. Come in. Take your masks off if you want."

Matt ushered them inside and introduced them to Stacy and the Gomez family, then went through the chore of again explaining what happened. It felt less official than Matt thought it would, and neither officer took any notes. He was relieved they were mostly there to support the families and offer any assistance necessary. But it was also obvious that the Corps considers their Marines both property and family. When a Marine is injured or missing, questions will follow.

"We will have an officer stationed at the hospital every day. That is standard. And the hospital is required to give us any medical updates we request. So hopefully we will be getting the same detail as you. PFC Gomez is a tough guy. We think if his body cooperates he can get through this. Please call us whenever you need to," Pearson concluded as she handed Matt a very official looking business card.

As they left, Matt exhaled a sigh of relief. They were less intimidating than he expected, and the inquisition he was expecting never came. He appreciated the steps they were taking to help.

The next day, in addition to his constant prayers, Matt began a daily ritual to send positive vibes to Jay. He committed to swimming twenty laps in their backyard pool freestyle, then to finish with a lap U Boat style.

Jay and Matt did U Boats in the pool when they were working out together before the accident. It's a sort of float on your back with your legs together and feet pointed toward the sky, out of the water, while swimming forward using only a pushing motion with forearms and hands. Matt committed to adding another U Boat lap each day until Jay was home.

The same day Matt started his laps, he placed a tablet of paper on the kitchen table and encouraged everyone to write on it. Their thoughts and prayers, expressions of worry and positive support, and messages directly to Jay for him to read when he got home.

The first journal entry actually came in the form of a note to me from Matt. As I watched the families make journal entries, it was clear how much they needed Jay in their lives. The love the group had for him and each other was compelling, but alone would not necessarily be the reason for me to save him.

6/11/20
Dear God,
Please take care of Jay. He is our world. We need him here. Please watch over him and bring him back to us. We pray for him constantly.
Matt

June 12th, one full week after Jay's admission to the ICU, and because no family were permitted due to the rapid spread of Covid, the hospital made arrangements for Jay to be viewed via Zoom.

The families gathered in the living room with Reagan's laptop on the ottoman. Before they knew it, the Zoom link showed Jay's body on the hospital bed. The group sprung up toward the screen, all now crying at the sight of Jay.

"Jay! Hey sweetie, it's Reagan. I love you. Please come back to us!"

Each of them uttered a similar expression, and although there was no movement and he still had tubes in his nose, he otherwise looked the same. There were several nurses in the room adjusting the machines near his bed who greeted the group.

Matt asked if the nurses could hear the group, and they said they could. He requested an update, and the first good report finally came when Dr. Stevens entered the room and joined the conversation.

"Good news is the bleeding has stopped and the swelling of his brain has started to subside. This is a good sign. He stirs in his sleep a bit so we have mittens on his hands so he can't pull his I.V. out. He's still on oxygen with the nasal cannula and he's heavily sedated from a number of meds, but he's no longer intubated. He's staying strong and we're hoping he continues to make progress."

At this, the entire group was crying and hugging. Reagan fell on the couch and buried her face in a pillow, heaving sighs that expressed the collision of pain and joy she was experiencing.

Later that night as everyone was getting ready for bed, Frank texted Matt and asked Matt to meet him in the kitchen.

Frank spoke in a lowered voice. "The hospital just called and said he opened his eyes after our Zoom with him. He opened his eyes! Matt, our boy is going to pull through! I just know it. Do you want to tell Reagan and the others?"

Frank was like a kid on Christmas morning, and Matt took pleasure in seeing Jay's dad positive about the status. Though still somewhat strangers, they hugged each other and smiled mutually for the first time since being together.

"How about we check again in the morning just to be sure? Then we can talk before the morning Zoom," Matt replied. He was happy but wanted to continue to guard Reagan.

That night Matt slept for most of the night, more so than he had for the past week. He prayed before and after sleeping, and awoke recalling a dream of Reagan and Jay walking down the aisle of a church at their wedding.

The dream was beautiful, except when the preacher declared them husband and wife at the end of the ceremony, then said, "All rise" to the congregation, Matt could not stand. He tried and tried, but it was like he was glued to the pew. Much as he attempted, he could not rise.

Matt rose well before sunrise and was surprised to find Frank already in the kitchen making coffee.

"Hey, up early?" Matt said, entering the kitchen so as not to startle him.

"Yeah. I'm used to getting up pretty early to be on my construction sites, but last night I hardly slept with the great news about Jay."

"Me too. Some mornings I get up early and just drive or walk over to Trails End to catch the sunrise. It's a great way to start the day. Looks like you're mixing up some breakfast."

"Hope you don't mind. I hit the store yesterday and thought I would cook for everyone this morning. Huevos rancheros with some authentic tortillas I got from the Mexican grocery. I plucked a few jalapeños off your plant out back as well, and Stacy made homemade salsa yesterday. Should be a nice spread for us to have before the big Zoom this morning."

Matt got excited seeing Frank's energy, and the inertia of it all pulled him in.

"Love it. How about I help. What can I do?"

"Heck, it's so early I think we have time. How about we grab our coffees and you show me your sunrise spot and we hit that before we cook?"

Matt was thrilled with the thought of having some alone time with Frank, then glanced at his phone and replied, "Great idea. Let's see, sunrise is in 23 minutes, so plenty of time. We can drive over. It's only about three minutes from here."

"I like it. I bought Horchata as a side drink, so I hope your family likes it."

"Horchata?" Matt replied, the word being totally foreign to him.

"If you like sweetened rice pudding, it's a sort of milky version of that. Delicious, especially with Mexican food. Damn Matt, you gringo!"

Matt laughed as he poured his coffee, "Totally true. I'll try anything once. Jay used to make some sort of butter and sugar on a hot tortilla and eat it before bed. I tried it, but it was way too sweet for me."

Frank laughed, then replied, "Yeah. That's his half-assed sopapilla. He did that as a kid at home too, but way too much sugar for me as well. *Debe ser agradable ser joven.*"

Seeing again his Spanish didn't register with Matt, Frank followed with, "Must be nice to be young!"

They pulled into the Trails End lot, and as usual a few local fishermen were using the boat ramp to start their morning fishing trips. A few people in parked cars faced the intercoastal waiting for the sunrise over Masonboro Island.

"This is one of the best kept secrets. I often buzz down here in the morning for my sunrise fix. Helps with the speed bumps throughout my day, if you know what I mean."

Frank replied, "Can we go sit on the bench at the end of the pier? Looks like a great spot for photos."

"You read my mind," Matt replied as he turned off the engine.

They made their way to the viewing pier as the sun began to illuminate the area. Matt could tell Frank was taken by the beautiful surroundings. Though certainly not his first sunrise, for many months between his work in Chicago and then deployments for construction assignments all over the country, it was clear Frank didn't make time for such experiences. But at this point in the visit and given his focus on Jay's recovery, it seemed like a perfect scenario.

"Matt, thanks for this. Wow, this is unbelievable," Frank said as his eyes scanned the area.

They sat as the boats slowly made their way off the ramp and toward their various destinations, and observed various birds in the water and air busying themselves as minute by minute the sky absorbed the brilliant colors offered by the rising sun over the Atlantic.

Several people boarded their SUPs and began to smoothly paddle out toward the heart of the waterway, easing over the wakes offered by the slowly passing fishing vessels.

"I really need to move to the coast," Frank said while sipping his coffee.

"True. I never get sick of sunrises. And no two mornings are alike. It's the best fifteen minutes of my day. Look at how the clouds are coming to life with the colors."

As they mutually enjoyed the beautiful dawn, they sat in silence for a bit. Then Frank turned to Matt to convey some thoughts it appeared he wanted to reveal before his upcoming departure back home.

"Paula and I just want to say thanks for what you have done for us, and for Jay up to this point. You probably know that Jay and I are incredibly close. He's my only son. But after he met Reagan and your family, he told me what great people you are. We were so worried about sending him to the Marine Corps for obvious reasons, but when he said he was spending his weekends with a family who are from Chicago, I thanked God over and over."

Frank lit a cigarette as he spoke, leaving Matt a chance to reply.

"Thanks for saying that. You and Paula should be proud of him. He's a great guy, and you raised him well. He and Reagan appear to be true soulmates. He's done as much for us as we have for him. I have used every prayer possible to get him through this, as any bad outcome would have been totally devastating for all of us. I hope you don't mind me saying, Jay is also like a son to me."

Frank smiled and replied, "Trust me, he's not perfect. But he's basically a good kid. And he adores you and your family."

At this, Matt could feel his emotions percolating, so he finished his last sip of coffee and maneuvered the conversation a bit.

"A few weeks after he and Reagan first met and went on some dates, Jay and I went out for a beer. And he was so sincere and so funny. He said to me, 'Matt, I really like your daughter a lot. And I think we might have a future together. But do you have any advice on how to handle her when she doesn't get her way? I mean, I've never been spoken to like that by a girlfriend before. I'm not sure I can handle it.'"

With this, Frank exhaled some smoke and burst into laughter, as Matt slapped his back and also gave a hearty roar.

"What did you tell him?" Frank asked, still chuckling.

"Are you kidding me? That's dangerous territory. I told him to go talk to my wife!"

They continued to share a laugh and exchanged other stories about Jay and Reagan from when they were kids. By this point, the full sun was above the horizon and setting on Masonboro Island, looking like a bright orange golf ball sitting on a fairway.

Back at the house, the others were still asleep as they continued talking while making breakfast. Frank was like a maestro, flying around the kitchen as Matt mostly stayed out of his way.

The smell of the breakfast items woke the others, and one by one they came to the kitchen to consume Frank's Mexican fare. Reagan and Harper were especially drawn to the white Horchata drink, insisting Stacy keep it on hand from now on.

As breakfast ended, the group prepared for the morning Zoom update with Dr. Stevens and his staff. The group viewed a nurse standing next to Jay's bed and saw Jay's head moving and his eyes open.

"Oh my God. It's Jay! He's moving. Jay! Jay can you hear us?" Paula shouted toward the screen.

"Hey folks. It's Doctor Stevens. Last night Jay started coming back. Only opens his eyes here and there, and he is trying to talk a bit. His throat is going to be very sore for a while due to being intubated for a week. But it appears he's coming back online so to speak. We still have CT scans and other tests to continue, but he's fighting hard. He's young and incredibly strong, so we are very optimistic."

As was the case yesterday, the group was in full tears as the words came from the doctor.

"Appears you speaking to him yesterday helped him reconnect. Go ahead and talk to him and see if he is able to respond," Stevens offered.

Frank looked at Reagan and said, "Go ahead, Reagan. Talk to your Jay."

"Hey baby. How are you? Can you hear me?" Reagan said.

After a short delay, Jay's head shifted to the side and he slowly replied, "YESSSSSS."

Reagan and the others covered their mouths in disbelief. There wasn't a dry eye in the room. Stacy held Paula's hand as they sat huddled with each other staring at the screen.

"We're here for you, Jay. It's your mom, We're all here for you together."

After another delay, Jay slowly replied, "Ohhh Kayyyy."

6/13/20

Dear Jay,

Today we got to see you speak for the first time on Zoom! It was such a relief to see your face, to see your eyes open, and hear a few words from you. When the nurse asked us if we had any final questions at the end, you said, "Nnnnoooooooooo!" I think we wore you out with our excitement over seeing you awake, but this made us laugh.

On the second Zoom today the nurse asked you to stick out your tongue, and you did. It was adorable and funny. I can't wait to see you again on Zoom tomorrow, but we are still very worried about you. There are hundreds of people praying for you around the clock. Your friends from Chicago sent us a picture of them in someone's yard raising beers to you. We love you and we miss you.

Love,

Reagan

6/14/20

Dear Jay,

You have so many people praying for you, because they love you and know how special you are. The Deweys have been great hosts to us, and your buddies at Lejeune check in almost every day. We know you are fighting hard, so keep getting better. We are devastated and need you here with us. You have so much to offer us and the world, and we love you. Please keep fighting and let your brain and body heal. We want to see you as soon as we can!

Love,

Mom and Dad

6/15/20

Dear God,

Thanks for all you have done so far. Jay can move his arms and legs, and his eyes are open. Now we need you to focus on healing his brain so he can walk and talk and think. There is only one Jay, and he is the Jay we need in our lives. We will help heal him if you just get him home to us. Amen.

Harper

6/16/20

Dear Sweetie,

Last night the nurse told us you recited your name and birth date, and you said, "Reagan is my girlfriend." This made me smile and cry. The nurse said you keep asking when I am coming to pick you up. I would be there right now if I could! I can't wait to see you again on Zoom tomorrow, and to have you home soon. Our lives are very empty without our Jay. I love you so much.

Reagan

6/17/20

Dear Jay,

It's been almost two weeks since we saw you in person. We are so proud of how hard you are fighting. Your parents got to finally visit you yesterday and were so happy. Because it's not clear how much longer you will be there, they are leaving in a few days because your dad needs to get back to work. But they plan to fly back as soon as you are released.

When your parents were visiting with you, we got to Zoom in and watched you walking around your room opening and closing doors and drawers. You looked like a caged mouse trying to break free. That's our Marine! Get home soon so we can talk music around the firepit. I might even let you beat me in a game of cornhole.

Matt and the Deweys

P.S.- The Cubs are in last place as usual, but the Bears report for training camp next month!

As Matt prepared his next journal entry, two weeks since the accident, he decided to share the snake experience with Jay.

6/19/20

Dear Jay,

Last night you were reportedly giving the nurses a hard time by trying to get out of bed. Of course, that's good news for us. I hope you're giving them hell. No doubt you are ready to get out of there, but please be patient and let your brain heal.

I will tell you more about this when you're here, but last week I went for a run in the pouring rain, listening to the classic rock playlist you made me. Along the way, I freed a scared little snake that was caught in some turf mesh. This was the first positive thing that I experienced since your injury, and several days later you woke up. I think God is listening to our prayers.

Fight hard and come home soon. I'm doing an extra U Boat for you every day, but not sure how much longer I can keep that up. lol

See you soon!
Matt

6/20/22
Hey Marine,

I went for another run today because your progress is giving me and everyone else new energy. The news yesterday that they are moving you to the surgical neuro floor soon and that you may begin eating on your own soon is awesome.

While I was running today and again listening to your playlist, the song Ventura Highway came on. As I listened to the words, it was clear that the song is about you right now. The words almost exactly describe your situation.

It was a beautiful end to my run. Even though the song is really about one of the members of the band (America) reflecting back to when he was a little boy and was standing on Highway 101 outside Ventura, California while his dad changed a flat tire, it was eerie how much the lyrics are a metaphor for you. When I got home I wrote down my interpretation of the song. I hope we all can listen to it together soon.

Matt

VENTURA HIGHWAY
(AMERICA)

Chewing on a piece of grass, walking down the road
[THIS IS YOU IN THE HOSPITAL DREAMING RIGHT NOW,
CAREFREE AND HAPPY.]

Tell me, how long you gonna stay here Joe?
[THIS IS ME ASKING YOU NOT TO LEAVE US.
YOU ARE JOE IN THE SONG.]

Some people say this town don't look good in snow
[REFERENCE TO WILMINGTON.]

You don't care, I know
[YOU WOULD BE HAPPY WHEREVER YOU ARE.]

Ventura Highway, in the sunshine
[VENTURA HIGHWAY IS HEAVEN. YOU'VE DREAMT ABOUT
IT DURING YOUR INJURY, AND YOU MAY HAVE EVEN
CONSIDERED GOING THERE BECAUSE IT APPEARS PEACEFUL.]

Where the days are longer, the nights are stronger than moonshine
[ALSO A REFERENCE TO HEAVEN. YOU LOVE THE LIFE
YOU LIVE, BUT YOU ALSO KNOW THAT WHEN YOU
GET TO HEAVEN IT WILL BE BEAUTIFUL.]

You're gonna go, I know
[THIS PART OF THE SONG IS TERRIFYING,
BECAUSE I KNOW YOU HAVE A
PLACE IN HEAVEN, BUT WE DON'T WANT YOU TO
GO THERE YET. SO WE'RE PRAYING HARD FOR YOU
TO STAY WITH US.]

'Cause the free wind is blowin' through your hair, and the days surround your daylight there [YOU ARE YOUNG AND
HAPPY AND YOU WOULD FIND HAPPINESS BOTH ON
EARTH AND IN HEAVEN. YOU ARE DREAMING A LOT OF
BEING HAPPY AS YOUR BODY CONTINUES TO HEAL.]

Seasons crying, no despair
[LIKE MY RUN IN THE RAIN, THE UNIVERSE IS SAD
FOR YOU RIGHT NOW. IN FACT, IT HAS RAINED
ALMOST EVERY DAY SINCE YOUR INJURY.
HEAVEN IS WEEPING BECAUSE YOU'RE HURT.
BUT YOU ARE TELLING EVERYONE NOT TO
DESPAIR AND TO BE STRONG.
THOUGH THE SEASONS ARE CRYING, YOU ARE
FIGHTING HARD AND ARE TELLING YOURSELF
AND OTHERS NOT TO BE SAD. YOU ARE USING
ALL YOUR STRENGTH TO COME BACK TO US.]

Alligator lizards in the air
[THIS IS A REFERENCE TO WHAT A FREE SPIRIT
YOU ARE. OUR MARINE HIPPY IN YOUR JEAN
SHORTS...YOUR LOVE FOR CLASSIC ROCK AND
BANDS SUCH AS THE GRATEFUL DEAD. THIS IS THE
PLAYFUL PART OF THE SONG, JUST LIKE YOU.]

Wishin' on a falling star
[YOU'RE DREAMING AGAIN, THINKING OF
REAGAN, THE GREAT LIFE AHEAD, AND WISHING
TO FULLY RECOVER AND COME BACK TO US.]

Watchin' for the early train
[THIS IS ABOUT THE TRAIN TO HEAVEN. YOU
KNOW IF YOU GAVE UP YOU COULD GET TO
HEAVEN EARLY, BUT YOU ARE FIGHTING TO STAY
ON EARTH. YOU HAVE MADE YOUR CHOICE,
WHICH IS TO BE HERE WITH THE PEOPLE YOU
LOVE. YOU STAND AND WATCH THE TRAIN TO
HEAVEN PASS BY, AND YOU DECIDE
NOT TO BOARD.]

Sorry boy, but I've been hit by purple rain
[GOD HAS OUR BACK. YOUR FAMILY AND
LOVED ONES AND I HAVE BEEN GIVEN THE
STRENGTH TO PULL YOU THROUGH. IT'S A SAD
TIME BUT BEAUTIFUL IN SOME WAYS BECAUSE OF
THE LOVE THAT HAS EMERGED TO GIVE YOU THE
STRENGTH TO FIGHT THROUGH YOUR INJURY
AND COME BACK TO US. PURPLE IS ALSO A
REFERENCE TO AMERICA AND YOUR MILITARY
SERVICE. IN FACT, IRONICALLY, THE FATHER
THAT IS REFERENCED IN THE ACTUAL SONG
CHANGING THE TIRE ON THE SIDE OF THE ROAD
WAS ALSO A U.S. MARINE.]

Aw, come on Joe, you can always change your name
[EVEN IF YOU COME BACK TO US A LITTLE
DIFFERENT THAN BEFORE YOUR INJURY, IT'S OK.
WE LOVE YOU AND WILL ALWAYS BE HERE FOR
YOU. YOU'RE OUR JAY, AND ANY VERSION OF
JAY IS GOOD ENOUGH FOR US.]

Thanks a lot son, just the same
[YOU'RE THE CLOSEST THING I EVER HAD TO
A SON, AND I CONSIDER YOU MY SON. EVEN
THOUGH WE WOULD ACCEPT A DIFFERENT
VERSION OF YOU, NO THANKS. WE'RE FIGHTING

TO BRING YOU BACK TO YOUR WHOLE SELF.
WE'RE GOING ALL IN TO HEAL YOU TO THE
FULLEST, AND WE LOVE YOU.]

6/21/20
Dear Jay,

We're so proud of you. The last 48 hours have been nothing short of a true miracle. Two weeks ago we were worried about you pulling through. That first week was so scary. We had everyone praying, and the Crew from Carolina Beach came by and we formed a prayer circle on the lawn and asked God for his power to heal you. You showed so much strength and progress that each day we gained a little more hope. We had some light moments with your folks here, especially cooking meals with your dad. The point you turned in a really good direction was when you entered rehab. You went from barely speaking at all to talking to us conversationally.

Then last night you started using your phone to text and call. The doctors said if you work hard you could get home soon and possibly be 100% within a year. Again, from where we were on June 5th, utterly amazing. This is because the world has big plans for you and Reagan.

We think we cashed in every favor with God and the universe, which we would gladly do again for you because you are such a good guy. Anyway, we're still all in to get you here. We love you, Marine. Hope you enjoyed Matt's interpretation of Ventura Highway. It sort of wrote itself.

Big Love,
The Deweys

Matt and the others continued journaling about Jay every day, resolute to document his progress and reflections about his journey of healing. Frank and Paula left Wilmington, and Matt promised to keep them updated and welcomed them to come back after Jay's release, and to help Jay with any trips back to Chicago when healthy enough to fly.

On June 27th, the call from Dr. Stevens came. The call they had been praying for since the night of the accident.

"Matt, it's Doctor Stevens. Jay is ready to be released, but he will need someone with him 24-7 for a while. We asked him who he wants to be released to, and he said Reagan and her family. He cannot return to work for now, and he shouldn't fly. And he needs to be somewhere where everyone is very careful in terms of Covid. Are you willing to accept responsibility for..."

Matt cut Stevens off mid-sentence. "Yes. Oh my gosh of course. Tell me what we need to do. When can we come?"

Reagan must have been listening from upstairs, given as Matt continued speaking to the doctor she flew down the stairs and was at Matt's side in seconds.

"Mom, Jay is coming home!" Reagan shouted, both legs jumping off the ground like a little girl jumping rope. Matt plugged his opposing ear in order to carefully listen to Stevens' instructions.

The pick-up would be the following morning, and Stevens gave a few directions but also said everything would be in writing. Medications, stretching exercises, sleeping arrangements, rules about not using stairs, diet, etc.

As Matt continued receiving details, Harper entered the living room covering her mouth with joy, then exposed a huge grin before Reagan tackled her onto the couch.

Stacy entered the room eyes to the ceiling, silently thanking me for any role I had in delivering their boy, their *Marine*, back to them. The dogs followed at Stacy's heels barking excitedly in response to the collective joy in the room.

Matt hung up with the doctor and embraced the group with the collective hug they hoped would eventually happen.

"Oh my God, we've got to get ready. Dad, what can he eat, where should he sleep, what do we do?" Reagan's words came faster than her ability to make sense of it all.

Stacy made a beeline to the fridge and poured a glass of wine, which Harper promptly grabbed and started to drink. Reagan followed after, grabbing her own glass, and the Dewey ladies cheersed to the wonderful news.

The rest of the day was a blur. They moved Jay's belongings down to the first level guest room, situated a television and his game station for him, placed additional pillows on the bed, and even moved the large JBL radio into the room given Jay's love of music. They wanted everything perfect for his arrival.

Frank, already back to work in Pennsylvania, texted Matt after receiving a similar call from Stevens, and thanked Matt for agreeing to move Jay in. Matt next texted the Crew, then the contacts from the base, and let them know Jay was being released but could not return to work until cleared.

The next morning came fast, though none of them slept much. It felt like a day that for a while might never come. In my mind, it was the day I had planned on giving them all along. The world needs Jay, and this was not going to be the way I would take him back up to Heaven. That day would come when Jay is old and gray, and lived a full life. Not at 22.

The group left an hour early for the hospital, even though it was only twenty minutes away. Reagan wore a U.S. Marines sweatshirt, and Stacy held the card that Jay's entire unit signed. They parked the car and waited in the hospital lobby for their boy. The minutes ticked by like hours, and they paced with anticipation. Even through their masks, they could see each other's smiles.

As the double doors swung open, Jay appeared in a wheelchair. Thinner than when they last saw him June 5th, but otherwise looking very well. He grinned through his mask as he made sight of Reagan, and she rushed onto his lap and nearly knocked him over.

"Thank God you are here, babe!" Reagan said as she wiped tears from her cheeks. The others trailed behind her waiting for her to let Jay up for air so they could each hug him.

"Heeyyyy." His speech was slow and bit labored.

"What's up, Marine?" Harper said as she patted him on the head.

Stacy was next, and gave him the card and a big hug. "I'm going to fatten you up, Marine. Hope you're hungry."

Matt tried to be strong, but the emotion of seeing Jay reunited with Reagan and the family welled up in him to the point where a large tear burst and rushed down his cheek. As Jay slowly stood from his wheelchair, he raised his hand to throw Matt a high five, followed by a huge hug.

Matt whispered to Jay as the group moved in to further consume him, "Your golf cart days are over Marine, but thank God you're with us. We're out of here."

As Matt said this, he glanced up at me looking down upon the group. While lots of people often say *Thank God* in various contexts, I could tell Matt meant it. He and the others truly were thankful for my decision to save Jay.

As I got to know Jay and listened to Matt and Reagan and others describe him, it would have been great to have him and his Oorah spirit up here with us. I think he would have fit in with the other Saints and angels, and right now we certainly could use his weird sense of humor, knowledge of classic rock, and ability to make us smile.

But it was clear his family and friends needed him more. Besides, my time and attention were being pulled in so many directions, and the prayer line from down below was nearly impossible to keep up with...

Dear God, My mom is sick with Covid...

Jesus, Please help my family...

Heavenly Father, We need your strength...

I continued to check on Jay as Reagan and her family nursed him back to health, as he returned to Lejeune to finish his military service, and as he and Reagan prepared to make their big move from Wilmington.

The last time I checked in on Jay just before their move to Chicago, I observed him and Reagan cuddling around the firepit on a beautiful fall night in the Dewey's yard, listening to Ventura Highway, and looking up at the stars.

Gazing up at the beautiful sky, Matt whispered over to Reagan and said, "The fact that millions of people are enjoying these same stars warmed by separate fires is very satisfying, isn't it?"

No answer came, as Reagan and Jay had already drifted off to sleep. Matt smiled at them, looked up to me, and- knowing I agreed with him- gave a thankful wink.

A PLACE TO DIE

"You know, I can't believe the year we've had. Putting Missy down was hard enough. Your mom finally passing and all those arrangements. Cleaning out her house, fixing it, selling it. If this is more than a flu, I'll be pissed," Sharon said, her hands squeezing the steering wheel for emphasis on the last word.

Sitting in the passenger seat and shifting in her seat uncomfortably, Jan's left hand clutched her abdomen as her other hand held her chin while staring out the window.

Grimacing, Jan replied, "Trust me. I'm ready for a positive turn. I mean, what else could we endure? And your mom in hospice in New Jersey right now, you flying back and forth to help her, and my brother passing just last year. I mean, really."

The recent cold snap and January Christmas decorations scattered around the Carolina Beach area dampened their spirits. The sun densely shone through thick clouds with a temperature in the low 50's. It just felt like the deck was stacked against them.

They arrived at the clinic for Jan's appointment, a follow-up to a visit two weeks prior after she first experienced persistent stomach pains. After the pain worsened, she thought it best to check back. Could be the flu given the time of year, or the increasing spread of the new SARS virus, or something else.

"I'll get the door for you," Sharon said as she parked, quickly exiting the car to make her way toward the passenger side.

Jan opened the door herself, then asserted, "Now I think you know better than that. After all this time together, you really think you're going to start coddling me now?"

With this, Sharon took a step back, but stayed close to her while allowing her to walk on her own. She thought about offering to grab a wheelchair seeing Jan's pain was worsening, but knew she would get the same response.

With Jan having been on the hospital board for two terms, they knew she would get VIP treatment. They checked in, were walked to an exam room, and the doctor entered almost immediately.

"Well, Ms. Dewey, I thought I told you to go home and feel better. Jan, Jan, Jan. You just don't listen," Dr. Carson said with his usual broad smile and chuckle. A portly, older, gray-bearded and bespectacled Teddy Roosevelt-type.

"Hell doc. If I would have known it would only get worse, I would have asked for a freakin' second opinion." As usual, Jan could go toe to toe with anyone. Men and women alike.

"Your temperature is a bit elevated, but your other vitals are fine. You've lost seven pounds since I saw you two weeks ago. Tell me about the pain in terms of frequency and intensity."

"She's in a lot of pain all the time, doc," Sharon interrupted, but stopped as soon as Jan shot her a disapproving look.

"Pain has been pretty steady, mostly in my abdomen and a bit in my lower back. Shooting pain here and there, and at other times just a dull ache, and I've been nauseous lately. Been treating it with Tylenol, and not eating much. Just been gradually feeling worse since my last visit."

"Got it," Dr. Carson said as he felt around her stomach area. "Any of this sore to the touch?"

"No. Not really. It's deeper than that."

"So we're going to schedule you for some labs, blood work, etc. I'd like to do that as soon as possible. This afternoon if you are available. If not, tomorrow."

"We can do it this afternoon," Sharon chimed in again.

"Yes, as my personal assistant slash pain in the ass roommate indicates, we can do tests this afternoon," shaking her head, Jan rose from the exam table to put her clothes back on.

"I'll tell you what though, if you make me wear a pink gown again next time I come in, I'm outta here." Jan had a way of using humor to help others feel better. As she spoke, she wasn't entirely convinced it would work on herself.

A day later Jan was back at work, much to Sharon's discouragement. But work was the best antidote for the discomfort of whatever this was, and a positive distraction for Jan. She always found great joy in her work, a forty-year college administrator, and currently the VP of Business Affairs at the local university.

The biggest challenge was appearing steady, masking any flare-ups of pain, and hoping the NSAIDS and pain meds the doctor gave her for now would keep her on her game at work.

Two days later, the news came that Carson wanted more tests done, specifically imaging and endoscopy. His phone call to her was his best attempt at optimism.

"Listen, this could be anything. Don't make any hasty conclusions. Let's just be thorough early on so we can pinpoint what's happening. The pain is persisting even with the meds I gave you, which is concerning. And your appetite is weak, which means your energy is going to be low. So for now I want you to rest and we will get your tests scheduled ASAP."

After a pause, Jan wryly replied, "Just when I thought the 'cone of uncertainty' ended with hurricane season. Thanks a lot, doc."

That evening after dinner, Sharon made an effort to help Jan relax. "Let's sit on the deck a bit. The weather is beautiful, and the dolphins have been running a lot," Sharon said as she cleared the table while Jan shifted to get comfortable on the couch.

Sitting on the rocking chairs on the upper deck looking out at the ocean was essentially a nightly ritual for them. Jan always occupying the one on the right, and Sharon on the left facing the ocean.

"Sounds good. But listen, I don't need a lecture on how to take care of myself. We will get the tests scheduled and I will keep working unless the pain is bad. That's the deal."

As Jan spoke, she winced a bit as the discomfort in her lower stomach intensified. She waited until Sharon wasn't looking to coil her arms around her mid-section, reaching for another pillow to try to get comfortable.

Sharon placed the dishes in the sink, holding off until later putting them in the dishwasher; she knew if she didn't capitalize on Jan's agreement to sit outside, the opportunity would be lost. Jan always dove back into her work after dinner. Emails, reading articles, making notes for upcoming meetings, analyzing spreadsheets. But tonight those priorities seemed less important.

As Sharon wiped her hands, she noticed Jan slowly walking through the sliding door out onto the deck. She waited for her to settle into her chair, then asked, "Can I get you anything before I come out? Did the doc say you're ok to have your customary gin and tonic?"

Sharon hesitated to offer this, but thought perhaps it would ease Jan's pain and give them some time to chat.

"Actually, yes, that's a fine idea. Bring me one."

Jan stepped away from her favorite drinks several weeks ago when the initial symptoms came, but figured accepting the offer might help Sharon worry less. And she also knew perhaps if she joined her for one, Sharon might relax a bit.

A few minutes later, Sharon emerged with Jan's favorite drink- Tanqueray and tonic, a splash of Rose's lime juice, and a lime on the rim, on ice.

"Ahh. Yes, this was a good idea. Finally some warmer weather and nice and quiet out here tonight," Jan spoke after her first sip. The beach area was especially quiet and quaint this time of year, with few renters or vacationers around.

The house Jan inherited from her uncle twenty-five years ago was their sanctuary, their home, as close to paradise as anyone could ask for. A two-story cape house with yellow, cedar shake dormers, 40 yards from the ocean with a pier leading through the estuary right onto the beach.

"If you're up for it, let's walk on the beach this weekend. We haven't done that since Missy passed, and the weather looks ideal," Sharon said, settling into her own rocker with the same drink as Jan.

Sharon continued, "Hey, I just want to say one thing, then we can enjoy our drinks. I know you hate for people to worry about you. But you know you're my world. We've been friends and lovers for as long as I can remember. Whatever this is, please let me care about you. Let me care *for* you. I don't have your mom to keep an eye on while you're working. I don't have Missy to take on her walks and keep me company. I sit at home and call mom up in Jersey, and worry about when I should schedule my next trip up there. So I need to feel like you need me. That's it."

This was as close to an emotional conversation Sharon would ever initiate with Jan. It just wasn't their style. They were best friends, lovers, companions, housemates. The labels on the relationship changed based on who they were around. But they knew the truth, which was they would always be there for each other.

Jan smiled and put her hand on Sharon's arm, then looking into her eyes for the first time in a while, said, "Of course you can care about me, as I care about you. You're the best pain in the ass anyone could have. Now sip your drink and wait for your dolphins to emerge."

Sharon grinned and said, "This view never gets old. I don't understand how anyone could not like the beach. It's so calming."

Jan's eyes closed as she listened to the sound of the waves meeting the shore. She replied with her eyes still closed, "I fell in love with the ocean the first day I landed here from Chicago. I knew I had to live near the water, and this house was perfect. For me the ocean is about cleansing and purification, and forgiveness. Like a blank slate."

Sharon quietly exhaled, settled into the back of her chair gently rocking back and forth, then rolled her head in Jan's direction.

"I suppose that's why we love each other," Sharon said. "This place has given us beauty and kept us balanced. Those perfect footprints we leave at the water's edge on our walks, they soon disappear, wiped clean by the tide. As though we were never here. Sort of like life, really. Beautiful but brief."

This made Jan smile, and though they didn't frequently have deep or philosophical conversations, she found their mutual affection for the ocean and beach to be an aspect of their relationship she always cherished.

After a pause, Jan looked up toward the sky as the sun made its final descent, and said, "I certainly have drawn strength from the ocean, and so many times it has given me peace and perspective, but also a sense of humility. When I look out on the horizon and the size and strength of the water, I know that I matter, that we matter, but I am also aware of how fragile we are."

Jan woke the next morning to dress for her appointment with Dr. Carson to receive her test results. Now nearly four weeks since her initial pain, and no sign of improvement, Jan had a feeling it was something bad.

She wrestled with herself on the range of possibilities. Sixty-four years old, overall healthy and active, no medical history of any kind, non-smoker, moderate drinker. Then there was the karma of it all, the recent set-backs with sick family members. Her mom's death. The passing of their family dog they had shared for twelve years. *No way the universe could be this unfair*, she thought to herself.

Carson was both their doctor for many years, so he knew how to speak to each of them respectively about their health. Sharon the more reactive and emotional, and Jan gruff and straight-forward. He especially knew not to sugarcoat things with Jan, as she would have no tolerance for such treatment.

"It's your pancreas. Tests were highly conclusive for cancer. We don't know what stage yet, but imaging suggests it's pretty far along. You're scheduled for a biopsy and cytology with Dr. Vasquez up at Duke in two days. He can provide his analysis and recommendations for treatment."

After a pause so they could digest the diagnosis, he continued, "Hard to say if the Whipple surgery is an option or not. But I think he wants to immediately schedule chemo if the labs confirm positive. It's a shitty scenario, but we need to stay positive."

Sitting beside her in Carson's office, Sharon's grip on Jan's hand tightened. But she resisted the impulse to cover her mouth and cry, using every ounce of effort to steady herself.

Even Jan had to pause a minute to respond. She wanted to be quippy and ease the tension in the room. She wanted to say something to make it better, mainly to calm Sharon. But she struggled to find the words.

"This Vasquez better be good, or I'm giving you back the service plaque you gave me for serving on your damn board."

Jan drove home at her insistence. In part to show that she could. In part to feel some locus of control. But mostly because Sharon's nerves were shot and driving at this time may have been unsafe.

"Is this what has to happen for you to let me drive once in a while? Really, you're not my chauffeur." Another attempt for Jan to lighten the mood.

"Very funny. I don't know what to say. And you're not saying much either. How is your pain right now?"

"The meds are helping. I just need to try to find something worth eating. Shit, I've lost fifteen pounds already. Where was this miracle weight loss plan five years ago when we were trying to get in shape for our fucking trip to the Bahamas?"

"When you're done making jokes, I'd like to know what you're thinking, Jan."

"I can't process through it that fast. Obviously I'll talk to this Dr. Vasquez later today, and then we will do whatever he says. He's the Chief Oncologist at Duke. That's all I can give you right now."

Chemo treatments would be scheduled for the month of February, and with the Wuhan, China flu spreading, they were keeping a keen eye on the news. Four treatments a week apart.

Vasquez speculated Jan was already at stage three or four, and that surgery would be unsafe given the contour of the cancer around her pancreas. But he insisted chemo possibly followed by radiation could have positive effects.

"Miracles happen," were his last words to Jan as they hung up, though she found this specious and assumed he often ended such calls with his patients the same way.

Jan sat at their kitchen table, looking out over the ocean as she had a million times before. Tempted to look away after a few seconds, she held her gaze longer this time; somehow attempting to capture the image, to enjoy it versus viewing it as the presumptive backdrop of their daily lives. Sharon sat across from her sipping a cup of tea as Jan's mind raced about their new reality.

"I've got to figure out how to tell the staff. This is going to suck," Jan finally uttered.

"Listen, we will develop a strategy. You get to decide who you tell, when, and what you say. It's all up to you. Just think it through like you always do. You've helped build that campus your whole career. You can do whatever you want now," Sharon replied.

"I know. But I have 180 people counting on me. You know how people talk. As soon as the news breaks, they will never look at me the same. You know how private I am. I just hate that I have to do this."

"Then don't do it now. Start the treatments and see how it goes."

"Then people will wonder why I'm taking days off, why I've lost weight. Why I'm edgy with them as I balance managing the pain with managing important decisions. That's not fair to them either."

They moved to the rocking chairs on the deck, talking as they always did to catch up at the end of the day. Sharon listening, but not trying to push her opinion too hard, careful to let Jan control it all as she did every aspect of her life, and usually theirs.

Lending her support by just listening and reflecting seemed the best approach for now. As darkness fell, Jan decided to go lie down. Before rising from her chair, she told Sharon how she would approach telling staff.

"I've got a full division meeting next Tuesday. I'm going to meet with the chancellor a half hour before, tell him, then tell the division in person. They will appreciate it coming directly from me. They've earned that."

Sharon could only muster the words she knew Jan wanted to hear- "Sounds good, honey. That sounds like a good plan."

Tuesday came and the chancellor took the news well. A matter-of-fact academician with a limited capacity for emotions, he mustered the same response Jan predicted would come.

"Sorry to hear. Let me know how I can help. Take all the time you need."

Jan knew he genuinely felt bad for her, but mainly that the bomb she just dropped would cause him to begin worrying about the impact on the university. The chief financial officer being out for cancer treatments. Who would stand in? What big decisions would need to be made in her absence? What was at risk for the leadership of the business side of the house?

But Jan knew she could coach him along step by step, meanwhile showing him and others she could still lead even while battling the fiercest of enemies. After all, she was a woman who ascended as a major campus leader throughout her entire career among men, silencing her sexual orientation to prevent any blowback within a conservative organization in a red state.

The battle scars she already survived prepped her for even the harshest of chemo treatments. Exiting his office and heading to the union to inform her people, she said aloud to herself, "You got this."

As she entered the ballroom, the usual familial atmosphere was at hand. People smiling and laughing, hugging each other and catching up. She had built an organization of trust and positive relationships, where people shared a common vision- provide excellent programs and services to college students to enable them to have the best experience possible.

While she was happy to see and feel the energy, she knew the news would instantaneously deflate the room like never before.

"Good morning, friends," her usual greeting using the microphone to carry her voice in such a large space. "Settle down. I don't want those stiffs in Academic Affairs to think we're having too much fun." The staff chuckled as they took their seats around tables facing the front podium.

"First meeting of the new year. I trust you all had a good holiday break. As usual, here in Business Affairs we are ready to do what we do, provide students at this university the best experience for the money. Thank you for your work last year, and thanks for all I know you will do this year for this outstanding university."

Heads nodded in agreement. Then, before a longer pause than usual from their leader, she delivered the prognosis.

"Listen, you know I love and respect you all. So I want to tell you something personally. This is the hardest message I have ever delivered to you. Some of you have been with me over 20 years, and some of you are brand new to this division."

The room got quieter than it had ever been for a monthly division meeting, many assuming perhaps an announcement about her retirement was imminent.

"You know I have been in and out the last couple of weeks. So, I want to tell you, and this is so hard... I have been diagnosed with cancer of the pancreas."

With this, the only sound in the room was the low hum of the lights above. Many staff grabbed their mouths in disbelief.

"We all know this is a terrible enemy. But you know who I am as a person and leader. I'm going to fight this with all I have. I can't tell you how far along it is, but they can't do surgery. I'm doing treatments soon, so I will be in and out of the office. Just continue to do your work, and do it as well as you always have. Continue to make me proud. I love you all."

Jan held her emotions with only the last couple of words coming across as a bit shaky. Versus staying for the remainder of the meeting, she had asked her assistant vice president to take over from there, and stated she had another meeting to be at.

Her AVP took the mic and said, "Thank you, Jan. We are with you as always," as she exited the ballroom. Only when she was outside the union did the emotion come, and it came hard.

She looked around to see if others were nearby. Only a few students in the distance passing to their next classes were within view. Then her breathing got heavy, and the tears welled up and covered her face, dripping off her chin onto the pavement.

No matter the final outcome, she knew nothing would be the same for her. *How I'm perceived as a strong female leader*

134

will vanish, kept running through her mind. The questions about how she was doing and how long she had to live would begin to morph her work, her reputation, and her accomplishments. This was as overwhelming to her as being sick.

She scurried across campus to where outside her office in the Volvo was Sharon, leaning over to open the passenger door for Jan's entry, eager to hear how it went and lend the requisite support.

Jan's face was flush and still damp with tears, and Sharon put her hand on Jan's arm as they pulled away. Knowing Jan would not want her colleagues to see her like this, they briskly made their way off campus toward the sanctuary of their Carolina Beach home.

The month of March was a blur for them. The Chinese flu was officially declared a global pandemic- "Coronavirus" or "Covid-19"- and Sharon made only one brief trip to New Jersey to check in on her mom and elected not to tell her the news about Jan for now. At 87 and diagnosed with congestive heart disease, she knew this would only cause added worry and stress.

Jan's pain persisted and the chemo was hell. Though she read up on how to best prepare for the treatments with rest, proper diet, and recovery, nothing mattered. The flu-like symptoms after each treatment were awful. Her weight was dropping more each week as she struggled to sustain her energy.

Watching their favorite episodes of Friends one evening after dinner, Jan continued doing her best to keep things light. From the couch, she spoke toward Sharon in the kitchen.

"Hey. I assume after my chemo ends we will go out for seafood? I'm going to need a new wardrobe if I keep losing weight."

Sharon replied, "I told you we're in this together. After you beat this we will go back to our normal, endomorphic states."

"Right. And if I don't have a gin and tonic soon I swear I'm going to kill someone," Jan efforted a half smile.

They continued to talk, and the mood seemed right for Sharon to present Jan with a proposal she was contemplating. Jan appeared comfortable with pillows and blankets positioned around her, her pain manageable now with a low dose of Vicodin that Vasquez provided.

"I know we both love Jennette and Aidan. They've basically been family since they took over as tenants downstairs. But I think with everything happening we need to tell them it's time for a change."

Sharon spoke while seated on the coffee table facing Jan.

"What for? Aid is never around now with his girlfriend and Vamonos Pest and school, and she's constantly at work," Jan shifted on the couch a bit as she spoke.

"Because these stairs up and down are not good for you, and we certainly don't need the income. We can give them a few weeks to find a new place, and let them rent for free for the last month. But I think it's time to make that a space for us."

Jan appreciated how Sharon was always looking out for them, though the notion of moving into the apartment downstairs and the hassle of doing so did not appeal to her. Ten years ago such a project would have been fun, but not now.

"I'm home most days now anyway, even working remotely here for now. You always do the errands and shopping, so I'm not really going in and out that much. Plus, with all this Covid stuff happening I need to be in the office a bit and keeping up with what's happening. We're requiring all students be tested, so I have to help with the planning. They're even seeking volunteers to help swab noses for crying out loud."

Jan hated to deflate Sharon's proposal as she knew her intentions were good, but Sharon persisted.

"From what I can tell, everyone will be working from home soon as Covid rates continue to rise. Plus, we both know things may change at any time with your health. And when it does, we should be ready. Let's plan ahead on this. I will do the work. You tell me what you want down there, and I will get Tim and his workers here to make it happen."

After giving her time to take it in, Sharon added, "And without those stairs, you can take more walks on the beach when you're up to it."

Seeing Sharon's preoccupation with the plan and in consideration of all Sharon was doing for them, Jan relented- "Makes sense. Ok, let's talk to Jennette right away so she has time to find something. And let's make sure Aidan is there. He's going through so much lately, so I want to be careful with him."

"Fine. Truth is, at 59 I'm getting too old to be carrying groceries up and down stairs anyway. So this is mostly for me."

"Hah. Whatever. Just make it nice. Money's not the issue. We have my retirement and mom's inheritance, plus the rent account from Jennette."

Sharon looked at Jan clutching the blanket around her as she spoke, noticing how the bones in her hand were protruding more visibly.

"I know money's not the issue, but I also know you don't want the Taj Mahal. Trust me, I'll make you quite comfortable down there, dearie."

The use of the word *dearie* for sarcastic emphasis made Jan laugh, followed by her final retort, "Well, *dearie*, nice for you to finally pull some weight around here. But how the hell am I supposed to be comfortable with you down there bugging me about making sure I'm comfortable? A bit of an oxymoron, don't you think?"

They both chuckled, followed by Sharon applying a kiss to Jan's forehead as her eyes got heavy and she quickly dozed off.

Sharon pulled the blanket over Jan's shoulder and left her a bit longer on the couch, then drifted out onto the deck to collect her thoughts. So much of her time was recently spent researching pancreatic cancer and trying to take care of her beloved Jan. She knew where all this was heading, and she wanted Jan comfortable every step of the way, especially toward the end.

They invited Jennette and Aidan for breakfast on Saturday to talk, though last-minute Aidan said he couldn't make it given his band Vamonos Pest- or "VP" as it was known by- had a gig that night. Having rented the apartment unit to such reliable tenants for nearly 10 years, they worried how this would impact them.

Jennette, fully sympathetic to the situation, immediately took the news well and with full support, even offering to immediately move back in with her sister in Leland in order to give Sharon more time to convert the unit for Jan's use.

Jan wouldn't hear of it, and in the end she insisted Jennette and Aidan remain until they found another place to live. But in just a week's time, Jennette texted Sharon to state she found the perfect place just two blocks away, and that Aid took the news well and totally understood their situation. The following Saturday they were gone.

They had let their handyman Tim know to be ready, and met with him outside on the deck the day after the apartment was vacated to clarify what needed to be done. Sharon was careful to require the few guests who came over to only meet outside in order to help prevent any contact with Jan.

"You tell me what you want and I will make your job a priority," Tim offered, speaking through his mask.

"Just pull your pants up when you work down there. I don't want to see your 50-year-old ass crack while I'm resting." Tim was also quite familiar with how much of a pistol Jan was, even while discussing serious topics.

The basement apartment was by most standards pretty nice, though old. The house was built in 1965, and renovated at least once before Jan moved in after arriving from Chicago in 1996.

After Sharon moved in several years later, they did the usual upkeep, paint-jobs in and out, and replaced the roof. The salt air wrought havoc on most of the outdoor fixtures.

Sharon worked to begin presenting Tim some concepts of how it could be redone on an accelerated timeline, and because Tim was like family to them he assured them it would be perfect.

By April 2020, Covid-19 was rapidly spreading, exceeding one million cases worldwide, and the decision to close the campus was made. The students would move out of the dorms, finish classes online, and staff would also begin working from home.

As Tim continued the work on the unit, Jan was tied up in online meetings all day related to plans for keeping the university running. Her pain was steady but the meds kept the more intense pain at bay.

Resting and a few naps between meetings each day kept her energy just high enough to focus on work, and the coincidence of remote work due to Covid was one of the few bright spots in terms of the timing of her illness.

While her staff attempted to pick up the slack, the demands on her as chief financial officer soared. Would the school have enough tuition and fees to keep running for the summer and fall, and was it even safe to do so?

Campus leaders discussed taking aggressive measures, such as fully closing for summer and planning for online only classes in the fall. As the work continued and intensified, Jan pushed herself to help bring the results to keep the campus financially afloat. She was determined to continue to work until the cancer would render it impossible to do so.

After concluding an online meeting, Jan said to Sharon, "Do you think I should continue to be on video for these damn Zooms? I look like a popsicle. I'm switching to audio only from now on."

"No one cares what you look like. You have cancer, and everyone knows it. They're just amazed you're still working at all, as am I frankly. And while it's not my place to say, I do think you should consider stepping away. Stepping away for good."

Passing Sharon in the kitchen as she spoke, Jan changed the subject with great intention.

"Are we moving all this kitchen stuff down there or just replacing it with new stuff? I know you've always wanted to go nuts at Bed, Bath and Beyond. Here's your chance."

Sharon worried with their joking all the time they were avoiding the real conversations about the future. About how much time was left, what Jan wanted in terms of her estate, the funeral service, the important stuff.

Though unplanned, Sharon's words came fast and firm, and without either of them prepared for such an emotionally weighty moment.

"Goddamn it Jan, I'm scared! I'm scared for you. I'm scared for me. I'm sad and angry at the same time. I can't believe this is how God operates. You've given your whole life and career for others, and this is what happens? I'm just not *ready* for this. I'm not ready to lose you, to lose *us!*"

As the volume and intensity of Sharon's words escalated to a crescendo, the last word was given added emphasis as she slammed her hands on the kitchen counter, now shaking in a way Jan had never seen. She spoke with a raw emotion blending fibers from her head, heart and soul, and her eyes filled with tears.

Jan slowly approached Sharon to console her, at first preparing to make a joke, to ask Sharon why she was crying when she wasn't the one dying. But not this time. Instead, she hugged her with all her strength.

"I don't tell you enough how much I love you. How much I have *always* loved you. How much I know I put you through, and now what I am putting you through. And how lucky I am to have you here, especially at this time. My job needs me, and you need me. But I can't stay home looking out at the ocean, waiting to die. I can't go out that way. I need to pitch in while I have my strength. I'll know when it's time to stop. You just keep focusing on making me a nice place to die, and we will finish things down there together."

As Jan finished speaking she pulled away and faced Sharon, now both with tears in their eyes and smiling at each other, each reaching to softly wipe the other's tears.

"A place to die. I hadn't thought of it just like that. But as usual, you do have a way with words." Sharon laughed as she reached for a tissue.

As Jan worked remotely, Sharon made the downstairs apartment project her priority, constantly checking in with Jan on her specifications and the set-up. Even widening the doorway in case Jan would eventually need a wheelchair for access.

A large picture window was added in place of the wall facing the ocean, and a second doorway toward the beach and patio beneath the deck was installed so they could sit out back on the ground-level porch as they always did on the deck above, watching the shrimp boats in the mornings and the dolphins and surfers in the evenings. Matching rocking chairs were ordered, just like the ones upstairs.

By May, Covid and its Alpha and Beta variants were rampant, so only essential services were open in the U.S., and Jan spent most hours providing financial forecasts for the school, using different scenarios for outcomes.

The chancellor needed to know how they would fare if the fall semester opened in a hybrid format, with some classes online; how they would deal with a drop in enrollment and its impact on tuition and fees; and, how they would make ends meet if they had to have a semester with only online classes where students wouldn't pay fees for campus services.

As was the case with the entire country, the outcomes were unclear so the solutions were tentative at best. Jan had guided the university on how to survive coastal hurricanes and stay afloat financially, but this was something different.

"Give me some good news today, doc. It's bad enough we're both wearing these masks and look like Bonnie and Clyde about to hold up a bank, so tell me something good."

Dr. Carson chuckled from behind his mask, his cheeks rising closer to his eyes to signal his appreciation for Jan's wit.

"Well, the good news according to Dr. Vasquez is it isn't advancing as fast as it could. The bad news is, it's also not remitting. Your T cell count is stable, but your weight loss concerns me, as does your pain. You're refilling your script twice a week. Are you sure Sharon isn't horning in on your meds?"

Sharon smiled from behind her mask, seated next to Jan in Carson's exam room.

"Listen, I would gladly stop the meds for my favorite cock-tail, but you continue to warn about mixing them. Gee, is it really going to matter in the long run?"

"Well, I can only tell you what I'm trained to tell you. What you do when you leave my office is, of course, your call. Use the meds to manage pain. More liquids, and force down those pro-tein shakes. And a short walk every day in the fresh air. Only on the beach when you have the energy, please."

"Thanks, doc. And don't get any ideas. We're not selling you the beach house any time soon. Sharon informs me she's plan-ning on opening a distillery downstairs after I'm gone."

Another broad smile from Carson as he turned to head to his next patient. As they walked out, they talked about the move downstairs scheduled for the weekend.

"Tim is ready. Let's take one last look tonight, then he has his crew coming Saturday to help move things, and make sure every-thing is set. I'm really excited about our new life down there. It will be a nice new start."

Jan shook her head in agreement as they exited the building holding hands. In the car, they continued their planning.

"Ten years ago we would have rented the top level for the extra cash. But I'm definitely not in the mood for hearing footsteps above us night and day. But I get to go up there when I want, to still view the ocean from the deck. I've always counted on that view to get me through the tough days," Jan said this only half seriously, as she doubted she would have the energy much longer to climb stairs.

Sharon replied, "Done. If I have to piggy-back you up there for that to happen, I will."

By early June of 2020, Jan's energy was diminishing. The requirement for social distancing kept her at home 24-7. No vis-itors, no trips out; even the beaches were closed.

She settled into her new digs and actually liked the new view of the sunrise, the birds skipping across the sand, and seeing a few redtail foxes scrounging for turtle eggs along the dunes. Especially the new view of the horizon out the large picture window and the new rocking chairs on the patio where coffee and the morning paper were enjoyed.

But she was down to 120 pounds, very slow in movement, and becoming forgetful. Her assistant at work did his best to include her on major decisions, but the pain meds made her groggy and her vision was increasingly opaque. She cancelled most morning meetings and late afternoon meetings, and began communicating only through fragmented emails.

Mid-June her staff invited her to participate on a last-minute Zoom about Covid, only to find out it was a surprise convening for Jan's 65th birthday, with staff and faculty from the entire university online to view a slide show of her and a recounting of all her major accomplishments throughout her career. New buildings, new recreation fields, new parking decks and landscaping. All the things she created that helped the university become a national leader in its business and service models.

While she had always dreamed of a big send-off to recognize her work upon retirement, she knew that was not in the cards now. The cruel collision of Covid and cancer saw to that. But she appreciated the effort and was humbled by the gesture. Short of a full miracle, she knew this would be her last birthday to celebrate.

Meanwhile, the effort to ease social distancing restrictions and reopen the economy sorely backfired, as the federal government raced to create a vaccine. By mid-summer, an uptick in cases and deaths resulted in a complete work stoppage.

Only gas stations and grocery stores remained open, and most people began ordering all supplies online and picking up their groceries curbside. The university finalized their plans to offer only online instruction for fall.

Other than the occasional call from the chancellor, Jan stopped checking in with the college. Her staff worked for her long enough to know what to do, and how to lead the business side of the university. Her healthy bank of sick leave would ensure her salary would continue through her remaining days.

Sharon woke one morning next to Jan and looked over at her, noticing how frail she had become. How shallow her breathing was, and how the liquid Morphine was increasingly sedating her, especially impacting her clarity during the waking hours.

They had been talking about the option of moving her to hospice versus home-hospice as a next step, but the widespread infections of Covid at nursing homes and in-patient facilities made their choice easy. Jan would remain in the house from here forward. A nurse began visiting to check on her twice a week, then every other day, and- by mid-July- daily.

On July 24th after they finished breakfast, Jan said, "Let's go upstairs tonight after dinner. It's been a while since we sat on the top deck. Those rocking chairs are getting dusty. I think I'm up for it and can be careful on the stairs. We can grab a gin up there and reminisce. It's supposed to be a cool night, and I'd like to have that view again."

Sharon listened and worked to provide a nonchalant response. "Sounds great."

Jan continued, "Good then. And I was thinking, let's get up early tomorrow like we used to and see the sunrise together. It's supposed to be a clear day. We can set the alarm for 5:45 and have our coffee on the rockers as the sun comes up."

Sharon wasn't in the position lately to push back on anything. She knew things were winding down. Instead, she simply made efforts to keep Jan comfortable. Helping her change clothes, finding the TV clicker she constantly misplaced, adjusting the font size on Jan's laptop so she could check emails, giving her a sponge bath and helping her to bed.

"That sounds awesome. Of course, we have plenty of booze since it feels like we've been living through prohibition around here. I'll run to the store for your favorite cheese and snacks," Sharon offered.

Jan knew she wouldn't eat much of it, but also knew it would make for a nice evening with Sharon. She enjoyed seeing how much Sharon wanted to make it a relaxing evening followed by a perfect morning.

After a dinner mainly consisting of salad and fruit, Jan picking at hers and only taking a few sips of her protein shake, they put on comfortable clothes, grabbed two blankets, and made their way up the flight of stairs to the deck.

Sharon stood behind Jan as she slowly managed the steps, making sure to be in position to catch her if she fell back, but also giving her enough space to do it on her own.

Sharon, not usually the one to crack the first joke, said, "Heck, if I would have known you could still climb stairs, I wouldn't have wasted all that time and money renovating the apartment."

Jan's response was quick. "Careful with that humor. I think after all this time, my snarkiness is rubbing off on you."

The evening was beautiful in every respect. Jan appeared unfazed in terms of pain; she was lucid and coherent and her energy was high. The temperature at sunset was a comfortable 65 degrees with a nice breeze off the water.

Though the beach was officially closed, a few surfers on longboards were catching slow, rolling waves for nice long rides, and above the horizon and over the shoreline the ocean birds circled.

A few brown pelicans did their usual straight-line plunge into the ocean with explosive splashes before coming up with fish. Tiny pipers and waders tip-toed along the sand also enjoying the view, before being shooed away by large, white albatross.

Just before dusk as the sun set behind the house to the west, tall shadows cast along the sand below as the ocean turned a brilliant, bright orangish-red.

A group of Northern Gannets hovered on the horizon in their view, and as they continued south one peeled off ascending high above the others, disappearing into the clouds.

As Jan got comfortable, Sharon caught her in long gazes at the scenes being offered by the beach and ocean, a view they had both enjoyed for many years together. Though there was so much Sharon wanted to say, Jan appeared content silently taking in the spectacular view and surrounding panorama.

Jan pointed out to the water and smiled, as a school of dolphins emerged at the surface like the dial of a clock slowly passing from 10 to 2, then submerging and repeating the same rotation several yards ahead.

"You know, I could never get tired of this view. How lucky we are to be here. How lucky we are to enjoy it together," Sharon replied after the extended space of silence.

"True. It's been great. You're not going to get too emotional on me I hope. I know how you are after a few drinks," Jan replied while looking over smiling, noticing how tired Sharon looked, but how much she tried not to appear so.

Jan continued, "Remember the night we had Tom and Kim here from Raleigh, and we were out here talking each other's ears off over mint juleps, and the next thing we knew we woke up and it was 4am and everyone was fast asleep in their chairs, wet with sea dew?"

Sharon was thrilled Jan could recall such occurrences, this one many years ago, then replied, "Yeah, and instead of waking them you threw beach towels on them and we left them out here until morning."

As Sharon finished speaking they were now in a full roar together, Jan coughing a bit between laughs.

"I was just worried the damn seagulls might shit on their heads!" Jan said, now laughing even harder, spilling some of her drink.

After their laughter settled, Jan looked over and placed her hand on Sharon's, and said, "So many great memories, and it all went by so fast. Feels like I just moved in here yesterday."

Sharon continued her focus on the school of dolphins, then squeezing Jan's hand said, "We will make some more memories *dearie*, don't you worry."

The full moon grew in brightness as a million stars consumed the sky above them, and the water turned a mix of dark blue and turquoise as the moonbeams bounced off the slow, rolling waves.

Staring out in the distance, Jan somewhat quietly said, "I think it's only when we lose our beauty that we can best appreciate the beauty around us."

Sharon worked to quell the welling of emotions in her chest, and enjoyed watching Jan finish her drink, ask for another, and continue to tell stories of all the good times they had over the years at the beach.

Several hours elapsed in the span of what felt like several minutes, and as they finished their second cocktail and the night air made for a chilly breeze off the ocean, Sharon noticed Jan's eyes getting heavy.

"C'mon girl, let's get you to bed. We're not sleeping on this deck tonight."

The walk back down the stairs was a little more challenging, after the drinks and with the night dew on the steps. But they took it slow and Sharon held Jan's waist tightly with one hand, her other hand clutching the railing.

Sharon helped Jan into her favorite pajamas that she bought her for Christmas last year. Teal in color with little German Shepard faces, similar to their departed Missy.

"5:45. Don't let me sleep through it. I'll make us coffee and we will be on those rocking chairs before the sun is up at 6," Jan said as Sharon pulled the covers over her.

Sharon smiled and caressed her hair as Jan drifted off to sleep, then whispered, "*I'll* make the coffee. Sleep well my love."

Sharon slept upstairs so Jan could sleep undisturbed. Unlike most recent nights where she tossed and turned, Sharon slept like a rock. A mix of pent-up exhaustion and contentment on such a great evening, and seeing Jan in such great spirits.

She woke at 5am recalling the dream of her and Jan as little girls walking on the beach, playing in the surf and building sand-castles, then the dream jumped to them riding in Jan's Camaro after they first met- top down and cruising to and from dinner at their favorite local restaurant followed by drinks on the deck. Happy. Carefree. Very much in love with each other.

It was still dark, so using only her cell phone for light Sharon made her way outside and down the stairs, quietly entering the apartment enabling Jan to sleep a few minutes longer.

She made her way to the kitchenette to get the coffee ready, meanwhile checking the weather forecast for sunrise. Appeared there would be no cloud cover, and dawn would be beautiful.

At 5:30 she quietly made her way into the bedroom and to Jan's bedside to turn off the alarm so she could sleep a bit longer. She stood over Jan in the dark room admiring how peaceful she appeared.

Making her way back to the window facing the ocean, she stood sipping her coffee thinking about the things Jan said she still wanted to do. A weekend drive to Charleston to their favorite B&B and restaurant. An upcoming performance of Grease at Thalian Hall. Catching the Steely Dan concert at Greenfield Lake next month.

Sharon had the dates blocked on her calendar, and tickets purchased. No matter the effort and no matter how briefly, if Jan were up to it, they would do whatever she wanted in the remaining time they had together. This was the labor of love Sharon gladly provided to her beloved Jan.

Around 5:45 she made her way to Jan's bedside, not initially noticing that Jan had not stirred an inch since she quietly closed the door moments ago. She reached to caress Jan's face and felt the coldness of her cheek.

"No. No. No! Not now. Not *now!*"

The words emerged involuntarily. They came from the recesses of Sharon's heart and soul, resonating with painful and expressive grief. She rolled Jan toward her and clutched her in her arms. There was no doubt, no bartering, no praying for another day. She was gone.

Sharon buried her head in Jan's neck crying profusely, clutching Jan with both arms and rocking her back and forth. Time stood still, and what felt like a few seconds was a number of minutes- the time marked by the sun coming through the front picture window inch by inch, gradually removing the darkness of the room from the floor to the bed, until it fully illuminated their faces.

She gently lay Jan's head on the pillow and folded her arms on her chest, then kissed her forehead. She held her hand on Jan's and sat with her as the sun, now half above the horizon, cast a magnificent glow on Jan's body, almost warming it back to life.

As the sun made its final push over the sea, the sky burned crimson glory as though the heavens were on fire, and Sharon walked out to the patio and sat on Jan's rocking chair, consuming the beauty for both of them.

INTERSECTION

"Aid, I know you are sad about Jan. Do you want to walk over to Sharon's later and spend some time with her?"
"Mom, I can't be over there right now. It's just too dark. It's hard enough getting through my classes at Cape Fear, and since VP split up I just want to find another band and spend more time with Colton before she heads back to school Sunday. She's about the only thing keeping me going right now."

"I know it's been rough. Keep pushing to finish your classes, then we can talk about you transferring to ECU with her. I know things are tough with Covid right now, but it will turn better."

Jennette tried to perk him up, but only two months since Jan's death, he seemed so withdrawn and disconnected. He pulled his disheveled hair back behind his ears with both hands, and paced in their kitchen while slamming a few drawers.

"Reilly's dad got laid off because no one is building right now. Fucking Covid. Reilly is freaking out about losing their house. All he has right now is me and our music. We're going to keep looking for another band. Tomorrow morning we're gonna surf so I will probably just crash there tonight so I don't wake you."

"Alright, sweetie. Surfing always perks you up, so have fun. I believe in you, and I promise things are going to turn good again at some point. I just know it."

"Cool mom. Live like you rock, right?"

Aidan lazily gave her the horns sign with his right hand, but without his usual smile. It just appeared lately he was carrying the weight of the world on his shoulders.

She left for work worried about Aidan, and about how with Jan's death yet another person he cared about left him feeling abandoned. As she departed, Colton pulled up and made her way inside; immediately sensing Aidan's tension, she threw her bag on the counter and approached him.

"What's wrong, Aid? You look sad."

"Basically everything. Everything is going to shit. Mom's hours are cut at the clinic, so she has to pull more shifts at the bar which I know she hates. But she pretends it's cool just so I won't stress about it. These stupid fucking community college classes, and we can't find a full band to put together. And I miss our apartment on the beach and I miss my talks with Jan. She and Sharon were like family."

Colton approached him from behind and put her arms around him, then pulled his long, gray hair back, removed her tie from her hair, and tightly tied his hair together.

Playfully tugging on the new ponytail, she whispered to him, "You want some braids, pretty boy?"

Aidan turned and hugged her for a long time, gradually feeling much of the stress leave him as was always the case when he touched her.

As he pulled away, he whispered to her in a somewhat desperate tone, "Right now there are a thousand talented artists punching their art onto a universal tablet. I just want to be among them."

Colton smiled and tenderly kissed him, then he said, "C'mon, let's go see what Reilly's up to. He said he's got the house to himself and the fire's going. He picked up a case, and I'm so ready for a few." Holding hands, Aidan grabbed his keys as they scooted out.

As the sun set over Reilly's house, things were unusually quiet. His dad Carl was out with one of a string of lady-friends, and Reilly's brothers were already at a party up on Dow Road.

Colton sat on Aidan's lap in the mostly dirt yard around the makeshift firepit, the bottom ring of a 55-gallon drum filled with wood scraps from the nearby lumber yard that Carl worked at before being laid off.

Reilly stoked the fire with a long stick, then brought its enflamed end to his face to light his cigarette.

Aidan sat quietly mesmerized by the flames and associated crackles; the usual cacophony of blaring music that typically emanated from the house was absent for a change. But the solitude and silence only made him more anxious, more focused on the heavy weight of his life and unclear future.

He tipped Colton on his lap a bit to fumble into his pocket for one of the pills he was considering taking, but instead stood and snagged a beer from the nearby cooler.

"Riles, your fire skills are for shit. Step aside," Aidan said as he set his beer down and grabbed a massive pile of nearby newspapers and tossed them onto the flames. Colton tugged on her vape and laughed as she exhaled.

"Nice Aid, the fucking newspapers are for kindling. Now we're going to be dodging soot all night," Reilly shook his head disapprovingly and tossed his stick atop the heap of smoldering papers.

As the edges of the papers caught fire, a million snowflake size ashes emitted into the air, now floating around them and showering them like a blizzard.

Colton looked up at the swirling specks and giggled, then Aidan began to chuckle a bit, put his hands on his knees in a full roar, then pitched his head toward the sky and yelled, "Fuck!"

His cigarette loosely dangling from his lips, Reilly raised both hands in the air as though dancing in the middle of a full whiteout.

Aidan followed suit, then began singing one of their favorite Green Day songs- "Another turning point, a fork stuck in the road. Time grabs you by the wrist, directs you where to go."

Colton and Reilly joined in, now all three singing at the top of their lungs while dancing around the fire covered in swirling ash- "So make the best of this test, and don't ask why. It's not a question, but a lesson learned in time. It's something unpredictable, but in the end it's right. I hope you had the time of your life!"

They partied around the fire, then crashed around 3am; intent on surfing, Aidan entered Reilly's bedroom around 6 and tried to wake him. Reilly muttered that his "bell was ringing" and needed time to nurse his hangover before possibly meeting Aidan later for some waves.

Though he too was beat tired, Aidan grabbed his board and made the several block walk toward Sharon's house where he could cut through her yard to access the surf.

Aidan could surf in any conditions… any condition of surf and any condition he was in. Happy, sad, hungover- it didn't matter. It was, other than music and Colton, one of the few things in life that gave him true joy. Not like the unrequited love he gave to his father and Marley as a child, but the kind of reciprocal love that few things in life ever offered.

As he cut through Sharon's yard, he looked up at her house to see the lights still off. Lights that for years illuminated happiness and joy between Sharon and Jan, and who shared their joy with Aidan and his mom as tenants and friends.

He strapped his leash to his ankle and stood alone on the beach pausing to stare at the house, thinking about all the great memories formed there- in every corner of the house, on the deck and on the beach.

Turning toward the water, Aidan noticed the red flag flying westward on the nearby empty lifeguard stand, the warning from yesterday that dangerous riptides were present, and for swimmers and surfers to enter the sea with the utmost caution. The same conditions that he gauged based on the turbulent surf were present today.

But Aidan had surfed in rough tide before. In fact, he had surfed about every climate imaginable. And though no other surfers were braving the surf this morning, Aidan was confident in his ability.

Despite his better judgment, for reasons not totally clear to him, he *needed* to be in the water this morning- not just for his surfing fix, but to cleanse himself of so much pain he was feeling.

His long hair flying into the wind, he took a defying running plunge into the surf which immediately pummeled him like a garment in a washing machine.

Reilly sat up, rubbed the sleep from his eyes, and popped a cigarette into his mouth. He reached for his cell phone- 11:11am. Scratching his head, he made his way to the bathroom recalling vaguely that Aidan tried to wake him much earlier, and that he took a pass on their session. He dialed Aidan and it went to voicemail.

"Aid. What's up bro. Sorry man. Needed some more zees. Hope you caught some good rides. Call me later." As he left his message, his phone vibrated showing Jennette's image.

"Hey Jennette, what's up?"

"Reilly, have you seen Aid?"

"No, actually I just left him a message. We were supposed to surf but he got up early and went without me. Did you try his cell?"

"Sharon called and said she found his cell and shoes under her deck, the usual spot he leaves them when he surfs. His board is on the beach near the water, but he's not around."

Reilly rubbed his forehead confused, trying to piece it all together, then said, "Maybe he finished surfing and just threw his board down to go talk to some people or walked to grab food. Let me drive over and see what's up. Or maybe Colton picked him up. Did you try her?"

"Yes, she said she was with you guys last night but left your house this morning after he went to surf. Definitely, if you can come help look for him. I'm a bit worried."

They hung up and Reilly drove to Sharon's to find Aid's mom and Sharon walking along the beach eyes peeled toward the tumultuous surf. With the rough conditions, there were still no other surfers in the water. The red lifeguard flag, frayed on its edges, rippled furiously in a swirling direction from the circling winds.

After walking up and down the beach for over an hour asking anyone and everyone if they saw a young man of medium height with long, gray hair surfing this morning, Jennette made the call to Carolina Beach Police. By the time they arrived, the CB Ocean Rescue team began to descend upon the area and entered the surf in an effort to find Aidan.

Sharon worked to try to help keep Jennette calm, with little success.

"Sharon, where *is* he? This isn't like him. He surfs for an hour, 90 minutes at the most. He's always so careful, and he's a strong swimmer. He never just heads places without giving me a call. My God, what is happening?"

Sharon worked to console her, and by now Reilly had called Aidan's other friends who made their way to the area gas stations and restaurants to ask around. Each showed anyone they happened upon a photo of Aidan, while inquiring if he were seen that morning.

By afternoon, the Coast Guard was in full force combing the nearby rough waters for any sign of Aidan. As rescue helicopters circled above, Sharon convinced Jennette to let the officials continue to search while they take a break up at the house.

Jennette looked out at the ocean through Sharon's sliding glass door; the torrential crashing waves and turbulent winds increased her despair.

She did her best to keep at bay the thought that a horrible accident befell her son, but the dreadful reality of what might have happened increasingly crept in. Her mind bounced between the hope of any minute seeing him enter the house and admonishing him for all the fuss, with girding for the worst.

By nightfall still no news came of Aidan's whereabouts, and Sharon insisted Jennette stay over so she would be closest to any updates that came.

Jennette's worry overwhelmed her, and around midnight in part due to exhaustion she fell into a light sleep on the couch. Her scattered dreams were a mix of visions of news that her only son was found and unharmed, with interruptions of terrible images of him as a little boy in their bathtub crying and reaching for her to pick him out of the water into her secure grasp.

At 2am the flashing red and blue lights from a line of emergency vehicles on the beach came streaming through the windows and woke her. She sprang up and made her way out the door and toward the water, already knowing the horror that awaited. This would be the day that her dream life with Aidan ended, and her nightmare as a mother began.

~ ~

The seaside memorial service for Jennette's former landlord and close friend Jan was beautiful. July 25, 2021, exactly one year after Jan's passing and 10 months since her Aidan passed, she wondered where the time went.

An amazing celebration of Jan's life and accomplishments- daughter of a Chicago cop, three sisters and a brother, she was a trailblazer in all aspects of her 65 years on Earth.

Jan's brother Matt and his wife Stacy from Wilmington, the next town over from Carolina Beach, helped Sharon get every- thing ready. As the others arrived throughout the week, they shared the news of their daughter Reagan's engagement to Jay Gomez, and that their other daughter Harper was getting ready to start graduate school in Richmond next month.

Jan's sister Susan, her wife Cat, and their daughter Rosie drove in the day before the service from Surf City, and took care of the catering for the brunch after the ceremony. Their good friends Britt and Eddie also came, as they had helped Susan so much during and after Cat's bout with Covid.

Kim Dewey-Walter, the youngest sister, and her husband Tom arrived from Raleigh several days before the service to also help get Sharon's house ready for visitors, and for the service that would be on the beach in front of the house where exactly one year ago Jan peacefully passed. As usual, Tom woke early each morning to go for runs on the beach.

Sister Jackie and her husband Neil from Illinois arrived last, Neil having just finished a show in Boston and needing to leave the day after the service for REO's next show two days from now in New York. Everyone doted over their new baby Selena, the first chance they all had to meet her, and of course congratulated Neil on his new gig as a professional touring drummer.

They sat on beach chairs and blankets on the sand at sun- rise, though the cloud cover masked much of the illumination typ-

156

ical for this strand of Carolina Beach at dawn. But it also kept the temperature at a comfortable 70 degrees.

After a brief ceremony by Reverend Kelterman, they pushed Jan's ashes out to the churning sea on a small raft made of drift-wood and adorned with seashells and tealights, and a photo of Sharon and their departed German Shepherd Missy.

Then they shared stories of Jan's childhood and high school, her college years at Michigan State, and her adult and career life in North Carolina. A friend of Aidan's played one of Aid's songs on acoustic guitar, a beautiful lullaby Aidan wrote for his mom and frequently played during their local gigs.

Matt described how when he and Jan were in high school and worked as lifeguards on Cal Park Beach one summer, Jan was reprimanded for driving the lifeguard truck because, as the chief guard put it, "Girls don't drive trucks."

Jan gave clear instructions before passing that after the ser-vice there was to be a gathering on the upper deck of the house looking out over the ocean, a celebration of her over her favorite mint juleps and gin drinks, while spinning her playlist of cherished hits from the 70s.

As the guests made their way back up to the house, Jennette peeled off to walk up the beach alone. Sitting in the dunes, she tried to clear her thoughts, staring at the waves crashing in much stronger than usual due to heavy on-shore winds. And louder than she preferred as she desperately worked toward attempting to calm herself.

She wondered what she might have done different if she could do it all again, if anything. As was the case each day now, she struggled to reconcile things and held the universe in contempt.

Separated from the others, she worked to rationalize the loss of Jan and Aidan. There was no hurry getting back to Sharon's house, though she knew the Deweys would embrace her and support her with great love.

She felt for them as well, given they waited a full year after Jan passed to do the service, this being the first chance everyone could travel as Covid restrictions loosened.

She thought about the last day she saw her son Aidan at their newly rented condo a few blocks from Jan and Sharon's house. As her memory took her back to that fateful day in September of 2020, she continued to stare, transfixed on the ocean.

So many times the beach and water gave her hope and strength. But today the sea appeared as an annoyance, rough and menacing like it was the day Aidan left her. She glanced at the life preserver hanging from the nearby lifeguard perch, further triggering thoughts of the day rescue crews searched for him.

The increasing cloud cover cast a pall on her already fragile emotions, and she wrestled with whether she worked hard enough to know all that her son did outside her view, and whether some clandestine existence contributed to his departure.

But even after his passing, she was confident in the deep love she always expressed for him, what she sacrificed to raise him right and protect him, and accepted that sometimes even the best parents meet the cruelest outcomes- when one of their children passes before they do.

After the initial shock of his death gave way to the monotony of life without him, there were good days when she felt like her normal self, and other days when the crescendo of life alone and the echos of his absence were deafening.

The scattered shell fragments on the beach mirrored her broken heart, beautiful as a whole but also shattered beyond repair. Like an orange being squeezed by a giant fist, the weight of it all was more than she could withstand, and she put her head between her knees and wept.

Thinking about one of the statements Reverend Kelterman made just moments ago at Jan's service, she couldn't help continuing to ask God why Aidan was gone. Though recent months she began to move closer to acceptance, today's service and the focus on Jan's departure exposed some unhealed wounds.

"Your worldly possessions may have been given to you, or earned. But they matter less than the things of true importance. All we really have in this world are our family and our reputation. When we take care of one, the other takes care of itself."

158

Kelterman's words were true, and resonated with her given she always placed high value on the things that really matter-faith, family, and friendships. Nonetheless, her only true treasure on the planet was gone.

As she continued to stare out at the churning sea, the high-lights of their time together as mother and son popped into her mind like slide show photos...

Remembering how her poker-straight hair turned curly after giving birth to Aidan. His first game in little league at 6 when he stood in the outfield and dropped his glove to chase butterflies. Their move from Nashville to North Carolina, his excitement over his first performance with his band Vamonos Pest, and the joy of performing in front of his mom and friends. Making new friends in high school and then meeting Colton, his first true love, his soph-omore year.

His relationship with Sharon and Jan who embraced him like a son, spoiled him, and surprised him with a new surfboard when he turned 16, and who with Jennette came to all his VP gigs. Their helping Jennette nurse him to strength after he broke a rib surfing, then cheering him on as he won the Tony Silvagni novice short board competition at Kure Beach at 17.

And after Jan got sick, how sad it was for them to move out of the apartment beneath Jan and Sharon, though they understood the need for such separation in the final weeks of Jan's life. Then how as the joy of childhood morphed into the pressures of adulthood, how Aid increasingly became lost, and combustible.

As she sat and reflected on how instantly her world fell apart the day he died, she wondered whether she would be able to keep alive all the great memories they shared instead of the dark-ness that shrouded her with his sudden departure.

Like the day just after he turned 12 and they left Nashville for the coast, Aidan seated next to her in their rented U-Haul carting their worldly possessions east for a new start...

~ ~

"Mom, are you ok?" Aidan said as he noticed her fidgeting hands on the steering wheel.

"Of course. Why?"

"Because you just seem a bit sad. Are you sure you want to move?"

Jennette looked adoringly at her son, astounded that he cared enough about his mom to make such an inquiry. Especially for a boy of 12.

"I'll miss my family, but they will come to visit. Your aunt says North Carolina is beautiful. I'm not sad. I just want everything to work out and for you and I to be happy."

"Don't worry mom, I'm happy to leave Nashville. You said I might be able to learn to surf, and maybe eventually get back to guitar lessons. So don't worry about me, I'm good. Remember what you always tell me- live like you rock!"

Aidan smiled and made the *long live rock and roll* gesture with his right hand in a fist, index finger and pinky extended as horns.

After Marley left, they had little choice but to move. The lack of good-paying jobs in 2010 and cold winters in Tennessee were motivators for a new start, and the economy was just coming back after the Great Recession.

So when Jennette's sister called and said she and her husband felt good about taking them in with them in Leland, North Carolina, it felt like a calculated risk worth taking. A leap of faith.

Because she and Mar never married, the separation wasn't too messy. Though he was a part of her and Aidan's life for five years, it just never felt like he was going to be a long-term presence for them.

Their first few years together after they met at the Sonic Temple Festival were a blast, and he seemed interested in giving it a shot. But a string of bad jobs, and his persistent drinking, became problematic over time.

Then one day, just like that, Mar was gone. She cried, but knew in her heart it was a blessing. She had grown up around addicts, people who can't discern the bright line between a harmless glass of wine with dinner versus five beers a night, binging on weekends, and spending their paychecks banging shots and hard alcohol with their buddies.

She and Aidan moved in with her sister for a few months while she looked for work, and got Aidan ready for middle school in the fall. As they got situated, Jennette made a number of calls for job openings. House cleaning, secretarial work, waitressing, online sales. She needed an income quick, but didn't want to settle for the first thing.

Then came an opening at the methadone clinic in Wilmington. She had taken some health sciences classes at the community college outside of Nashville, so though she didn't have a degree she was at least able to speak the language a bit. And being raised around friends and family with addiction issues, her sense of empathy for clients would be informative and useful. Her sister, three years sober, was a welcome change from the Music City party scene.

After a few paychecks at the clinic and because accommodations at her sister Patty's place were a bit cramped, she began looking for rentals in and around Wilmington. The middle school near where Patty lived was not great, so she focused on neighborhoods associated with some of the better school districts.

Apartments.com showed many options, but most out of a comfortable price range for her current income. That's when Sharon and Jan came into her life.

"Hi. I'm Jennette. I saw your ad for tenants in your unit. Is it still available?" Jennette held the phone as she finished making Aidan's scrambled eggs in time for her to drop him off at school on her way to work.

"Hi, Jennette. Yes, we are showing it to a few prospects this weekend. It's a modest unit, about 800 square feet, but with two bedrooms and a full bath. Would you like to make an appointment to see it?" Sharon replied.

"Uh, yes. But how much will the rent be?" Jennette said, given on one income she was on a strict budget.

"The last tenant was paying $500 a month. We're consider-
ing increasing it a bit but it just depends on who we rent to. The
unit is on the ground level of our house on the beach, so we need
to make sure it's relatively quiet, no pets, no parties."

"The beach. Wow. Well, I'm a single mom who works and is
saving to go back to college, and my son Aidan is 12 and will be
starting 8th grade in the fall. He's a good kid, keeps to himself and
likes his laptop and video games. It's just the two of us, and I can
promise we would take great care of the place."

The thought of having a place on the beach, though a bit
expensive, would be perfect for them. Aidan being able to play
on the beach, possibly learn to surf, and Jennette being closer to
her job versus making the commute over the bridge from Leland
each day was ideal.

Sharon scheduled an appointment for Jennette to see the
unit on Saturday, and they hit it off from the start. Sharon leafed
through Jennette's application as they toured the apartment
overlooking the ocean.

"I see you work at the clinic in town. How's that been?"
Sharon inquired.

"I'm surprised for how small Wilmington is that so many people need treatment. I guess coming out of the recession I shouldn't
be, but it's of course sad that so many people struggle with addiction. I don't have those issues, but I come from a family with a
history of it, and my boyfriend who left us in Nashville was a heavy
drinker. So I feel compelled to help the people who come for con-
sultation and their meds."

"That's very noble work. Your son will be going to Mosley
Middle School, then to Ainsley. You will want to keep an eye on
him especially at Ainsley as they tend to have their share of drug
issues there."

This caused Jennette pause, but she figured the same was
true for most public schools. Plus, she still had a year to worry
about prepping Aid for the pitfalls of high school.

"So as long as you can put down a month's deposit, my
roommate Jan and I would be happy to rent to you for a year

and see how it goes. We can agree to the $500 I mentioned, as long as the terms of the lease are met. One car only in the driveway, no pets, and quiet after 9pm. The floors are a bit thin and Jan works at the university and gets up early."

Aidan bounded in from outside beaming with excitement.

"Mom, this place is so cool! I found some awesome shells on the beach. Can we really live here?"

Sharon smiled and said, "I think so. With that hair, I think you will be the hippest surfer on the beach."

"Thanks Miss Sharon." Aidan extended his hand to Sharon to shake, which she wasn't expecting.

"Well all right then, a young man with manners. All the better." Sharon laughed as she shook his hand and walked them back to their car.

"Aidan, I have never seen a boy with such amazing hair. Gray with those beautiful streaks of pink. Is that your mom's handiwork?"

Aidan smiled at Sharon and said, "She does it once a month, any color I want. Someday I am going to be a professional musician, so I'm getting ready ahead of time."

After moving into their new digs at the beach, as they ate dinner together Aidan revisited a topic he had broached with his mom before leaving Tennessee. The urgency for him was growing since making some new friends at school.

"Mom, remember what I asked you in Nashville, about starting guitar lessons again? Do you think we can make that happen now?"

"Sweetie I just have to make sure we can afford it. This is the most rent I've ever paid on my own, and we have to pay a bit of utilities too, as well as car insurance, gas, groceries…"

Aidan interrupted while pushing his food around his plate, feeling the same rejection as last time he broached the subject.

"Got it. It's just that I met some guys at school who play instruments, and I told them I started lessons before moving here then stopped, and they said if I get a guitar we can jam together."

Jennette knew Marley's departure and the move was a tough adjustment for Aid, recalling how he left in the middle of the night without so much as a goodbye to Aid or anyone associated with their friend and family circle. So she felt compelled to try to ameliorate his disappointment.

"Tell you what, give me two more paychecks to catch up on some bills, and meanwhile I will start looking on craigslist and some pawnshops for a used guitar. Then if you practice on your own for a bit, I will see if we can afford to resume lessons. Ok?"

Aidan seemed happy with his mom's answer, given this was closer to a yes than he had before. The following month, Jennette picked him up from school and surprised him by driving to a pawn shop where she purchased a used red Ibanez guitar in exchange for him promising to keep up with some basic chores in the apartment as well as stay on top of his homework.

"Listen, remember Sharon said no noise after 9pm, so even after we get you an amp for it, you cannot use it in the unit. You will need to just play it acoustically until you can find somewhere to plug in, or perhaps during the day when Sharon and Jan are out of the house. Deal?"

Several days later as they were both leaving for work, Jennette bumped into Jan in the driveway.

"Morning. Hope you and Aidan are settling in and like the place. I can hear the faint twanging of a guitar downstairs. Is that you or Aidan?"

"Oh my gosh, Jan, I'm so sorry. I will tell him no more unless he sees you are both out of the house."

"Goodness, of course not. My brother Matt played drums in a garage band for years in Chicago, and my parents loved it. Really, I can barely hear it. No biggie. Tell him to keep practicing!" Jan said, much to Jennette's relief.

"Will do. He is saving up for an amp but he knows that will be strictly something he plays either at school or at a friend's house."

"An amp. Interesting. Listen, tell him to come upstairs and knock on my door Saturday and perhaps I can dial him up with some chores to help him earn some money. Sharon and I hate keeping up with the weeds and shrubs around the property, so we would gladly pay him to do a few things for us if that's ok with you."

Saturday came and as promised Jan gave Aidan what would end up being his first paying job. She laid out for him the tasks that needed to be done, where the supplies were kept, and how much she would pay him.

Jan, herself from a blue-collar, Midwestern upbringing, knew the importance of teaching kids early about work ethic and the value of a dollar.

"Thanks, Miss Jan. I will come see you if I have questions." Aidan left with the list of chores and excitedly returned downstairs to tell his mom.

"Mom, Ms. Jan is so cool. And if I do everything on the list for a month, I will have enough for a used amp. Fucking sweet!"

"Aidan Logan! Do not use that language! Just do a good job, and say thank you each time you are paid."

"Sorry, mom. I just got excited. Everyone in school swears though. Worse even."

"What do you mean worse?"

"I just mean, this isn't like school in Nashville. Kids smoke cigarettes and weed in the bathroom, and you can buy stuff after school if you want."

With this, Jennette escorted Aidan to the kitchen table and sat him down. The whisps of purple and pink that she died into his thick gray hair were increasingly resting on tiny whiskers on his cheeks and chin. *My little 12-year-old is growing up too fast*, she thought as she looked at him.

"Aid, you and I have always trusted each other. You had my back when things got bad with Marley, and I have always protected you as my only child. Please make good choices, and please *always* tell me anything you need to. I'm not naïve, but I grew up seeing what drugs and alcohol can do to people and their families. I don't want that for you."

Aidan squirmed in his chair a bit with the weight of the conversation, and with the awkwardness of the topic and emotional tone that his mom delivered it with.

"No problem, mom. I'm not into all that. I just want to learn to surf, play guitar, and maybe meet some girls."

Jennette laughed and playfully put Aidan into a light headlock, tussling his messy mane of hair which Aidan now rarely combed.

A month later Aidan approached Jennette about the amp. A friend from school was selling a small Fender that his older brother gave him, at a rate better than any they had seen online. When Aidan and his mom went to pick it up, she got to meet Reilly and Clark, Aidan's closest friends from school.

"Hi Reilly. I'm Aid's mom. Thanks for selling him the amp," Jennette said as she entered the small bungalow behind the Fat Pelican dive bar where Reilly lived with his dad and two brothers.

"What's up, Aidan's mom? Cool to meet you. Aid says the music scene in Nashville is sick. This is Clark who plays bass. Mike is coming over later with his drums, so we're gonna jam in the garage for a bit. Is it cool if Aid stays?"

Jennette was excited Aidan already had a core group of friends, and that they shared a common hobby. But something about the house and Reilly already troubled her. She couldn't put her finger on it, but it perhaps was a mix of not seeing any adults around, the condition of the house and the surrounding neighborhood, and Reilly appearing a bit fidgety and forward. Nonetheless, she trusted Aidan and didn't want to be the stick in the mud given his excitement for finally getting an amp and a group to jam with.

Jennette craned her neck around the space a bit, then asked, "Are your parents home?"

"Uh, mom's been gone, like *permanently* gone, but my dad will be home from work later. My older brother Pete is here. He's a senior at Ainsley. I think he's out back with some friends. We can get a ride home for Aid if you want, or we can walk him back."

She raised her voice a bit as the radio in the rear of the house increased in volume, now blaring, and replied, "Thanks. But that's ok. Aidan, text me when you are done. No later than 8 please since it's a school night."

Jennette drove home and tried to make sense of the inter-action and the impression it left, but also reminded herself of how she was at that age. Sneaking cigarettes from her mom when her girlfriends were over, trying on make-up and skimpy outfits for fun, and later skipping school and drinking cheap beer in her basement when her parents were at work.

But she balanced the stark reality of adolescence with what she knew too well about the pitfalls of addiction. Alcoholic family, a sister who used meth until she finally got into treatment, and an ex-boyfriend who couldn't keep a job because he constantly partied. Her life was a crash course in substance abuse.

Aidan texted her at 7:45pm, and she returned to Reilly's house to get him.

"Where's the amp?" Jennette asked as Aidan threw his guitar in the back seat.

"I'm just taking the guitar back and forth because I can't use the amp at the apartment anyway, and this way when we rehearse here I won't have to lug it back and forth," Aidan said as he hopped in.

Jennette saw how happy he was, perhaps happier than she had ever seen him, and agreed that was a good plan. "Rehearsal, huh? Are you going on tour soon or what?"

Aidan smiled and looked at his mom with great affection. He understood at a deep level the connection they had, what she had been through up to this point in her life, and how much she cared about him.

Though he never really got to know his real father, the few stories his mom shared about him painted enough of a picture for him to have a true sense of how tough his mom's past was. Marley was also a mess, and didn't turn out to be the father-figure he needed. So she was his world, and he was hers.

Jennette and Aidan's new life on Carolina Beach was by all accounts a fresh start. While she had chances to date, she instead took a second job at a nearby restaurant bartending a few evenings a week. The extra money made it easier to cover their expenses, including weekly guitar lessons for Aid and the used surfboard he begged her for and which- with the money he earned on his chores for Sharon and Jan- he pitched in for.

He continued working for the "landmoms" as he called Sharon and Jan, and forged a tight relationship with them almost as he would with aunts. They asked him about school, about his band- Vamonos Pest or "VP"- and how his surfing was coming along.

Jan, who forged a career around young adults as a college administrator, especially took Aidan under her wing. He frequently came home after school to see if she was sitting on the deck above, and he would join her for a Dr. Pepper and talks about many different subjects. On Saturdays, Aidan would frequently peer into their sliding glass door until Jan invited him in for pancakes.

That fall Aidan started high school at Ainsley, the same place the guys from VP were attending. As Aidan spent the bulk of his time other than chores and homework at Reilly's house with the band, Jennette was increasingly guarded about his comings and goings.

Several weeks after his freshman year began, they went out for burgers one evening.

"Aid, I'm really proud of you. You kept your grades up while devoting yourself to your music, you learned to surf, and you made a group of pals. I just want you to remember what we talked about, that you can trust me and come to me with anything."

Aidan's response was not what she was expecting, though she was glad he came straight with her. He finished the last bite of his cheeseburger, then swigged down a gulp of soda. Pushing a thick strand of hair from his face over his ear, he exposed the features that Jennette always adored- prominent black eyebrows over beautiful brown and green eyes.

"Mom, I know you vape when you're working at the bar. You don't have to keep it from me. It's better than cigarettes, and I'm cool with it. But I'm going to be honest with you, when I'm at Reilly's we vape there and some of the guys smoke cigarettes and even drink a bit. Reilly's brothers smoke a lot of flower."

Jennette knew enough to think on her feet and not react negatively to Aidan's admission. After all, she asked for honesty and trust, so this was the form it was taking.

"Aid, thanks for telling me that. I wasn't hiding it from you, it's just I promised them there would be no smoking or vaping in the apartment. That's why I only do it at work. It's still a bad habit though, and one I wish you wouldn't start. But I'm not going to be with you at school or when you're with friends, so please be careful. A little vape pen is one thing, but trust me, cigarettes are a nasty habit. I smoked for a while and it's hard to quit."

Aidan grabbed a handful of fries and nodded his head affirmatively.

Jennette continued, "As for weed, that's a hard no. That leads to other shit. Please be careful, and I want to know more about what goes on at Reilly's. Absolutely no drinking or drugs at your age, otherwise the band stuff is over. Does that make sense?"

"Yes Cruella," Aidan said as he laughed nearly spitting out a mouthful of fries. He called his mom this whenever he wanted to mess with her, a reference to their favorite movie they watched together when he was little.

Jennette grabbed Aid's mane of colored hair and pulled it down over his face, now long enough that it draped well below his chin and shoulders.

"How about a color other than gray for a change? Black? And how about a haircut, little man?"

"Nah. I dig the gray, so do the chicks. And rock stars don't cut their hair. You're lucky I shower any more. Live like you rock, remember?" Aidan said playfully throwing fries toward her.

Jennette's evening and weekend hours at the bar increased as she emerged as one of their more reliable and talented bartenders. But she routinely called Aidan on her breaks to check in, whether he was doing homework or practicing at Reilly's.

Most nights she picked him up on her way home, and some nights he used an Uber or got a ride from one of the older kids hanging out with VP.

Close to the holidays, Aidan approached Jennette as they were getting ready for bed one night regarding something he and VP were cooking up.

"Mom, so VP is going to do a few sets of music at Reilly's and it would be cool for you to come check it out. Do you think you can get the night off next Saturday?

"Wow, Aid. That's great. Sure, let me check. So this will be in Reilly's garage?"

"Actually his dad let us set up in their living room last month since it's getting colder out, so it will be inside. Everyone is inviting people and we're pretty stoked to play some of our stuff. We've got some originals and a few covers."

"Sounds great. Of course I would love to be there. I will check tomorrow with work and I think it will be fine. I haven't asked for a single night off since they hired me."

Saturday came and Jennette couldn't wait to see Aid perform. Other than hearing him in their townhouse in Nashville when he was a child taking beginner lessons, she really had no idea of his playing ability.

Aid got picked up earlier in the afternoon to help set up for the party, and for a pre-party rehearsal. Several hours later, Jennette pulled up the street to Reilly's house where the cars were already lining the curbs. She found a spot a few blocks away and, along with throngs of teenagers making their way in the same direction, headed toward Reilly's.

As she made her way in, she was reminded of the age gap between her and the kids who were all around her. *Apparently, I'm gonna be the oldest one here*, she thought.

But the scene was really not unlike when she was their age. Kids huddled with each other outside on the lawn, drinking out of red solo cups, sharing clips on their phones and smoking cigarettes and vape pens.

Jennette pushed her way through the front door and caught sight of an older man standing in the kitchen smoking a joint, circled by a group of high schoolers. Given he seemed about her age, she assumed this was Reilly's dad, and made her way toward him to introduce herself.

Though the band hadn't started, loud music cranked from the PA, requiring she raise her voice. "Hey. Sorry to interrupt. I'm Jennette, Aidan's mom. You must be Carl."

Carl exhaled a cloud of smoke and pulled Jennette in for a hug which she was not expecting, one longer than complete strangers typically exchange.

Rocking in his stance a bit and now awkwardly holding her wrist with his hand, Carl yelled back, "Janet! Nice to finally meet you, girl. Reilly and Aid and VP are gonna kill it tonight. How about a drink?"

His breath emanated a strong odor of alcohol and weed, and he motioned to the kitchen table which was stocked with alcohol bottles of every kind.

She considered correcting him for getting her name wrong, but figured he wouldn't remember by morning anyway.

"Ah, thanks. I'll just grab a beer."

Carl motioned toward several coolers in the corner, and turned to continue his conversation with the kids. Notwithstanding her observation that other than she and Carl, every person at the house was not of legal drinking age, she figured she would stay for a few songs then slip out.

Aidan intersected her path and snuck up to give her a kiss on her temple.

"Mom, I see you met Reilly's dad. Thanks for coming."

Aid's eyes were a bit glassy, and he drew a long pull from his pen after speaking.

"I can't wait to hear you guys. Have fun. Don't be nervous."

Jennette was careful not to overly dote on her baby in front of his peers, but she was enamored at how happy he appeared.

With that, Aidan headed toward where the band was set up and strapped on his Ibanez. Reilly grabbed the mic and yelled, "Attention all patrons of Vamonos Pest! We have assumed control!"

Throngs of teenagers from outside and other parts of the house crammed toward the space where VP opened their first set.

Jennette couldn't believe her eyes and ears. The band was incredibly tight, high-energy, and started with an original song that sent the kids into a frenzy. And all eyes were on Aid as he ripped into several complicated and incendiary riffs.

As their set continued, it was obvious to her and everyone in the room that although VP was a solid band, Aidan was the heart pulse. His mop of gray hair with swatches of pink, purple and green hung over his face as he shredded on guitar and had everyone eating from his hands.

After a 30-minute opening set, the band concluded its last song. Then Reilly spoke to the crowd- "Thank you! That song, Tortured Dance with Fate, was written by Aid. We'll be back for set two after we grab a drink!"

They stopped to take a break and the place went nuts; by this point the party was at full volume. Aidan unstrapped his guitar and made his way into the crowd as boys and girls hugged and high-fived him.

Jennette stood off to the side, beaming with pride as he approached her.

"Oh my God, Aid! What happened to my little boy taking his first guitar lessons off Lower Broadway? You up and got real. That was amazing!"

Aidan pulled his hair back and tied a rainbow-colored scrunchie around his wet mane, exposing his still boyish but increasingly mature and handsome face which, dripping with perspiration, never seemed happier.

"All good, mom. I owe it all to you. All you do is work to take care of us, so I just want to make you proud."

She was surprised he pulled her in for a huge hug as she knew most teenagers found it highly uncool to be seen with their parents, much less hugging them, in public.

Aid didn't care. She was his best friend, his protector, and he knew he was lucky to have her watching over him. They exchanged a kiss on their cheeks and she peeled herself from him now with tears welling in her eyes.

"I'll stop embarrassing you now and go home. It's past my curfew. Have fun, and slay your second set. You make your mom proud."

Smiling and looking into her eyes, he gave the horns sign with both hands raised high above his head, then shouted, "Live like you rock!"

THE RUN

don't know why the obsession came. It started gradually but came on strong. Gripped me like dope grips an addict needing a fix. Started to consume me even though the rational part of my brain knew it was an absurd idea.

Growing up and over the years, I ran a lot. I guess it was around 5th grade when it all started. Perhaps a ploy by my parents to get me out of the house more and help burn off some of my nervous energy. Hard to totally recall, but the original edict from my mom probably went something like this- "Thomas, it's a nice day. Why don't you go for a run outside?"

"A run? What do you mean?" Sitting Indian style in front of our small black and white television in the living room, I looked up at her.

"You know. Take a jog around the block or something."

By most standards I was fairly normal for the average 10-year-old boy; at the time my priorities were watching cartoons and the Three Stooges, and playing baseball and football at the park at the end of our block. But just running for the sake of running didn't really appeal much to me at the time. Didn't compute.

"I'll go with you today, and then you can go on your own next time," my mom said, starting to lace up her rarely used, white canvas house sneakers.

Now 44, the best I can recall about that fateful day was that mom all but insisted I take a run with her. Thinking back, I'm still not exactly sure why. We walked out the front door, walked up the street for a bit, then started into a slow jog together.

Having been born in the house and lived there my entire life of ten years already, as we passed each house on my block- twelve homes total, same as every block nearby- I could recite the name of every family member living in every house. Didn't even need to think about it. They just registered with me.

The Drakes- Kenny and Tracy; the Johnsons- Marty, Sue and Frank; the Gateleys- Steve, Martha, Rick and Randy; the Anthensons- Bruce, Mary, David, Wendy and Judy, etc.

Everyone knew everyone. Kids played tag and rode bikes until the streetlights came on, girls played hopscotch on the side- walk, and the boys gathered for whatever sport was in season at the park, including hockey in the winter.

The adults gathered on front stoops and porches over coffee in the mornings and beer in the evenings, discussing adult stuff as the kids begged for five more minutes of play before supper.

So looking back on my first "official run," I recall we slowly jogged to the end of the block, around the corner, back up the block behind our house, through the park and back home. Probably three blocks total. No big deal. But that's how it started.

From then on, whenever I was bored or mom deemed I needed to burn off some energy, I would run. No stretching. No thought. Just shoes on, out the door, and running.

Though I may not have known it then, later I would appreci- ate how good running was for the senses. The scent of roses and lilies in front yard gardens in the spring; blue jays, cardinals and robins nesting and chirping among the canopy of oak and syc- amore trees along the streets; squirrels nesting and scurrying into boxwood and evergreen shrubs.

The hot sun baking my skin during summer runs, and the turn- ing of the Midwestern colors each autumn. The feel and sound of different surfaces beneath my feet. The enjoyment of strapping on my clunky Sony Walkman to jam to my favorite bands along the way, and the daily clanking of trains in the nearby railyards gave credence to what our little suburb was a bigger part of- Chicago.

An idyllic little town south of the Chicago border, Draven was where families left the big city for in the early to mid-20th century to start a new life, a better life for many.

Where in 1965 for around $18,000 you could own a brick home with three bedrooms and 1.5 baths, a fenced yard and a garage. With parks, little leagues, scouting, churches and good schools, and a parade, carnival and fireworks each 4th of July. A great little slice of Americana where kids could be kids.

But by the 1980s the secret was out. This wasn't just a place where White people could flee the high cost, high crime and congestion of Chicago. This was where *everyone* could start over. Blacks, Latinos, everyone.

By age 12, I was extending my distances and changing up my routes. One day I ran straight up my street, Ellis Avenue, to Kmart and back, or to my high school, circling the track a few times, then running home.

Another day I would zig-zag through different blocks in obscure patterns. Other days I ran past the homes of girls I was interested in, hoping they may catch a glimpse of me in my "athletic prowess."

In the winter I ran with long johns under my grey sweatpants, knit hat, scarf, gloves and a thick jacket. In hindsight, I likely looked like a teenage version of Ralphie's little brother being chased by bullies in A *Christmas Story* (of course, in my mind more like Rocky Balboa running up the steps of the Philadelphia Museum of Art, arms raised in victory after reaching the top). Different days, different runs, different sights and sounds.

The point is, I ran. I ran like nobody's business. I ran while my mind raced about people and things and problems. I ran to wind down and sometimes to wind up. I never really got tired. I rarely got winded. I just ran.

In middle school after class let out each day I ran to the local greasy spoon, Chris' Coffee Shop, along the expressway where I worked as a busboy. Pretty cool gig where for a few hours after school each day I would sweep and mop the floors, wash dishes, take out the trash, and let the waitresses flirt with me as they were being checked out by the truckers stopping along I-94 for a quick meal.

The truckers were a hoot, and always good for some colorful language or a dirty joke. They dropped their various loads of cargo in the city, then stopped in Draven making their way through the various interstate tendrils on the way to the Michigan and Indiana provinces they called home.

For slightly longer runs, I headed toward our version of "downtown," where the Draven Cinema, Vintage Village store, Pano's Candy, Joe's Boots, and a few corner bars donning beer signs and other mom and pop shops sprinkled Chicago Boulevard.

One day I ran downtown to catch the end of the Nat's Pub 5k race, only to turn around and run home, twice the distance of the actual race itself. I never joined the track or cross country teams, and I didn't compete in races as a kid. I ran for myself.

As a four-year starter on our high school wrestling team, running was also an ideal hobby due to the need for strong cardio. Our coach ran us to death. We ran outside at the start of practice, we ran the basketball arena bleacher steps in the middle of practice, and we ran wind sprints at the end of practice.

I went off to college in 1995, still running regularly to manage the stress of college classes. So jogging in college was just a continuation of the habit of running. I still liked how it made me feel, and how it gave me time to clear my mind and think.

But each time I came home from college I noticed my hometown changing. White people moving out, mostly to northwestern Indiana. Families of diverse races and ethnicities moving in. Fewer familiar faces greeted me as I ran my neighborhood over breaks and summers home from school. No hostility, just less familiarity.

Old man Golden, who typically threw me an apple off the tree in his yard as I passed his house running, had passed away. Ms. Smith, sitting on her porch smoking Newports and reading the paper, a usual friendly wave as she looked up through her own exhaled plume of smoke, moved out. Kitty and Pauline Carlson, the little girls I used to babysit, no longer there.

Then in 1999 after graduating from college, the words came from my dad one evening at dinner... "Thomas, we're moving this summer. Dennis is done with high school, David is moving after he finishes in the Army, and Todd is already gone, so there's no reason for us to keep the house."

As is the case with most people when they learn the house they grew up in is being sold, the words came hard. Holidays, birthdays, nightly supper, jostling with my dad and brothers in the living room, shooting hoops in the yard, pitching a tent on the small swatch of grass next to the garage and gazing up at the brilliant stars at night. All the stuff you do as a kid in the tiny footprint of a house and yard that you call home, over.

I spent that last summer making the rounds saying goodbye to friends, neighbors, classmates, teachers, and coaches. Saying goodbye to the town. I kept running, though the runs had a different feel, a different purpose; perhaps they even felt a bit desperate.

I was acutely aware of every step, every crack in the familiar sidewalks my shadow engulfed. Some days a longer stride to match a personal best time, and other days a slow jog enabling my eyes to document things with greater detail. Trying to capture and retain the special images so I could call them up from the recesses of my brain later in life. Many years of running to reflect upon, and 21 years in this little town.

Assigning the names of the inhabitants of each house on my block was more challenging that summer. Some were gone, and some I didn't know. Subtle changes to the houses I passed became starker.

The lawns looked less green. Some of the screen doors had new locks on them, appearing to be changing from doors that opened to warmly pull others in, to doors meant to shut people out. Strange cars and strange music. Strange faces and fewer waves as I passed. Obscure and different in ways that were obvious and other ways hard to describe.

I can't remember the last run, but it was probably around July of 1999. In fact, I likely didn't declare it as such. I just ran one day, then got busy as I prepared to help with the move, and lost time to run again before leaving. That was it. The childhood and house I knew and loved faded in my rearview mirror as I pulled away for the last time.

As happens to most people, the years after I left my home-town just flew by. A year of teaching high school, two years of graduate school, a move out of state to start a family and a new job, then more graduate school, and more jobs, and moves that took us farther away.

But the running continued. Some years less so, and some years more intense. My first 5k at 25; my first 10k two years later. Then in my thirties, half marathons. About three a year for a while. Running and running and running.

Running to think about how to be a good husband and father. Running to deal with job stress and money worries. Running to get a break from the kids. Running to shed a few pounds. Admittedly, the same reasons that most people run. Except also running to think about where the running started…running in Draven, then running away from Draven.

The muscle memory made it easy, and many runs brought my brain back to the early runs through my childhood neighborhood. Deeply embedded and vivid images of my block, the houses, the familiar cars and yards. The people, even the sounds and smells.

It was all right there in my mind. So clear I could almost tran-scend myself to change backgrounds from the current to the past. Now taking my runs in bucolic Raleigh, I occasionally wondered about how the old neighborhood looked. Then one morning, Kim brought up my hometown and how it had dramatically changed.

"Tom, have you read what they are saying about Draven? Worst crime rate in the state." My wife slid her laptop over to me at the breakfast table. "Hard to believe. It used to be such a nice town," she added.

Having frequently talked about Draven's decline with friends and family, I didn't stop to look at whatever she was referencing online. But I couldn't resist my usual, somewhat defensive response.

"That's because everyone bolted. There are no jobs there, and all the good teachers left. Damn shame." I believed in my heart we are all prisoners of our upbringings, for better or worse, so while I was disappointed that my hometown's reputation weakened over the years, I was empathetic to the reasons why.

As I left the kitchen, I struggled a bit with how I really felt about what I continued to hear and read about Draven. Part of me wanted to defend it, part of me wanted to write it off. After all, what did I care? Everyone I knew growing up there as a kid had long since moved out, moved on, and mostly moved up.

I blinked and 15 years passed since my last visit. I think it was for a friend's dad's funeral in a nearby suburb of Draven, followed by a brief drive through the old neighborhood. I was 29 when I last passed through the area, and life with a busy job, wife and two kids accelerated time. As they say, "life took over."

Aside from a few minor injuries, I was still running. Fewer races, a slower pace, but still lacing them up most mornings and getting out there. "Pounding the pavement" as runners call it. Getting my miles in.

For reasons I can't pinpoint, my recent runs had me more fixated on Draven. On the town, on memories of growing up there, and on the streets I ran in my youth. So whether it was curiosity, sentimentality, or just stupidity, I can't say. What was coming to be was first just a passing notion, then a curiosity, then- a plan.

Having just returned to Raleigh from my sister-in-law Jan's memorial service on Carolina Beach, I finished my morning run through our neighborhood- four miles just to get the blood pumping. Kim was clearing the dishes after breakfast, so I saw my opportunity to pitch the idea to her.

"Sweetie, I have a conference to attend in Chicago in October. I'm thinking about staying on an extra day to run Draven."

"To run to Draven? What for?"

"No, not to run to Draven. To run Draven. To run the town."

A dish slipped from her hand and clanked in the sink, and she looked at me with a look I had seen a thousand times before. The one that follows any statement made by me that exits my mouth before my brain has completely processed it.

Her long pause before speaking felt longer than usual.

"Are you out of your mind? You want to first go there. Then you want to get out of your car and go for a jog? In the hood? In the ghetto?"

"Nice. We haven't used the word ghetto in this country since 1975. Yes, the town has changed. Yes, it's unsafe in parts. But it's still my hometown. I just feel like I need to reconnect with it," I said with limited conviction, busily wiping the counter in order to avoid eye contact.

"Tom, I love you and I know as a sociology professor you are studied on all this, but as you well know, even years ago when we went back there it got worse and worse. The annual summer carnival was shut down because of fights. There was the shooting at your high school two years after you left. And the news of the gangs and drugs there. Sorry Tom, but it's just a really stupid idea. Plus, why would you take that sort of risk anyway?"

"I know. I hear ya. Just something I have been thinking about since I'm going to be in the city anyway. I'll just think on it some more. Just thought I would run it by you."

My volume trailed off as I walked out of the room, my best attempt to retreat but not totally declare defeat on the subject. But she was on to me, and followed me into the bedroom needing to be heard. Needing to clearly go on the record to emphasize her concern about what I pitched to her.

"Tom, please, I'm telling you, and I know how you are once you get an idea. Do not stop in Draven during your trip. Do not even think about going there much less running there. Sorry, but my emotions are a bit fragile right now with Jan passing and everything."

Now standing face to face with me with her hand on my arm, making direct eye contact, she showed a serious side she rarely revealed.

"I hear ya. I don't want to promise I won't, because if I do it you will say I lied to you. So let me just leave the idea alone for now, and if it gets legs I will let you know. Really, it was just a thought."

I started to pull away from her but her hand tightened its grip on my forearm.

"And I'm telling *you*, you're not Neddy Merrill attempting to swim the fucking Lucinda River in some novel. This is real life, with real consequences. And I'm not raising two kids on my own because of some weird victory lap you half concocted on a whim," her voice raised in intensity and volume as she turned away, getting the last word after all.

I knew I had underestimated her reservations, and despite my attempts to convince her otherwise the initial exchange had no effect on making her believe I wasn't seriously considering doing it.

To the contrary, after nearly twenty years of marriage she knew my every thought, intention and plan from the moment of inception. And she knew my soft peddling the idea to her really meant I was trolling for her support, and that I was in fact serious about it.

This worried her all the more. But she decided to leave it alone for now. There were still two months before the trip. She would have another bite at the apple in due time.

The following week, news continued to focus on the continued presence of Covid. August of 2021 was seeing the C.1.2 variant and mutations of the original strains spreading, causing Americans continued stress.

After returning home from work one day, my phone rang and it was my best friend Jeff, also among my classmates from Draven who had long since fled the area and was comfortably perched in Richmond.

"Jeffrey, what's up, how are you?" the call started innocently.

"Good Tommy. Same as usual. How are things at State? Oh, and so sorry to hear about your sister-in-law, Jan. How's Kim with all that?"

"Hanging in there. The service on the beach was beautiful, and we got to see family which was nice. Can you believe Neil is fucking touring with REO? We *must* stag some tickets and go. Otherwise, just watching the Rona Virus stuff as usual," I replied.

"Yeah, I'm so over it. Listen, Kim texted me about you thinking about going back to Draven. You're not serious about that I assume."

Before I could reply, he continued.

"You know they say it's not safe to even drive through there anymore. The old crew even stopped going to the annual fish fry at the lake. Even from within the fenced area you could hear gunshots in the distance, and cars were being vandalized and fucked with. I'm pretty sure Steve's car got stolen one year actually."

"Really? It's *that* bad? I simply told Kim I have a conference in Chi-town in October. It's been a while since I checked out the old neighborhood. So I was thinking about a drive by since I will be there anyway."

Too early in the conversation to introduce the full plan but, like Kim, I sensed he was on to me already.

"Dude, what's wrong with you? You can't fucking say *drive-by* when you refer to Draven. You're pretty sick you know!" he said, laughing a bit.

"Actually, you know how I did a lot of running growing up and I still run a bit. I was thinking about running the old neighborhood."

The familiar pause before his response suggested he now understood I wasn't joking. Like Kim, he knew me too well.

"Thomas, are you out of your fucking mind?" His response was worse than I predicted it would be; perhaps the only time I ever heard him use my formal name, and coupling it with an F-bomb meant he was dead against it.

"I mean really, are you serious? First, for what purpose? Second, no way Kim would ok this. Third, do you know how dangerous that town is now? I mean, they are comparing it to the worst parts of Chicago and East St. Louis. You absolutely cannot even think this is a good idea."

"I hear ya, but this country is in such disarray right now. There is such hyper-partisanship, and people can't even listen to perspectives other than their own. Some are saying the political pendulum between the Obama and Trump eras has swung farther apart than in the history of one political party following another into office. This country is splitting like it did before the Civil War."

Jeff cut me off a bit as he sensed I was getting on my usual soap box about the genesis of racial strife in the United States.

"Listen, you and I have talked before, and I always agree with you that race is the persistent unreconcilable challenge in America, but what you propose isn't going to change all that."

I replied, "I know. It would definitely require some plan…" He interrupted me even faster this time.

"No. It requires no plan. There is *no plan* that makes it sensible for you to go to Draven, Illinois, get out of a perfectly safe vehicle, and go for a leisurely jog. Nothing. There is nothing smart about doing it. Dude, I don't even think the few people who live there go for runs anymore."

At this point, I was regretting having the conversation with him at all. Jeff was always my phone-a-friend. The guy whose common sense and logic matched his intelligence. He could rewire your house, fix your car, make you a homemade meal and give you investment tips all in the same day. He was a new world man, and he was rarely wrong. Maybe never actually. And I always valued his perspective, and *always* took his advice, and was always glad I did.

Nonetheless, I could tell my persuasion of the plan was having no effect on earning his endorsement, nor was his discouragement of the idea changing my mind. Paradoxically, I think it only fueled my resolve, though I also knew in the back of my mind I might be biting off my nose to spite my face.

"Tom, I just Googled Draven. Have you seen the headlines that come up? 'Population below 10,000.' 'Chicago's suburban blight.' 'Draven officials charged with fraud.' 'Draven, Illinois tops shot spotter data for discharged firearms.' One headline ever reads, 'Do not take the two Draven exits off the expressway unless you live there.'"

"Jesus. Why do you think I call it the *noosepaper?* The media in this country are half the problem, Jeffrey. Trust me, I will think it through. I appreciate your concerns, and I appreciate Kim letting you know. Hey, I gotta take another call. Talk soon."

We hung up though no other call was waiting. Much as Jeff's perspective on things made total sense, after the call it seemed to have the opposite effect on my thought process.

Later that evening another call came. This one from another friend who also called Draven his hometown and whose career as a Chicago cop was winding down.

"Tom, Jeff texted me about your notion of coming back to Draven. At the risk of repeating what he said, I think that's a risky proposition."

"Hey Walt. Hi to you too. Tell me how you feel."

"Dude, it's no joke. I know you are more left-leaning than the rest of us, and that's all good. The thing is, Draven isn't really safe for anyone. It's not about being unsafe just for White people. There are some elements there that don't discriminate. It's unsafe overall. Trust me, I feel for kids who don't have a stable upbringing, and who get lost along the way. The only family they have sometimes are drug dealers and gang members. But I've seen some shit that most people have only seen in movies. There are some heartless souls out there with bad intentions. You need to really think this through."

As always, I appreciated Walt's perspective given his stellar career in law enforcement in one of the toughest city's on the planet to be a cop. Similar to Jeff, I always considered Walt's advice on point. And similar to my conversation with Jeff, I knew this wasn't something worth debating.

"Walt, I can't argue any of that. It's really hard to state why this thing matters to me. Whether it's my need to affirm or disprove Draven's reputation, or to somehow convince myself it's not as bad as people say. I mean, most of what we read online is crap."

"I get all that. But promise me you aren't catering to some twisted martyrdom here. Promise me you will be the Tom we all love- the guy who has always been dead center on issues and decisions. The rational one. Don't fall from the center of the see-saw to the far end. Trust me, if you fly off, it's gonna hurt."

Despite the input from three of the most important people in my life, from that point forward, the idea morphed into a full-blown plan. It occupied the space between my ears every day for two months. It permeated my dreams at night. It excited me, and it scared me. It gave me a dose of adrenaline similar to the runner's high I felt in the middle of my half marathons.

I used Google and Google Earth to intensify my research on Draven. Demographics, crime rate, what was shut down and what was still open. I used social media to see who still lived there. Were any names familiar? Was anyone I grew up with still living in the area? An empiricist by trade, I wanted to make a decision informed by data, not hyperbole.

I had a feeling what I would find, but I looked anyway. Political corruption, drug busts, assaults in the schools, not enough cops, drive-by shootings, hardcore gangs, boarded-up shops and homes, vacant lots, burned-out buildings, curfews to curb crime and keep residents off the streets at night.

Every Internet search rendered the same findings- a shell of the town it used to be. Not safe, and especially not safe for visitors. And not a single family I knew still lived there; not a single child-hood friend or business owner's family. No one was still there. All moved on. All gone.

Census data also told the story. Founded in the early 19th century by George Draven...a place everyone wanted to live. The decade I was born, the 1970s, around 19,000 residents including 99% White. 1990, peak of 25,000 residents, 59% White. And by 2020, under 10,000 residents, 10% White. The correlation between the town's decrease in White population and the decline of the town made be both sad and uncomfortable to reconcile.

Paradoxically, all the research I conducted just fueled my resolve. A junky with only one thing in mind- I would prove them wrong. I would pull it off. I would visit and see that it wasn't as bad as people said, and I would live to tell about it.

I would run my hometown and awaken the dormant images of my childhood. Our house, the homes on the block, the streetlamps and street signs, my church and schools, all of it.

I continued to map out the details of my plan. Taking breaks at my desk at work, I plotted the run. About 4 miles in total including the three main roads and my street. Sibley Boulevard, Chicago Road, 142nd Street and Ellis Ave. I knew the route well in advance.

I planned to park in the old Kmart lot on Sibley, a public spot at a major intersection that would be safe, mid-day of course. Safer than other areas at least. That would only be three blocks from my high school, then I could turn toward the downtown area, then past my middle school, then past the lake we swam and fished in each summer, the hot dog stand I worked at on weekends, the penny candy store, the baseball fields and driving range, then a straight shot up the street I grew up on, then a few more blocks back to the car. No alleys, no side streets. A solid plan and in broad daylight.

The conference was in late October, so the weather would be fine. My last session was scheduled to end on a Monday. So I would rent a car for a day, drive the thirty minutes from the city to Draven, make the run, then have the rental back to O'Hare before my flight that night. Easy plan. Rental insurance for sure, but my belongings would be safe in the trunk. Mainly a few suits and my laptop.

Each week as the trip got closer, my confidence and excitement grew. I pictured every detail of the run and thought about whether I should take some pictures along the way.

I decided against it, given someone who looks like me running through Draven would be strange enough, much less doing so snapping photos like some giddy tourist.

Several weeks before the trip, news continued about the spread of Covid variants, but aside from the requirement to wear a mask on the plane, the public was inching closer to normal operations.

The image of the run was now occupying my every thought, awake and asleep. It invaded my conscious thinking, and permeated my brain even as I tried to focus on other things.

It occupied the space between closing my eyes to sleep and sleeping, and was the first thing that popped into my head when I woke.

Meanwhile, I ran more frequently, ate well, and stepped away from the weekend beers. I needed to be ready. I wanted to be in good shape in case I needed to accelerate away from harm. Of course, my preparations made it clear to Kim what I decided.

I put off talking to her about it about as long as I could, but several nights before my flight she took the bull by the horns. Waiting for me to exit the shower, she handed me a towel as I opened the curtain.

"Clearly you're doing this. So I'm not going to ask you to lie to me. I just want you to know I'm against it, and I think it's a scary thing. In fact, I think it's stupid and self-centered. This isn't some sociological experiment to inform your next lecture in class, Tom. This is our life. Thanks for making me worry the whole time you're gone."

"I know. This is really selfish of me, and I can't quite explain why I have to do it." The words came with limited conviction, but actually did make me feel like a prick for disregarding the impact of my decision on her. But it was nice to hear she would worry.

"Promise me you will consider aborting at any point if something goes wrong. You have always had good street smarts and instincts, so listen to them when they come. If you back out, it doesn't mean you've lost. It means you tried and it didn't work out. Doing this run isn't going to bring your hometown back, Tom. You lost it a long time ago."

She spoke in a much calmer tone than the first time we discussed it, perhaps acquiescing that a tone of care might have a better chance of reaching me now, or the day of the run, than an emotional plea.

"A hundred percent. I hear you. If I see trouble, I'm out. I will call you as soon as I am back in the car."

As we hugged, the reality of what I was doing set in. This really was risky. This really could end badly. I had so much going for me- her, the kids, my job. Could this just be my failed management of my first significant mid-life crisis? But I was too far gone now. This was going to happen.

The three day conference was interesting, but truthfully just a distraction. I was no longer in town for professional development. I was in town for the run. It was the only real purpose of the visit. Heck, it was increasingly my purpose for existing.

Leading up to the trip, it became an all-consuming obsession. The sex addict desperately seeking a hooker. The alcoholic or gambler swindling his kid's college savings on a weekend bender in Vegas. This was all those things. This was where fear and hope collide to produce total exhilaration.

Each morning before my conference sessions I ran along the Lake Michigan shoreline and up Michigan Avenue just to gear up, and because I always run cities when visiting as a means of sight-seeing.

Different scenes and sounds and colors, smells and contours of the surfaces, interesting architecture, the challenge of dodging city traffic, and how the shadows of the skyscrapers engulfed my own shadow for most of the run, making me feel humble.

I thought about calling Jeff one more time, but decided against it. He texted me a few times leading up to the trip, inquiring as to whether I was going through with it. My limited and vague responses to him provided the answer he was hoping against.

Monday morning I was up early brimming with excitement. I downed a quick breakfast in the lobby, threw on my running gear for the trip, and made my way to my rental car waiting out front of the Drake hotel.

Downtown traffic was heavy as expected, but the estimated arrival time to the corner of Sibley and Greenwood in Draven was 10:15am. Too early? Too late? I guess these details were left to fate at this point.

A flood of childhood memories consumed me on the drive out of the city and toward the place I called home. Over twenty years of memories. Friends, sports, first kisses, first sex, playground fights, relatives and friends, first car. Most of it very fresh and clear, as though it all happened just yesterday.

Then the sign for Draven entered my view. As I clicked the blinker to pull off the highway, I knew there was no turning back. I had returned to the place where there was to be no returning.

The off-ramp from the expressway circling me onto the main boulevard into town looked the same, dumping me toward the first intersection where a few cars were stopped.

"No way it's been 15 years," I said aloud before pulling to a stop at the light.

I found my sixth sense heightening immediately, just as I hoped it would. Visual cues began to feed my brain data. A boarded-up gas station, the White Castles restaurant closed but not boarded up. Chris' Coffee Shop replaced by a mega hardware store. Graffiti sprayed on the facade of the bowling alley, which though decrepit appeared to still be in business.

Cars alongside me with drivers who did not look like me. Some double-take looks toward me, but nothing menacing. Their glances described their thoughts- *Probably just some guy lost. Got off the wrong exit, or maybe just passing through to South Holland as a shortcut. Not smart, but whatever.*

Three blocks up to the old Kmart lot. My mind already downloading the images of what I should see block by block between here and there. A Wendy's restaurant. Dunkin Donuts. Vanberg Elementary School. Jewel Grocery.

Very few cars on the road, and as I proceeded forward it was clear why. The previous burgeoning boulevard of thriving businesses from years ago was no longer prosperous.

Wendy's, gone- a vacant prairie where it once stood. Dunkin Donuts, gone- replaced by a boarded pawn shop covered with creeper vines and spray paint. Jewel Grocery, gone- appeared to be a grocery by another name, now also boarded up. Some old semi-trucks parked out front on a lot left unpaved for years.

The elementary school was still there, the playground now a muddy, weed-filled lot. The jungle gym and monkey bars and swings I played on at recess, missing. Two basketball poles with no backboards. Several windows of the school boarded-up to cover broken glass.

My research had revealed that the Kmart lot I was planning to park in had been occupied by a car dealership that had also gone under, but that a small mini-mall across the street was still active- a dental office, a pawn shop, and a hair salon. As I pulled in, it looked the same as I saw online weeks before. This was the first small victory of my arrival. I picked a good spot to park, as close to the intersection as possible.

I sat in the car for a second scanning the corner where the two streets met. The same intersection I crossed a thousand times in my routines as a kid. Mid-point of the one mile walk from my house to the high school, riding my bicycle to see friends on this side of town, riding my dirt bike along the railroad tracks, and just cruising my car on weekends.

It all looked so familiar, yet so different. Smaller, and stranger. Glancing in my rearview mirror, now squarely centered and reflecting back in my eyes was the word DRAVEN on the faded, black and white striped water tower. Same tower, different colors, but with less pride than I remembered, even somewhat apologetic now.

A few cars stopped and started at the intersection, but no drivers looking my way. I locked my wallet and cell in the glovebox, exited the car, locked my suitcase and laptop in the trunk, and zipped the key in the front pocket of my running pants.

My habit before any run was to stretch for at least five minutes before starting out, but that seemed somewhat futile this time. I raised my arms in a circle around my torso, gave a few twists and a quick bend at the waist to touch my toes, and exhaled.

I looked up to view the altocumulus cloud bank hovering under the expansive powder blue backdrop- beautiful but a bit ominous. Like scattered cotton balls resting on a large plate of glass directly above me, the tops white and reflective of the autumn sun, and the bottoms offering darkened shadows almost within my reach. Temperature-wise, not bad for late October in northern Illinois- around 65 degrees.

191

I started with an initial pace not unlike the many 5k races I ran after leaving Draven, where my adrenaline drove my initial speed. I made a quick jaunt across the intersection and over the railroad tracks, recalling the drive-up restaurant that was there when I was a kid, where the waitresses came out on roller skates delivering burgers and shakes right to your car. Other than a few rusted steel girders protruding from the earth, now just a gravel lot.

After a block or two, I decided to cruise a bit, remembering this would most assuredly be my last race here. I transferred the energy to my brain's hard drive which was consuming data from every sight point, reminding myself, *slow down. Take it in. This is your town.*

Overgrown grass and weeds consumed the cracked sidewalks. Empty mini-malls and mostly shuttered storefronts on each side of the street. Tired houses in need of paint and new windows and shingles, landscapes overgrown.

Many houses devoid of life. Vacant lots where homes used to stand, and a few houses that caught fire and were left charred and uncleared. Expired embers that gave way to ashes, emphasizing the town is essentially burned out and dead.

A block up on the left, my high school came into view. Relatively similar as it was when I left it in cap and gown over twenty-five years ago. A flood of memories began to haunt me as I settled into an even lower gear, almost slowing to a fast walk.

My eyes worked to take a panoramic snapshot of every image of the place where my youth was fastened. Where it was cool to be cool, and where life still pulsated with new images and sensations... classes, sports, clubs, buddies, girls, plans for weekend keg parties in basements, rock music blaring in our ears. The trials and tribulations of youth.

But this was also the place where I was first exposed to kids who looked nothing like me. Black kids, Latino kids, Queer kids. All with different customs, different languages, different dress styles. High school was my indoctrination into learning to get comfortable around people not White, and which as I traversed my adult life in diverse circles, I was grateful for.

192

Scanning the area, still not much human activity. Even the houses that appeared still inhabited showed no signs of life. No one outside chatting up neighbors. No one mowing their lawns or washing their cars. No one looking out their window to see the world.

A few cars passed by on what used to be one of the busiest thoroughfares. I caught the drivers and passengers glancing over at me, but no waves, no long stares, but most importantly, no stops.

Average cars, the kind you would buy used from a second rate gas-station-turned-dealership. Some rusted out a bit, just as many cars that traverse the salted streets during Chicago winters tend to become.

Now just two blocks from the next intersection, I was making decent time and feeling good about my excursion. Getting to see the old haunts, a mix of memories and curiosity about the current state of things, and a bold confidence that the run was going to go as planned.

Turning the corner north from Sibley onto Chicago Road at the next stop lights, again I paused to view things. The Italian restaurant that for years was the top spot for food in town, boarded up. Its oval sign with the old Italian man's face on it that lit up the corner, his broad smile and expressive gray mustache, completely gone.

The gas station on the opposite corner, where most people got their gas and cigarettes, and had their oil changed by old man Nick wearing a silver coin changer on his belt, now just a vacant lot with a few piles of bricks and concrete scattered about.

Again, almost no cars at the intersection. I wondered what the few remaining residents did for work. Work from home? Take the train into the city? Retirees? Did no one drive much, or was it just not safe to be out and about? By now had to be close to 11am.

The next stretch was about eight blocks of residential neighborhoods starting with a lot that used to be Dairy Queen, leading to downtown Draven. Bones of the old building still there, but under a different name. Hard to tell if it was still open at all.

Hart's Car Wash across the street somewhat resembled what I remembered. Still operating as a self-serve, but overgrown with trash and weeds. The rusted mechanics of the washing and drying and vacuuming machinery suggested most bays were out of order. *No people, no cars, no need for washing them.* My brain continued forming conclusions on what my eyes observed.

But most homes on this block appeared inhabited. Some kept up better than those I had seen so far, though by my calculations going on between 70-100 years old now. Cookie cutter with one of four or five basic designs, some with brick facades and clapboard siding of various faded colors.

I wasn't tired, but I found myself drifting off a bit during this stretch, thinking about all the people who lived in each home since it was built. Who built each home, and what were they doing and thinking at the time? All long since dead. What were their lives like, their joys and pains? Did they take pride in their work, and did they realize they were architects of shelter for generations to come? The White families who bought them in their little suburban utopia in the 1950s, who then rushed to sell them to non-White families during the White flight of the 1980s.

The sociologist in me drew rational conclusions, and whether they knew it or not, they were all integrally part of a bigger universal fabric that is woven into every little town in America.

I chuckled as I passed a house with a bunch of cardboard Halloween decorations on the lawn. Little ghosts, goblins, and grim reapers mocking my every step. *A good sign though. Must be kids still here doing kid stuff.*

While the passing cars were few and far between, in the distance behind me I could hear the loud muffler of a slowly approaching car. I kept on, focusing ahead, trying to appear like just another local out for a morning run, knowing however that nothing about the image of me here now could render such a guise as plausible.

After what felt like a long time, a car slowly passed by me without stopping. Again, trying not to seem nervous, I used only my peripheral vision to capture the image. Chevy of some sort, maybe an older Monte Carlo. Red. Chrome rims, body elevated, and dark, smoked windows making it impossible to see inside.

A deep and thumping bass sound resonated from within. It slowed ahead, then made a gradual right turn several blocks up.

This made me tense for the first time since starting out, but I convinced myself this was to be expected. *I'm a middle-aged White guy running through a town with very few White residents. Of course I'm going to draw some attention. I'm a quarter through the run now; just keep going.*

I passed the turn where the car pulled in, and no sign of them. Two blocks up was the start of the downtown area. Or, what I used to know as downtown.

My brain created a sketch of what was supposed to be in place across the three block stretch of downtown Draven. A large Wal-Mart type store on the left, originally called Vintage Village. A series of small stores on the right including a Mexican restaurant, a jewelry store, a pharmacy, a music store and a shoe store.

Then on the left, two small pubs both with neon Old Style signs in the windows, then the cinema, and on the right a corner restaurant at the end of the block. The Draven Bank where I intentionally used the drive-thru as a teenager to flirt with the teller girls would surely still be there.

This was the slowest part of the run so far, as there was a lot to take in. A lot to process. I jogged in place in the middle of the first block and did two full turns trying to make sense of the images.

The large department store on the left was supposed to be there, but showed only a barren field of trees, weeds and trash. The stores on the right were now part of a strip of sealed tenements with spray paint and broken glass. No sign of any of the previous businesses existed.

Even the Draven Bank seemed long gone, appearing to at one point have been a pawn shop, which was now shuttered- its front entrance totally encased by sturdy, crisscrossed metal security gates.

Up ahead, the marquee for the cinema was still visible, with the word DRAVEN vertical from top to bottom. Empty dotted holes where yellow lightbulbs used to blink, circled the town's name. This was the hot spot where many nights throngs of teenagers lined up to escape their parents and see movies.

The front glass encasements that highlighted posters of the coming attractions and currently running movies were devoid of anything but empty liquor bottles, cans and cigarette butts.

I stopped to stare up at the marquee and shell of the building, wondering when the last movie was shown. Perhaps in the early 2000s? Not recently by any stretch.

Jaws. My first movie there with dad and David. Couldn't sleep for a week. I smiled remembering the number of times my brother got up to use the bathroom during the film, coinciding with every time the tense music signaled the shark's next attack.

By all accounts, everything gone. One single pub appeared to perhaps still be in business, discernable mainly because the bars on the front door appeared to be new, and a handwritten sign in the window read, "NO LOITERING. CALL AHEAD FOR PACKAGE ORDERS."

A small service bay that appeared more like a bullet-proof teller window was added to the side of the building for selling six packs and cigarettes. A large rat ran across the front, startled by unfamiliar human footsteps.

I slowly carried on, turning to capture one final image of the abandoned theatre, assuming the nearby library, liquor store and middle school around the next corner would show some semblance of life among the crated and dilapidated downtown where businesses and community once thrived.

Still no cars. Had a tumbleweed blown by me, or perhaps a coyote jot out in my path, I would not have been totally surprised.

Is this some sort of prelude to the post-Covid world or is this just Draven today? I wondered while viewing the somewhat apocalyptic surroundings.

At the next corner, I looked up the block toward where I knew the police and fire station and city hall to be. I elected not to go off course though. They would certainly still be there, and likely if seen by Draven's cops I would be encouraged to abort the rest of the run.

The liquor store was still there, as was the library. Somewhat the same, though both unkept and overgrown. The liquor store was blocked off by a security fence along its front, the kind that got wheeled open and locked shut each day.

Several cars were parked in the lot, and the large painted sign of the store's name on its brick side had long since faded away. The recesses of my brain offered thoughts I had not recalled for many years, such as parking there with friends waiting for older kids to buy us booze, and where I got up the nerve to eventually test out my fake ID created by none other than my old pal Jeff.

A block up on Lincoln Avenue on the left was my middle school- The memories started downloading... *Class president, and scored a whopping total of five points across two seasons on the basketball team. Wrestling team. School band. Two girlfriends. Two fist fights at recess...1-1.*

I drifted off to an image of the entire staff of my old teachers, my principal, and my Logan Middle School friends standing out front, the school band playing and cheering me on, holding a huge banner celebrating my homecoming run- "Welcome Home Thomas!"

I chuckled to myself, and in clear view now the school looked to be in decent shape and in session. I recalled hearing it had been renovated a few years back given its deteriorating shape. Built in 1900, a full 65 years after Draven was founded, it was one of the oldest schools in the county. No clue how many students were currently enrolled, but a few cars and several school busses scattered in the lot suggested it persisted despite Draven's demise.

Across from the school set a vacant corner lot that used to inhabit the town's best bar, Nat's Sports Page, where the annual 5k was run. Though I never ran it, my cousin Billy won it one year, several years before he succumbed to cancer. I wondered whether all the competitors still ran as I did, but in races in better places.

At the corner where throngs of runners and supporters gathered for the start and end of the race, today stood just me, running my little solo 5k.

On the next corner sat a gas station at the same spot a different one stood years ago. It was open, and 2 cars were pumping gas. One, a young boy, jeans hanging low around his waist, ball cap on and in a fresh white tee shirt, talking on his cell without paying me attention. The other, a Black woman of middle age with two kids in the car tussling with each other in the back seat, looked across the street at me, did a double take, and shook her head.

I was tempted to stop and talk to her, but I was able to read her mind without any dialogue- *Damn fool, running through here.*

About halfway done now, the clouds increased overhead and the wind picked up. Remembering how close I was to Lake Michigan and the impact it had on the weather, I thought for a second about the snow days and occasional blizzards I got to enjoy as a kid. Snowball fights, building snow forts, and playing football in the snow. Every little boy's paradise.

This last stretch down 142nd would be the longest straightaway, before the final run up my block, Ellis, which would lead back to the lot where the rental was waiting.

I aborted the gas station stare down and became excited about next seeing the area of town closest to my house. The area I covered a thousand times during my runs, on my Schwinn ten speed, and later cruising my Ford Fairmont with buddies.

The lake I fished and swam in, the little food stand I worked at, the penny candy store where I spent money earned mowing lawns and shoveling snow. The neighborhood I grew up in from birth until I left for college.

I quickly glanced for traffic and, seeing no cars in either direction, picked up my pace on the sidewalk on the left side so I could see any oncoming traffic and so I could get the best view of the lake.

As I usually did on runs, I reminded myself to use all five senses for full impact. I remembered the butterscotch candy factory just east of the middle school that emanated such a sweet smell to accompany my final two-block walk to Logan Middle.

Already I found myself disregarding the new normal that was everywhere I looked and stepped- cracked sidewalks, weeds and litter, broken bottles, vacant lots and boarded and burned out homes, shuttered businesses. A wasteland.

This area of town being closest to the Chicago boarder, the familiar sound of nearby railcars persisted. A sound so frequent during my childhood that most days I never noticed it.

In just the twenty minutes of the run thus far, I shifted my paradigm to reconcile the image of my new surroundings against the backdrop of my memory.

Several cars approached and passed me slowly, seeming to almost stop and with all occupants looking at me with surprise, or concern, or perhaps both. My brain tried to make sense of what this meant. Black and Brown drivers, but none appeared threatening.

I came upon the fencing around the south side of the lake, not yet offering a view of the water given the thick shroud of overgrown weeds and vines, making the fence itself nearly invisible.

By bodies of water standards, Lake Cavalier was fairly small. Maybe three city blocks across by five city blocks wide. Big enough for fishing in small boats though, and was always stocked with some really nice catches. Bluegill, crappie, bass, perch, and the occasional northern pike or muskie.

I recalled the many nights we snuck under the fence, throwing cold chunks of hotdog on our hooks to reel in large catfish which my mom would fry up back at the house.

Approaching the parking lot to the gated entrance for the lake, I spotted only two cars. It appeared to still be open, but the main building which included a bar and clubhouse was desperately in need of repairs and a facelift.

A few tattered and rickety rowboats with chipped paint tethered to a small rickety pier that looked impassable bobbed up and down like the red and white bobbers we used with cane poles as kids. Baby white caps briefly emerged and expired from the water's surface, like paparazzi camera flashes in my direction. I again slowed to get a closer look.

The trees along the entire lake, including many weeping willows along the shore, were sadly overgrown, some toppled in the water left for dead and unremoved. The weeds along the banks and lily pads consuming the open water suggested little or no boat traffic churned the lake.

The tiny strand of man-made beach outside the clubhouse was now just a small dirt plot, creepers encroaching most of its terrain. No sunbathing pontoon floating in the nearby shore as it once did. No swimming buoys establishing the swimming perimeter. No lifeguard stand. Certainly no throngs of laughing and smiling kids enjoying the spoils of lake life as I once did.

The 8-foot chain link fence surrounding the entire lake was now topped with curly cue barbed wire.

I looked down to see my feet had stopped running. They were planted, informing my brain of an image that required a little more time.

I slowly approached the fence and involuntarily my hands gripped it, not unlike a prisoner jealously peering out to the free world. Through the fence links, my eyes gathered an image I was not prepared for. A man standing on the shore fishing. A White man.

My brain quickly digitized a number of variables and conclusions on this sight. The first White person I'd seen today. Fishing no less. In a locked and fenced-in area. Fishing at a club that always only permitted White members. Could that possibly still be the case? A town that is almost entirely devoid of White residents but with a private club that still only admitted White members? *Impossible.*

Though he was within earshot, I did not shout to him. He turned to bait his hook, and his peripheral vision caught sight of me. He nodded to me, and turned to cast his line back out.

I couldn't tell if as he turned back to his task whether he shook his head back and forth a bit, perhaps in disapproval of my presence much like the lady at the gas station. But either way, here was a White guy in Draven, who appeared entirely calm with his surroundings, albeit inside locked and wired fencing. Was he prisoner of his surroundings, or was I?

A few more frame shots to store for future diagnosis or rationalization, then I turned and continued on. I was confused whether seeing him was good, bad, or meant nothing at all.

The dirt path along this stretch of the fence outside the lake where people walked and kids road bikes was gone, thickly over-grown with trees, weeds and shrubbery. Unlike the nearby road, impassable. I jotted onto the roadway, hugged the curb despite the lack of traffic, and picked up my pace.

The accumulation of images, people and gestures was somehow weighing on me more heavily than I expected, and for the first time I was looking forward to getting back to the car.

The little roadside hot dog stand I used to work at was next on the left. The core of the building was still standing, but under a dif-ferent name. Some sort of chicken joint now- once striped orange and white, now blue and white. It appeared to be open for busi-ness but only one customer sat on a stool at the window eating.

Across the street where once stood a rental hall where friends had graduation parties and my annual family reunion was held each year was a vacant lot. A bungled fence surrounded it, donning a weathered "FOR LEASE" sign.

On the opposing corner, once the largest factory in Draven and which employed thousands of residents for many years, Mise Paper Plant, was totally dilapidated and vacant. Its little square windows each shattered, its large parking lot now a junkyard of some sort.

The stoplight at the intersection where I sat in my car a thou-sand times waiting for it to turn green, was now a four-way stop. *Not enough traffic to warrant lights anymore*, I thought to myself.

The gas station that used to sit on the opposite corner was gone, though half its structure was still in place as though it was recently still in business. But presently appearing as more of a shanty used for cover by drifters.

Past the station up Cottage Grove Road, a single car approached in the distance. I kept moving with just two blocks before I would turn onto my street.

Approaching Ellis Avenue off of 142nd street, on the left were the remains of the golf driving range and baseball fields where I played little league. A small group of kids were riding their bikes in a field where the baseball diamonds once stood. The concession stand was still there but boarded up, and all the backstops and bleachers were gone.

The rows of homes opposite the baseball fields were as cookie-cutter as I remembered. Some boarded-up, most in bad shape and overgrown, and a number with tattered FOR SALE signs on barren lawns. All with thick and sturdy screen doors with metal bars and locks, and many also with bars on first floor and basement windows. *With no one around how bad could it be?*

I knew I was about three-quarters done now, with just the four-block run up my street leading to the block where my house stood, followed by a few more blocks to the car.

I was compressed with feelings of sadness and joy, but still exhilarated. My research was leading to a conclusion I hoped not to reach... the once bucolic little town I grew up in was long gone.

My thoughts turned to calling Kim from the car, telling her it all worked out and that she worried for nothing. Then jumping on Facebook to share the journey and experience with the old crew. And, most importantly, that I bravely went back and ran Draven.

Then it happened. The car approaching in the distance down Cottage Grove suddenly pulled up from behind me just as I rounded the turn onto Ellis Avenue. The same red Chevy, the same dark tinted windows, and with the front passenger window slowly rolling down.

Continuing to run didn't seem the best play. At 44 and no longer familiar with my surroundings, no chance of outrunning them. I stopped as they had, waiting for the exchange.

The passenger looked about 20, seated next to a driver a bit older. This wasn't the Bloods and Crips stereotypes perpetuated by Hollywood. No red or blue headbands, no gold grills on their teeth, no machine guns. The driver just stared ahead casually smoking a cigarette as an R&B song played.

The passenger laid things out for me.

"What you doing here?"

"I used to live here. I'm just going for a run."

At this, the driver looked over, and chuckled. The passenger continued, "You running? What you running from?"

"Nothing. Just wanted to come back. Look around."

"You like what you see?"

My hands on my hips, breathing heavily, and now seeing some shadowed movement in the back seat, I wasn't sure what answer to provide.

"You know where you are, right?" he asked, his hands too low in the car for my view, but conceivably fidgeting for something.

Before I could answer he asked again, speaking with greater emphasis, "Mother fucker, I'm talking to you. You know where you are, right? This ain't your Draven. This is *our* Draven, bitch. You left this mother fucker years ago. I see you too old or maybe too stupid, but mother fuckers getting killed here all the time. What make you think we won't smoke you?"

"I got it. Listen, I grew up on this block. I ain't causing nothing. I'll just head back to my car and get back on the road." I was careful not to patronize them, but I had limited cards to play. I felt my heart rate elevate and my legs weaken.

The driver took a long drag, smiled with another light chuckle, and uttered his first words toward me. "You think your car is still there, up on Sibley?"

The street smarts I thought I gained growing up here were trying to resurface. But they had been weathered over time, not unlike this town. This place. Weakened by years in safe towns, clean neighborhoods, and good schools. Limited by lack of use. And it was too late to hone them again. Like a body builder who hasn't touched a weight in years. Like a runner who stopped running.

Just then the rear window rolled down a few inches, enough to reveal the face of a kid in the back seat. Wearing sunglasses and a ball cap, but clearly Caucasian.

The guy nearest to me in the front seat looked down toward his lap, appearing to hold both hands together on something, his arms in the shape of a triangle. It became clear to me how indiscriminate they were approaching me and the entire situation. Then he spoke while looking ahead.

"Here's what's up. You're gonna get the fuck out of my town. This ain't Disney. We making a quick stop 'round the corner, then we're rolling back this way. If our eyes meet, you finished."

The last several words trailed off as they slowly pulled away. There was no yelling. No show of force. No finger in your face argument. No mediation. There didn't need to be. This wasn't a negotiation, this was an edict- *You're not wanted here. We don't give a fuck if you grew up here. This isn't your high school reunion. Get the fuck out.* And though I didn't see any guns, no doubt they were there.

Like a coach searching for the best play to run as time on the clock expires, my mind raced to consider my options. No cell phone. Car about a mile away, and who knows its status given what they said. No others in sight. Hadn't seen a single cop car the whole time. Could knock on a door and ask to borrow a phone to call the DPD for a ride to the car.

As these options emerged, my legs did the thinking for me. I was now running again. Brisk jog, then long strides like the ones used during my half marathons, then a borderline sprint. Running for my life? Not yet, but possibly.

I could knock on some stranger's door, but I might get the same reception. Shot on some stoop as a suspected intruder. Though I knew this to be my hometown of Draven, this was *today's Draven*.

The exchange occurred on 142nd and Ellis. My house was on 145th and Ellis, three blocks up. The car was another four blocks. Ten houses per block- I knew all this rote from years of running here. Long gone were the neighbors waving as I passed. There was no waving, and there were no neighbors.

My eyes met those of a little two-foot concrete lawn jockey on a porch, in the shape of a Black carriage man in a red coat holding a lantern. Not unlike the Halloween decorations in the early part of the run, still mocking me. Certainly not lighting the way toward anything now. Kim, Jeff and Walt were right- there was nothing to see.

Now sprinting onto the 143rd block of Ellis, my brain counted down the houses as I passed. Into my mind popped the flash of a scene from a movie I watched in high school that I had not thought of for years... *Occurrence at Owl Creek Bridge.*

Its main character a suspected traitor, freed from the snapped rope he was about to be hung from on the side of a bridge, now running to evade his capturers while envisioning himself falling into his wife's arms as he got close to his estate. Then just as his dream of escape ends the noose tightens around his neck, ending his life.

Now onto the 144th block. Starting to prepare for the image of my street. My neighbors' homes. *My house.* But there would be no stopping as I had planned. A quick glance at best, and then the final sprint back to the safety of the car.

Now another movie image collapsed around me, permeating my mind even as I had no interest in being distracted by any thoughts other than an escape route. Ricky- *Boys in the Hood.* Shot from behind running down an alley in Compton.

Just then a flash of fur and a loud growl met my eyes and ears followed by a striking pinch on my calf. Out of nowhere from behind, a large dog clamped down on me. Instinctively, and of course joggers are no strangers to menacing strays, I turned and flailed my arms, yelling and kicking toward him. He reared back and retreated, snarling and appearing for another lunge.

After a brief stand-off the mange darted across the street, its tail and hindquarters hunched low and its back hairs pointed straight toward the sky. A black and white mutt of some sort. No collar. No leash. Just anger. *Even the fucking dogs don't want me here.*

No choice now but to dart ahead, hoping that like the dog the guys in the car might feel they made their point and moved on. Looking down I could see two fang-shaped indentations on my calf, one bleeding but not severe enough to stop and deal with.

Still bigger problems right now. And again, in an effort to distract me from my current dilemma, my brain jumped to the memory of a surfing accident I had two years ago in the Outer Banks. I fell off my board and scraped my thigh on some coral, resulting in blood in the water.

When you learn to surf you learn the basic rules. Know the depth of the water, never fall in head-first, neutralize Jellyfish stings with your own urine, and when bleeding- *get out of the water.* Blood attracts sharks, and sharks don't like humans.

I snapped back to my reality. *This isn't time for pithy analogies. This is the time to enact a plan. Keep moving.*

Now on my block and sprinting as fast as my legs could compel me, I felt my sweat drenching my clothes. The sound of my own panting permeated my ears, mixed with the accelerating rhythm of my shoes hitting the pavement like the sound of a heartbeat through a stethoscope.

As was the case for most blocks in the neighborhood, on each corner of a new block sat a large boulder. Apparently, these were placed there to dissuade cars from cutting over the edges of the curbs.

Though my initial plan was to stop and touch it for good luck as I did when I was a kid, I barely glanced at it as I raced by. As I caught a glimpse of it, the structure that once seemed enormous now appeared to measure barely above my knees.

Earlier in the run, I assumed by this point I would slow to a leisurely walk of my street to reminisce and recall the neighbors who inhabited each house. Pulling back up the memories of each one I connected with in my youth, whether asking for $2 to mow their lawn or shovel their snow, or getting lectured by them for riding my bike on their lawns.

I recalled the number of Monday nights in the fall I would knock on the Robinsons' door next to our house, peer inside, then plead to Ms. Robinson, "My parents are watching Carson. I see you have the Bears game on. Can I come in for a bit to watch?"

Given my fight-or-flight instinct, all final aspects of the plan were now abandoned. This was no longer a stroll down memory lane. This was a race to survive.

Then mid-block at 14521 Ellis, the place I was born and raised, my heart overruled my mind. At any risk, I had to stop for a moment. I had to stand and take it in.

Just as I stopped, hands on my hips catching my breath, there they were. The Chevy rounded the corner a block behind. This time revving the engine with purpose. With fury. With a final plan of their own, and with no regard for my plan. With no regard for my run.

Like an avalanche of images flashing by just before a car accident, it hit me. *Shit. Kim was right after all.* A lifetime of "I told you so" was imminent. Like the main character who freezes to death in *To Build a Fire*, remembering as he's about to take his last breath that the old prospector who told him it was too cold to venture out on the Alaskan trail at forty below zero was actually right.

The only thing worse than a shitty decision is regret. The end of our last conversation when she dropped me off at the airport coming back word for word...

"Tom, remember we live in a place where people leave their doors unlocked. Where we still wave at strangers and say please and thank you. We've become accustomed to relative security at all times. You're going to a place that is devoid of any of this. Where teachers quit their jobs out of concern for their own safety. Just be careful. Be smart."

Not even the irony of being killed standing right in front of the very house I grew up in would have been worth such a fate.

Before I could process my options, the door of my house suddenly opened. The same wooden door with the doorknob in the center that my hands pushed open and closed behind me a thousand times.

The silhouette of an old woman emerged, looking at me on her sidewalk, standing and staring at her home. She slowly unlocked the screen door and opened it.

Glancing to her right, seeing the car now rapidly approaching, and my feet now instinctively moving toward her, she pushed the screen open with one hand and the inside door open with the other, arms spread like the Christ the Redeemer statue in Rio.

"Why don't you come in and sit for a bit?"

No words, I hopped the familiar five steps of the porch in two bounds and was in her living room. She closed the screen door, turned the lock, then closed the other door, followed by the twist of two locks. As she turned toward me I peeked through her blinds to see the car slowly pass.

"Thank you," I said, now feeling like I was in a strange time warp, caught between reality and fiction.

I could feel the beads of sweat starting to drip off my chin, so I wiped them with my sleeve, then put my hands on my knees. My vision got blurry and I thought I might pass out.

"You've let a complete stranger into your home, which I appreciate."

"Your leg is bleeding. Here." She reached for a tissue from the box on her coffee table and handed it to me, then I used it to dab my punctured calf.

"Well, you don't look too threatening, right?" She said as she stood near the door, a comforting tone and her warm smile upon me. Around 65 or 70 years old, she wore a house dress and slippers, and appeared to be alone. A small dog began barking from the kitchen, in much the same way our own dogs did over the years when people entered here.

"Hush now, baby, it's going to be ok," she projected back toward her little yapper, though I sort of hoped the words were meant for me.

She continued, now making her way toward an end chair and motioning for me to sit on her couch, "That car that passed. Those boys got trouble with you?"

"Well ma'am, I'm not sure. But I ran into them up on 142nd and they weren't exactly welcoming."

"Uh-huh. Surprised about that?" Her calm tone and demeanor were reassuring to me, and I sensed that maybe I was the closest thing to a visitor she had seen in a while.

"I guess not. No."

"You don't live here I suspect? Can I get you a glass of water?" She said as she stood up, not really expecting an answer to the first question. I meant to answer only the second, though the answer was the same for both, "Yes."

As she left for the kitchen I debated whether to tell her the truth. If so, how exactly? As I settled in and scanned the room, I was flooded with images and memories. Here I was after all these years, sitting in the living room I grew up in. Different of course, but the same. Smaller, but familiar.

I caught glimpse of the corner table and small ceramic pumpkin glowing with tealights inside, in the same place I used to play with my favorite erector set as a kid. I decided to come clean.

"I grew up in Draven. I grew up in this house actually. But I've been gone many years. So I decided to come back and go for a run here."

The end of my statement greeted her as she emerged from the kitchen, holding my glass of water. She paused under the familiar archway between the two rooms.

"You grew up here? In *this house*?"

"Yes ma'am. Pretty weird, right?" I wasn't trying to be a smartass, but being saved by her in the very house I grew up in was starting to seem somewhat cosmic to me.

"You've been gone, so you know what Draven is now. But you decided to come back here for a visit. And you decided to jog around town. Is that right?"

I felt a bit like I was in therapy, what with her repeating what I was saying, somehow trying to help me make sense of it. I could tell she was wise, and it all made sense to her. Not good sense, but she knew exactly what my motivation was.

"Well, how was your run then?"

I loved that she wasn't judging or lecturing me, but I assumed this last question was more rhetorical. Instead of answering it, I asked her, "Where are you from, ma'am?"

"Oh, not here. I grew up in the South. Deep South. You know those parts?"

I loved the answer. Having now lived in North Carolina for many years, I was amazed that I could spot southern hospitality even when I wasn't in the South. Even in my own living room.

"I left Draven after college. My parents sold this house. Then my wife and I moved to Raleigh. That was around 20 years ago. I haven't been back in many years. But I think about this town a lot. My childhood. This house. For some reason, I had to come back. I had to see for myself."

"And what have you seen?"

"Well, certainly not the way I left it."

"My husband and I bought this house 15 years ago, when I was hired to run the bank and he had a good job in the city. House is plenty big for us and our rescue Pearl, and Robert is from this area and has family here. The bank closed five years ago, then Rob passed suddenly. So it's home for me. Too old to up and move. Would you like to look around a bit?"

Assuming I had nothing but time to kill and still needing a plan to get to the car, I was thrilled with the offer.

She showed me around from room to room, and the bones of the house were unchanged. Different furniture, wall colors, etc., but every inch as I remembered it. Each room brought a flood of memories that emerged from the deep recesses of my mind. Memories I didn't even think were still there.

As I rounded each corner, I pictured my parents and brothers standing right before me, as the family we once were.

The time I popped out of mom's closet to scare her. The time my brother and I passed notes from top bunk to bottom in the room we shared, only for them to be found by my dad in the morning warranting a stern lecture about the use of four-letter words. The time we streaked in front of our babysitter. The time my brother and I skipped school and ran through a case of dad's Stroh's beer. The times we snuck girls into the basement. All the stuff that made American suburbia great.

My host was gracious, and the tour was quick. It all seem so much smaller than I remembered, but still felt like the same space where once the whole world lay out before me.

As we came up from the basement, her right hand moving slowly along the same wooden banister that we never used to steady ourselves as kids, I peeked out the backdoor window into the yard.

The concrete patio spanning around 15 feet to the garage where for years hung my basketball hoop, also seemed tiny. Where every night for years every kid in the neighborhood met to play basketball. The Jordan years. The only sport worth playing if you lived near Chicago.

Somehow reading my mind, she said without turning back, "I bet you used to shoot hoops back there as a kid."

"For sure. Was the backboard still up when you bought the house?"

"No, but Rob spent some time patching the roof after the last family took it down. So we knew there was one there. I'll bet you had a good time here as a kid. Good memories."

It occurred to me suddenly we hadn't exchanged names, yet we already seemed to know each other very well, what with us trading places and all.

"And I'm so sorry, and you've been so kind. I'm Tom Walter. I didn't even get your name yet."

Now standing in the kitchen, she turned and extended her hand. Beautiful, brown hand with manicured nails, and very soft skin.

"Priscella. Priscella Barefoot. Grew up in Mississippi but lived all over. It's nice to meet you, Tom Walter. I guess I should really be saying, welcome home."

Her smile and warmth was that of a grandmother, or favorite aunt. I could have spent the entire afternoon with her, talking about her life over tea, the house, Draven, or 50 other topics. And she most likely would have equally cherished it.

"So you'll be needing a ride to your car then." She didn't pose this as a question. This was a statement. This was non-negotiable.

"Well, much as I would like to finish my run, I'm thinking that is probably the safest play."

Pearl, now having accepted me as a welcomed guest, was no longer barking and trailed behind Priscella somehow knowing a car ride was coming and expecting to be included.

"Hold on. Let me get my things."

"As she left the kitchen for the back bedroom, the room where I vividly remember my parents' hideous green, velour wallpaper, I walked to the middle of the kitchen, stood, and did another visual panoramic of the space. Was going to ask her to email me a few photos since I had no phone, but didn't want to bother her given all she'd already done for me.

I entered the front living room again to check the street for the Chevy. All clear.

"Don't worry. Those boys not gonna mess with you now. Thing is, Draven is in bad shape. But most days people are out, nice to each other, some kids playing in the streets. Gangs got bad a while back but they mainly go after each other. They won't bother me, and my kin come and check on me on weekends. And my Pearl lets me know whenever someone comes near the house."

"I can't tell you how nice this has been. How lucky I was you let me in, I really..."

She cut me off for the first time, her phrasing of the next statement seemed to be something she wanted to get out before I left her.

"Things happen for a reason. You needed to come back. You needed to see. And it needed to be seen, hard as that is. Now it's done, and now that you've been home, you can go home."

Her car was tucked in the back of the driveway on the side of the house, right where my first car sat all through high school and during visits home from college. She unlocked the back gate padlock, and relocked it after we passed through. Seemed everything in Draven was locked down.

Pearl followed behind, her little tail wagging, excited about the ride. Maybe excited there would be two people in the car this time.

As we pulled out we talked about the house, about the neighborhood, and about Draven. Having told her I was parked in the old Kmart lot up on Sibley, she knew exactly where to take me, and I knew every inch of road as she made her way.

Still taking in the images, what was gone, what had replaced it, and how things looked, I meanwhile nervously kept my eyes peeled for the Chevy.

As we spoke and I scanned the blighted area, I was careful not to negatively react to how things appeared; but she was wise to the world. She knew who I was, she knew who she was, and she knew this place. Best yet, she identified with my purpose.

As we approached the corner where the lot was, I could see from a distance the car was trashed. I felt for the key in my pocket that I had long since forgot was there. As we pulled up to the rental, I was relieved that it was even still there.

Broad daylight. The windows on both sides smashed and the trunk open. Priscella uttered a few responses as she pulled next to it.

"Oh my," she said, as Pearl hopped on her lap for a closer look. "Do you think it can run?"

She stayed in her car as I exited, and watched me approach the car in disbelief. I first checked the trunk and found my suitcase including my laptop was gone. Next the glove box, which was popped open and empty- my cell and wallet also gone.

I tried to close the trunk but needed to slam it several times as the lock was damaged. She waited with her window rolled down and Pearl spinning on her lap as I inserted the key in the ignition. Thank God, it started. I left it running as I hopped out.

"I'm sure they didn't want the car, fortunately. Just your stuff. But it started. I guess that's what's important," she said, now getting ready to pull away. "I really don't have to run. Do you want me to follow you to the police or something?"

I made my way over to her. The condition of it aside, just gracious that the car I originally needed to get me back would now be used just to get me out. One last glance around the lot and intersection so I could safely spend a few minutes thanking her.

"I'm good. I will just head out and get to O'Hare and deal with it there. I really can't thank you enough, Priscella, really. I think you were the angel put in my path today. The only thing that helped me on this weird journey."

I would typically offer to pay a stranger who helped me, even without a wallet, promising to send them a check or something. But the bond we formed in our short time together somehow negated all that.

I continued, now placing my hand briefly on hers as it rested on the steering wheel. "Good news is, I've got your address memorized. So expect a nice thank you letter from me when I get home."

"It was my pleasure. Where I grew up, we did nice things for people. Even strangers. But you're not a stranger. Thanks for seeing the place. It made my day. Come back any time."

The last part made me smile, though while I'm sure she would welcome me back, I think she was making fun of me a bit.

As I stood and waved, and she waved back, her last words confirmed for me her brilliance, or her wit, or merely how she was making sense of my day- "Run along now!"

I turned back to view the smashed rental, and with my protector now gone, I hastily got going. The skies darkened and a storm cloud rumbled in the distance as I threw the rubber floor mat on the driver's seat over the broken glass.

With the menacing Chevy nowhere in sight, I eased down the street and resumed my focus on the town, highly convinced these would be the final images to take with me for a long time. Maybe forever.

No doubt Kim would be freaking out given I hadn't spoken to her since last night, but without my phone that would have to wait. I chuckled to myself thinking about the last time I made a collect call from a pay phone. Probably the last time I was in Draven.

Aside from the added hassle of checking the rental back in and making the claim for damages, then dealing with how to board a plane with no ID, I was able to get to my gate at the airport about an hour before takeoff. The airline even let me use a desk phone at O'Hare to call Kim who was hysterical.

"Tom, oh my God! What happened?"

"Sorry babe. Long story, but I lost my phone and just now was able to call you."

"You lost it? What happened? Are you o.k.? I've been going nuts!"

"I'm fine. Seriously. I'll tell you all about it when I get back tonight, but I made it. Basically made it fine and I'm already at the airport."

"So you did it? You ran? I can't tell you what was going through my head when I didn't hear from you."

"I'm sure. Sorry, Kim. I will fill you in tonight. I'm good now. Everything is good. And I made a new friend I can't wait to tell you about."

Shortly after hanging up the announcement came- "Now boarding flight 1026 to Raleigh, North Carolina, gate 27." I glanced around me out of habit for my bag and laptop, forgetting they were long gone. Probably bouncing around in the back of a red Chevy in Draven, along with my phone and wallet.

I settled into my window seat and exhaled, looking down at my running shoes and wondered whether I should keep them for posterity or burn them. Whether it was the trip, the run, or the intensity of today's experience, just after takeoff I quickly nodded off. The images of the day bounced through my head followed by a deeper sleep than I ever had on a plane.

I began to dream about Kim, the girls, sitting on my rocking chair on my front porch in Raleigh with a glass of wine. Suddenly, the vision was interrupted by the image of me running in a full panic, right past my old house on Ellis, the Chevy closing in on me as the sound of gun fire rang out. And in order to escape, I did what I always do during a nightmare. I opened my eyes. And the plane was gone.

~ ~

The inside of the plane was replaced by the usual image of my alarm clock next to my bed, chirping to remind me it was 6am. As usual, the chirp was followed by the sound of sparrows singing in the crape myrtle tree outside our bedroom window, the sun beginning to shine through the white plantation shutters.

Kim's arm rested on my shoulder as usual, and the dogs at my feet were in their usual not-ready-to-get-up-yet curl. My running shoes, shorts, and tee shirt sat on the antique trunk at the foot of the bed, placed there the night before as a failsafe reminder of my morning ritual.

As my feet hit the carpet, my brain downloaded last night's dream. *Very strange... I went back to my hometown and went for a jog. Impossible.*

I shook my head and smiled as I dressed to head out for my run.

CPSIA information can be obtained
at www.ICGtesting.com
Printed in the USA
BVHW011704100223
658305BV00022B/1008